the baby lottery

a novel

Kathyrn Trueblood

The Permanent Press
Sag Harbor, New York 11963

Library of Congress Cataloging-in-Publication Data

Trueblood, Kathryn.
   The baby lottery: a novel / by Kathryn Trueblood.
      p.   cm.

   ISBN 13: 978-1-57962-151-3 (alk. paper)
   ISBN 10: 1-57962-151-1 (alk. paper)

   1. Women college graduates—Fiction. 2. Female friendship—Fiction.
   3. Women—Psychology—Fiction. 4. Choice (Psychology)—Fiction.
   5. Abortion—Fiction. I. Title.

PS3570.R767B33 2007
813'.54—dc22   2007002103

Printed in the United States of America.

The Permanent Press
4170 Noyac Road
Sag Harbor, NY 11963
www.thepermanentpress.com

For my brother, Andrew, with gratitude.

Acknowledgments

I'd like to thank the valiant women who shared their considerable life experience with me: Sarah Ivy Benjamin, Karen Broberg, Kathy Buck, Sara Burnaby, Mary Byrne, Ellen Byrne, Jackie Brown, Laura Cairns, Meredith Cary, Sara Clarke, Laurie Evezich, Diana Knox, Laura Kalpakian, Shaun Kelley, Liz Marshall, Jan Miller, Caroline Mitchel, Cecelia Meintel, Julie Ann Sullivan, Victoria Vickers, and Carolyn Worth.

I'd like to thank and blame my writers group: Margi Fox, Sara Stamey, Gary McKinney, and Paul Piper. (The cafés where we meet would also like to thank and blame us.) Thank you also to Donald Cairns for helping this techno-peasant. Additionally, I'm indebted to Gregory Macdonald for his many talents and relentless cheer.

Finally, I offer a special thanks to Gundars Strads for his steadfast presence in my life.

Table of Contents

NAN

∾

The Baby Lottery

The hospital looks like a 1968 *Star Trek* mock-up. It's a cream-colored cement concoction with strange architectural features—Bauhaus block patterning for the central building, long submarine-like wings to the north and south. Nan Shay crosses the grounds, which are mounded and humped like a golf course, a softened landscape. Intentional, she knows. Ahead of her lie twelve hard-boiled hours under the fluorescent lights of obstetrics. At the electric doors, she pauses by the plaster statue of Mary, her head bowed and hands clasped, icon of medical mystery. Mother Mary, captain of this mish-mash of modernism. Nan salutes her before stepping on board.

The truth is she wouldn't want to work anywhere else; St. Mary's is a non-profit hospital founded by the Sisters of Peace. The early registration books inventory ax and saw cuts, bone fractures, consumption, near drowning, alcoholism, and later the polio outbreak. No one was turned away. That's what matters to Nan.

It's Christmas time in the cafeteria, and the same wreaths appear on the back wall, big fake bows slightly flattened by storage. The gigantic interior columns are wrapped in velveteen ribbon, and even the dust-gasping palms are strewn with tinsel. Nan appreciates the effort; it probably would look good if she hadn't seen it for ten years in a row. But the cafeteria is the only place in town where you can get a salad bar for under four bucks—on one plate a full meal and dessert if you count that Ambrosia fruit salad made with coconut and marshmallow sauce like the one her great aunt in the Midwest still makes.

Her shift runs 7:00 AM to 7:00 PM, and first thing she does is get the report from the off-going shift and check the boards. This morning Nan has a twenty-five-year-old woman who came in at term, concerned because she hadn't felt the baby move since yesterday. *Josie Peeler, accompanied by sister, unmarried.* At 5:00 AM, the chart records there was no fetal heartbeat. The woman has been prepped, the papers are signed, and it's time.

Nan sits with her awhile before applying the prostaglandin gel to her cervix to get labor started. Josie is a moon-faced girl with chipped teeth and her hair in a ponytail. "This is just tough and unfair," Nan says, "any way you look at it."

"Thank you," the woman whispers. Her lips looked chewed and she's hugging herself by the shoulders, up high, away from her belly. Nan gets the doctors' orders—Pitocin drip in her I.V. and they're out of the gate. Josie will "ride the pit monster," as the nurses call it. Induced labor really is harder—double-peak contractions—though some of the docs insist that the statistics don't support it. "Merely anecdotal," they say. Nan is glad to get the real pain started, so Josie won't have to wait and think about the opening and closing jaws of contractions, about the pain and the pushing to deliver a dead baby. Labor will take her beyond thought. Soon. Nan wants it to be soon.

But it's six hours of labor. The woman has a cervix like a Goodyear tire. Half a day to dilate a few centimeters, then booming contractions for the last two hours. Nan checks on her, preps some meds, checks back, throws some blankets in the warmer, checks back, delivers a meal tray for a nurse on break, checks back, changes an I.V. bag for another patient, checks back, wheels someone to ultrasound, checks back. The hours pass.

At first, Josie refuses the Fentanyl Nan offers. Her sister keeps coming out in the hallway and begging Nan to do something. Josie is thrashing back and forth holding onto the birthing bar. Nan has heard women yell, "Kill me," and she understands why. She puts an ice pack on Josie's sacrum and starts rubbing firmly, strong strokes. "Listen," she tells her when she is sure she has Josie's attention, "no one is going to feel any differently about you if you take the pain meds. You're already having to be braver than the rest of us will ever be."

Through gritted teeth, Josie tells her, "I didn't come in for prenatal care. Not till the sixth month."

"That's not what caused your baby to die, Josie," Nan says. "Listen to me."

She nods, hanging onto Nan's shoulders and groaning with the next contraction.

When Josie finally agrees to the meds Nan knows they aren't going to take the pain away, they'll only help her stay above it a few inches. The baby is born at 1:14 PM into the wan winter day, poor little thing the color of a Beluga whale.

"What was it, what was it?" Josie cries out.

The doctor, thinking she is asking about the cause of death, answers, "There was a true knot in the umbilical cord. I'm very sorry. No need to do an autopsy."

"No," the woman cries out again. "What was it?"

"A girl," Nan answers, comprehending all at once. "A little girl."

Josie is suddenly silent, staring at the mirror over the dresser, one of the homey touches of the birth center suites. Her face is immobile, unnaturally placid, as though she has submerged beneath the cool, silver film of the mirror. Nan is sponging the infant and wrapping her, so she just gets glimpses in her peripheral vision—Josie still staring, trancelike. Her sister is leaning against the windowsill by the bed, her hands pressed in a prayer pyramid over her mouth, eyes brimming with tears. It's a gesture Nan has seen before, as though hands cupped could contain a shriek and release it later in some gentler form. The doc leaves the room. When he comes back in, he asks Josie if she wants to see the baby. "No," she blurts as though she'd just tripped over the word and fallen.

Later, after the monitors have been shut off and the room is quieter, Nan stands near the bedside with the bundle in her arms. "Josie," she says, feeling the weight in her arms and the weight in a name. "Josie," Nan says as though she'd known this woman all her life, "you have to see how beautiful she is. You have to see."

Josie turns toward Nan, her expression like something ripped open. "Nan, you bring her to me," she says. She settles her baby against her side, then looks at her, so perfect and still. She traces the baby's eyebrows with the tip of her finger, strokes the tip of the infant's nose, the cleft above the tulip mouth. Nan has her arm around the sister who is at last crying, too. She can't help but wonder where their mother is, if this is supposed to be a banishment or a secret or a punishment in some other woman's mind. Josie surprises them both, wiping hard at her eyes and speaking firmly.

"Get the camera, Jill," she says to her sister. "We're going to take a picture, and we're going to give her a name, and we're going to give her a proper burial."

When Nan leaves Josie and her sister, the Team Charge Nurse tells her the early labors are already assigned, so she's put on mother-baby rotation, one nurse to four moms and new-borns. That's one of the reasons Nan chose Labor & Delivery when she passed her RN Boards, because the numbers are sane; you can stay human. Her first lady is a V-BAC—vaginal birth after cesarean—and there are always a few more concerns. This woman, Marietta, has had an extended labor, but Nan meets the doc as he's heading out and he gives her a thumbs-up. Marietta is snuggling with her baby boy, skin to skin while the father looks on. She's in her late thirties, pale red hair and those hazel eyes that look like polished tortoise shell. The dad's plain goofy, taking close-up pictures of the baby latching onto the mother's breast. Who can blame him? The labor nurse explains to Marietta that the husband is going to bathe the baby, and then they will take him off for his eye ointment and the routine tests. Nan places a hospital beanie on the little fellow's head before he's whisked out of the room. The mother beams at Nan, so enraptured she seems to give off a light all her own. But then it's time to start massaging the fundus and that's Nan's job, get that uterus contracting.

At first, Marietta bleeds heavily, which is to be expected, and the other nurse, Elaine, changes the pads while Nan moves her hands over the woman's belly. Pretty mushy. Marietta leans back against the pillows, grimacing. Nan apologizes the whole time. "I know, this isn't fun," she says, then she hears the other nurse make a noise between her teeth, "Shew."

"What is it?"

"She's bleeding good, Nan."

"Call Anderson. And start weighing the pads."

Elaine slings the sodden mess onto the scale, then heads for the wall phone. She's practically snorting when she comes back to the bedside.

"The doc recommends waiting twenty minutes."

It's pretty predictable, but the guy is probably stuffing stale muffins in his mouth in the break room, trying at this very moment to bring his own blood sugar up. Nan applies more pressure but doesn't feel the uterus contracting at all. She's afraid this is what the docs call "friable"—the tissue of an overextended uterus. Marietta struggles up, her face beading with sweat. "I'm cold," she says, "I'm really cold."

"We'll get you warmed blankets right away." Nan hits the nurse call button on the bed panel because there's no way she is leaving this lady's side till she feels some movement. Then Elaine makes her noise again, emphatically.

"Shew, she just gushed a liter, Nan, I swear."

They both look down. "Call Becky," she says.

"I'm on it."

Becky, the team charge nurse, rockets in with Dave, the only male on staff, and he starts transfusing blood right away. Nan can hear Becky on the phone with Anderson from across the room. "We've got a hemabate, Doc. We're talking liters here." Then a pause. "You get your ass to the O.R. now. This here's an emergency hysterectomy." Becky is tougher than pressure-treated wood, that's why she's Team Charge Nurse . . . and the docs know her assessments (they're not allowed to say diagnoses) are always on the mark.

By the time they start wheeling Marietta down the hall, they've transfused two units already. It's clear that the patient has heard everything because her eyes are wild with panic. Becky tells her, "We're taking you back to the Operating Room so the doc can stop this bleeding." But Nan is the one walking at the side of the bed, not Becky, she's down at the end. Marietta grabs Nan's wrist, her red curls a pillow storm behind her. She's so terrified and shocky her lips have gone gray and her eyes are dilated.

"Nan," she says to her hoarsely, "am I going to die?"

Nan's brain is running stats. She's thinking weight of the pads and volume of loss and rate of hemorrhage; she's thinking the patient has got a 60/40 chance, but in an instant Nan clears all that away, and looks Marietta in the face, steady now, and tells her what she needs to pull through.

"No, Marietta, you are *not* going to die. You're going to have breakfast with your baby in the morning."

Three hours later, Nan looks in on her. Of course she's sleeping, and her pallor looks like the white winter sky outside the window, but her lips are pink again and her vitals are good.

Sweet Jesus, Nan says to herself, not sure if it's a curse or a benediction, because she has seen women come to Labor & Delivery in the peak of health and leave by way of the morgue. It's rare that mothers die, but it happens. Though the statistics docs give are based on the law of averages—1 in 1000, 1 in 250—nature likes to cluster, nature likes sets of freak waves. People have forgotten that what happens within the body is a part of nature, too.

Sometimes that's how Nan feels at work—like a crew on board a vessel. And same as maritime, certain conditions can combine unpredictably, the fetch of a wave unbroken for 2000 miles delivers its force in the here and now. Last summer she watched a thirty-four-year-old woman go into cardiac arrest in the middle of labor and die. Freak wave.

Then there are the uncharted islands in this same sea, the places you can shipwreck safely. That same summer, there was a baby born dead after a faltering heart rate and crash C-section, a baby resuscitated whose Apgar scores were zero. Yet two weeks later he was out of the incubator and at home, suckling at the breast, doing reassuring things, making those reassuring noises. Whose stats can account for that? Nan thinks fleetingly of her friend Charlotte, thirty-eight years old and pregnant with her first child.

When she goes off shift, it's not her feet that hurt. At the desk, there's a message for Nan from Virginia. "See you for debriefing at my house." Even though the twelve-hour shift is brutal, Nan makes an effort to stop by Virginia's when it's girls' night out, if only for an hour of wine and unwinding. She met Virginia in college but became even closer when their pregnancies coincided: Virginia's first, Nan's second. But because Nan had never had anyone to share in the burden and the glory of parenting her daughter, her son Luke seemed like a first child too, albeit in an all-new way.

In their pre-natal yoga class, Nan used to catch Virginia smirking when the instructor handed out little angel cards for them to meditate on with words like *peace, surrender,* and *serenity* written on them. Virginia would smile back, her open and rueful smile. Looking around that circle of women, Nan knew there might be a baby among them who perhaps wasn't blessed. Whose mother might be wondering why she'd been cursed. The dropout rate in the class was predictable. And with each dropout, in a few days some news. Healthy baby, happy mommy. No deformity, no disability, no damage.

But smiling though they were, truly joyous for those lucky mothers, the god of statistics went on making his demands. So even as they were praying please God not my baby, it felt like they were wishing it on someone else. You start to long for some ritual appeasement to this god, wish long ago you'd made small blood-lettings a regular part of your life, as though you could avert this merciless wondering, this inescapable self-centeredness of prayer, because it had to happen, it had to happen to someone. The baby lottery. Virginia and Nan were among the fortunate; they delivered healthy babies.

Tonight Nan surprises herself by opening the door of the hospital chapel. A small plaque at the entrance gives its due to the original sisters who emigrated from Ireland after the potato famine of 1879 and founded a frontier hospital. The chapel isn't particularly inviting—a blower from somewhere in the bowels of the hospital ventilation system makes it sound like a plane about to take off. There's nowhere to kneel, no pews, just convention center chairs, and these big spiky plants backlit on either side of a huge cross. The wall outlets are painted red for some reason and the abstract stained glass over the cross looks like a nautilus caught in seaweed. Nan turns to the open chapel book on the stand and begins reading:

> *God,*
> *Seth says you carry his picture in your wallet.*
> *I beg you watch over him.*
> *Signed, Renee*

> *God,*
> *Please help my sister Lacey breathe better.*
> *Love, Maynard*

> *God,*
>> *We tried so hard and for so long to have Tony.*
>> *Please send a guardian angel.*
>>> *Please don't take him from us now.*
>> *Yours forever, Cindy and Richie Patton*

She notices that the word angel is spelled angle on most of the entries. It makes her remember the pictures in her children's Bible, the ray of light upon which Gabriel descended. She doesn't know what she believes anymore. Everything and nothing? She believes in that which gives comfort. An angel, a certain angle of light. What does it matter?

She keeps her entry simple (she writes the same thing about twice a year).

> *Lord,*
>> *Keep me strong,*
>> *Let me be glad.*

And then she writes her initial, *N*, and draws a circle around it.

JEAN

❧

In the Frame

In the unopened pile of mail she keeps in a tarnished toast
holder, Jean Neville finds a letter from her ex-husband,
addressed in that balanced architect's script of his. The letters
kneel shoulder to shoulder the way gymnasts do to create a pyramid. She skims most of it until she comes to the information she
wants: their baby was born November 11th, Frank Cameron Neville, 6 lbs. 9 oz. Since the divorce this fall, she has been debating
whether or not to return to her maiden name, Brovak, and, now,
reading the name of this baby who shares her surname but is no
relation, she feels the plates of her skull slowly pulling apart. She
goes back to the beginning of the letter and starts slowly: "Jean, I
hope you have been able to reconstruct your life."

"You wish," she whispers, looking up at the smoke-stained
and boogery ceiling of her apartment. Why should she recover?
Jump right back into the fray to please him? But it makes her
wonder if she is refusing to get out of the ditch on purpose. Some
fantasy in which she can hold Timmy accountable, in which she
can ruin his newfound happiness with Wifey Two and Baby Boo
by being the disaster he must feel responsible for. She will attempt
suicide, become an outrageous alcoholic, fax him at work, call
him ten times a day, become one of those Victorian victims
whose mind has come unhinged, whose soul is rent.

Of course not. But this is the swerving cave of her brain, the
stench of guano in it. Even as she goes to market, collects rents,
reads the classifieds, and calls her mother, her brain is on obses-
sive replay. Nan stopped by yesterday, emptied all her ashtrays,

and forced Jean to go for a swim. "You have to forgive him, or you won't be able to stop this." Wise girlfriend talk, if you're not the one who has to do the forgiving. Jean flops back on her bed in a funk and studies the crusty craters of her ceiling.

What Wife Two has with him is this baby, the salve for the great big wound she and Tim made in each other. But on Jean's side of the scale are the adventuring years of his life, all those trips they made—camping, hiking, kayaking—and Eliza won't be able to do any of that now, that's for sure. Still, Jean knows her condescension is pathetic.

When she was in her twenties, coming home from college meant attending baby showers for her high school friends. Women she saw as poor distended creatures with foreclosed futures who wore those giant T-shirts that said Baby and had an arrow pointing downwards, as if a person couldn't tell. It seemed vaguely grotesque, since their intestines already purged in that direction.

Then there were the insipid party games: like unscrambling the words *layette* and *stroller* spelled backwards, or guessing the girth of the expectant mother, or racing to a kitchen timer while pinning diapers on doll babies. Next it was time to identify a series of items collected in a blue baby-wipes box as a mock parenthood preparedness test. Things like Lipton tea bags—the old remedy for toughening nipples with tannin—one of those bulbous booger snatchers, a bottle liner, a freezable nubby gum soother, a plastic wall socket cover, a hemostat for extracting mashed Cheerios from a child's nose, an inflatable hemorrhoid cushion. When it was Jean's turn, she pulled out the hemostat and said "roach clip," waving it in the air and laughing.

She seemed to feel keenly embarrassed for women who weren't embarrassed at all. Once she was given a little tiny diaper at the door to pin on her shoulder with a big plastic stork pin—everyone was given one as a way to determine who'd get the door prize. At the end of the party they'd all had to open their diapers and see who had gotten the B.M.—a dab of peanut butter. That was the worst. And Tim heard all about it. They'd both escaped small towns in southern Washington and regaled each other with the stories.

Yet Jean never told him how she felt about buying the shower presents, how she stood in the aisle of the J.C. Penney's her father managed and spread her fingers inside a layette cap to illustrate for herself just how small an infant's head was. She was clandestine about it, looking over her shoulder, as though letting anyone know she felt that way might be dangerous. She didn't want to wake up one morning in Aberdeen and find out she'd never really gone to college at all. When she found herself pregnant in her sophomore year at the University of Washington, she hadn't hesitated. She'd gotten an abortion the next day.

Ten years later, when Jean and Tim started the fertility treatments, she'd sometimes say in despair, "You need two wives, Timmy," and she wonders now if her flip remarks didn't give license to his affair and the rushed marriage that followed their divorce. She hopes jealousy will visit his new wifey when Tim goes off to hike the west coast of Vancouver Island or kayak off Kauai and leaves her to the nappies and the squalling. That's when it will be Eliza's turn to think of Jean.

There really wasn't anything the matter with their marriage besides the fact that Jean couldn't have a baby. "Secondary infertility," it was called, since the aborted pregnancy made her a proven conceiver. But conceive she did not.

In the first year, she and Tim were comrades and made light of the infertility treatments. After all, they didn't believe they would need reproductive assistance for long. They were confident it would work for them. So they sketched satirical portraits for each other.

The first time Tim went in for a "sperm analysis" the receptionist turned out to be his former travel agent, and they both made out like they didn't know each other. What was either supposed to say? *Oh Hiyee?* Jean wondered if Dr. Daubresse's office would have a sort of lounge, considering the deed at hand, but no, just a bathroom with a bunk and a basket full of *Penthouse.*

"I flipped through one for the hell of it," Timmy said. "But it was just gross—women stretching their labia's out like bat wings—where's the turn-on in that? I wasn't even sure I could do it."

Jean was unable to stifle a laugh. "Honey, wasn't this the moment all those years of jacking off in high school were supposed to prepare you for? Back when bumping into a wall could give you a hard-on?"

"Hey, I managed it," he said evenly. "Eventually. I could hear the nurses talking through the walls in those namby pamby tones and after awhile one of them actually called through the door, 'Everything all right in there?'"

"God, I'm sorry."

"Yeah, they had this little form in case you couldn't get yourself under control: 'Did you lose the beginning of your ejaculation, the middle of your ejaculation, the end, none, check one.' Fuckin' A."

Even though she was laughing again, she felt a little prickle. "So did you?"

Timmy looked at Jean blankly.

"Did you lose any?"

"No, honey. I joozed right into their little cup. Then I put it in the brown lunch bag and handed it to the nurse who looked more embarrassed than I did. Okay?"

Jean went over to where he was sitting on the couch and slid between his knees, and they hugged each other, the kind of a hug you sigh into. Even now, nobody can tell Jean that Timmy doesn't love her. Nobody. But three years later, when Timmy was administering Pergonal shots at home, black humor didn't seem to help. You don't want your husband "administering" anything, but you bare your ass anyway and penetration—by needle, by penis—it all starts to feel like a "procedure."

Strangely, but as their efforts to conceive intensified, she dreamed long love-making dreams about other men—her high school English teacher, for instance, who didn't look as he had then but as he would have now, twenty years later, a man who'd aged beautifully, and the gap between a woman of thirty-eight and a man of fifty-two silly and insignificant, which it wasn't when she was sixteen and he was thirty. Ah, time . . . she'd always wanted to hug him, and in her dreams she got to do so much more. Then she dreamed about the son of a woman she used to visit as part of her caseload in the county. His mom had multiple sclerosis and was wheelchair bound. Her husband seemed always to be walking through the rooms on his way to somewhere else. But her teen-aged son sat with them, and asked Jean questions, and later when his mother's speech blurred, he translated what she couldn't make out.

Jean scoffs aloud to the ceiling. Even in dreams we evade. She is the one with defective organs, yet she dreamed as though it were Timmy's fault, and somebody else might be *her* opportunity—perhaps that smooth-skinned boy shining with the gloss of good heath, creamy and delicious, like a soft-serve ice cream.

After the dreams, the psychosomatic pregnancies set in. During the second half of each cycle, she felt exhausted, nauseated, dizzy—she looked up pregnancy, "early signs of," over and over in her books about expecting. She had enormous appetites and justified snacking, snarfing, and stuffing until she'd gained twelve pounds. Not that it showed much on her high metabolism frame. Then she went on health benders—brown rice, tofu, yogurt, kasha, millet, carrot juice. Timmy never knew what hairpin turn their diet would take. Back to despair? Burgers, baked beans, French fries, potato chips, diet Pepsi, frozen carrot cakes. Jean had to have something to bargain with.

God, if you give me a baby I'll give up all this crap, I promise. See, I've done it. I know you're waiting until I prove to you that I can be healthy before you give me a baby, but I can, really and truly, really, truly, really, truly, really, truly. Gasp. I know, you're waiting for me to submit on the deepest level. TOTAL SUBMISSION. That's the best I can do. I don't have the serenity for surrender. I can only submit after a struggle. Okay this is it. I've given up every bad thing. Every good thing? No, every bad thing. I don't even eat popcorn at the movies anymore because it's fake, it's that partially hydrogenated stuff, trans fatty acids. See, I know that's not good for me, not good for the baby, and that's all I think about now.

Then it wouldn't happen. Day 27 or 28 would come around all the same. Her neighbor or her mother would call and say, "Sweetie, you just need to relax and forget about it. Then it will happen." Ever notice that relax is a very unrelaxing word. It has the word *Ax* in it, which is what she wanted to do to all of them. *Relax Ax Ax Ax.* Instead she did what she could: Toffee peanuts, Rocky Road ice cream, frozen burritos, gallons of Chablis.

At some point, after reading about the possibility of side effects with in vitro—"hyperstimulation of the ovaries can in rare incidents lead to stroke"—Jean decided they had to have a will. So she set about using a do-it-yourself "Last Will and Testament Kit." After typing five hundred times "and if not surviving, I name . . . and if not surviving, I name," who wouldn't be desperate for descendants? Just thinking about it, she could hear her grandmother's voice, peppery as a hot cup of chai, "The Ten Commandments were heard, not only by those alive, but by all generations yet unborn." To Grandma Sophie's dismay, Jean turned out to be a secular Jew, not even a Reform Jew—the generations yet unborn didn't seem to speak through her.

Even for her girlfriends, it was hard to admit that they had reached the age of wills and funeral plans and ovaries like charcoal briquettes. Endometriosis, that was one of Jean's conditions. She didn't grow children; she grew cysts and adhesions. She has been roto-rootered, scoured clean by lasers, cheered on by everyone in her family. Through it all, no one seemed very concerned about her health—minimally yes, when she brought the subject up, but they were quick to assure her, "It will be worth it." Add to the first "condition" (endometriosis) the fact that her period was irregular, and she might as well have been a carnival game on the fairway rigged to make men lose. "Step right up, take your aim, three tries a dollar." Make that forty thousand dollars. And then there was Tim—totally normal while the medical texts on her condition vaguely incriminated the type A personality, the Caucasian college-educated woman prone to stress. Whatever that means, thought Jean. Try and find an ambitious woman who isn't prone to stress. Then she'd go back to social work.

Well, even if the chances of her getting pregnant via in vitro fertilization were remote—about 80% of the women who came in didn't—their check in the mail was a sure thing, and the fertility specialists knew you felt better doing something than nothing. Jean went three rounds of I.V.F. for Tim's sake. She felt less like a woman trying to conceive than a drug addict. First, the combination of Pergonal and Metrodin, the follicle-stimulating hormones, a shot every morning for eight days, fifteen times the normal levels of estrogen surging through her body. Her scalp tingled with heat, as though she had a hot plate on high at the back of her head, and she suspected everyone of emotional conspiracy. She'd accuse Tim of talking to her sister about their problems. When he pointed out to Jean how unlikely that was, given the truth (he didn't really like Jean's sister), she'd rage at him for that even though she'd required him to take her side in the family feud for years. Finally, she'd collapse in a soggy sort of contrition, sorry for what she didn't know, just everything.

Each morning before work, she showed up at the fertility clinic, and waited with a whole room full of anxious, obsessed forty-ish women to have an ultrasound and her blood drawn. At the perfect moment, as perceived by the doctor, she went in and had her eggs "retrieved," as the euphemism goes. Dr. Daubresse gave her a final shot of something called H.C.G., human chorionic gonadotropin. "What a relief," Jean told the doctor. "I'd be worried if it was *alien* chorionic gonadotropin." Truth is, the whole thing felt like an alien abduction, and whenever she tried to talk about it she had the urge to add details like salamander silver men with red slits for eyes and the cyclotronic spinning of the ship when they whisked her away. Then she'd only have to hint at "all the terrible things they did to me on the operating table."

Anyway, thirty-six hours after the H.C.G shot, the doc stuck an ultrasound probe into her vagina—Jean loved the way he said, "I'm going to introduce the ultrasound probe now." Introduce? The probe was like your basic dildo and if Mr. Probe and her vagina were introduced under different circumstances . . . well . . . they might have had themselves a mighty fine time. At least Mr. Probe wouldn't expect Jean to get pregnant.

"Okay," she squeaked. After a little scouting around in there, they put her under general sedation and threaded a needle up through her uterus and inserted it into her ovaries so they could suck out the eggs. And while she was conked out on the table, Timmy was supposed to be jacking off somewhere else in the office, which he wouldn't be able to do if he thought for a moment about what Jean was doing. Perhaps it was a practice that became a hazard—picturing someone else while he took himself over the top.

After the weekend, she went back in and had the now fertilized eggs "transferred" back into her body. Though she prayed for feelings of fullness, she felt the way she did now staring at the topography of her ceiling—blank and barren. Once she had hoped, until those first little drops of blood came. Three rounds of I.V.F. were enough—sitting in that office with her ovaries swollen like mushy plums and listening to a bunch of women she'd feel sorry for if she weren't already one of them:

"We rolled over our IRA's to pay for it his time. But you know what they say, Three times is a charm."

"We took out a second mortgage. No other way. This kid is definitely going to have to work her way through college. See, I talk like I'm already raising a kid."

"That's the thing, isn't it? I've got thirty thousand dollars on my credit cards, but it doesn't change the way I feel. Not my husband either."

By the time she and Tim knew the results, Jean felt she had to break membership with the infertility sorority. If she'd added anything to that conversation, she would have ended it. She would have told them that she wished her husband didn't have an inheritance to squander on her womb; she wished they'd quit sooner, before his desire became a fever that withered up their love.

Here's the funny part of forgiveness: you never know if you mean it or not. That morning, in the blush of a new day, while the belief in possibility is still strong, Jean calls Timmy's *new* number. She has really worked herself into a state of forgiveness; she is positively frenzied with it. When she got up off the bed, she drank two strong cups of coffee and ate half a pound of gummy bears. Now she stabs at the phone buttons like the Red Baron trying to keep his biplane from going down. Timmy's *new* wife answers and at the sound of her voice, Jean's heart threatens to turn to ice, arteries choking on ice crystals. Isn't that something that happens to evil stepmothers in fairy tales? But she persists, even though Eliza says "Tim?" when she asks for "Timmy," as though she otherwise wouldn't have known whom Jean was calling for. Yes, Yes, have his name, Jean thinks, whatever little piece of ownership you need. Timmy has his I-can't-talk tone on. He has sounded like that ever since he moved in with Eliza. Jean wonders what else a baby will make you do besides give up meaningful conversation for the rest of your life. She tells him she has gotten this new job managing an apartment complex, not permanent but a hiatus since she isn't going back to social work, really it's OKAY for the time being, actually she was very unhappy at her last job and she's sorry if she took that out on him because she's doing better, less angry every day, and she wants him to know that she's forgiven him and can move on now. There is a pause on the other end before she hears his breathing come back, like maybe he was checking the oven timer or the barbecue coals or something truly important. "Yeah, well, thanks, that's nice," he says, as though he'd opened a present containing silver ice tongs or a cigar slicer.

"You're very goddamn welcome," she says and slams down the phone, drenched in humiliation, waterlogged with it.

She looks around the apartment for something to save her from this near drowning. Typical 1970s bad taste: orange carpet, faux antique brick washed with black and white paint, the sinks and toilets that mustard yellow euphemistically called "harvest gold." She feels queasy. No photos on the countertops. What do you put in the frames when fourteen years of marriage dissolves? Your parents who just passed their forty-fifth wedding anniversary? Then Jean remembers the snapshots on the fridge: with Nan and Tasi at graduation; with Tasi and Virginia at Charlotte's wedding; further up are some cute and dorky school photos of Virginia's son, Milo, and Nan's daughter, Irene. Jean has to stop and think: Why are her girlfriends always stuck on the fridge with magnets? Why did her husband get to be in the frame? She goes in search of the old photos; she knows right where. And she starts ripping Timmy out of the frame and putting her dear friends in.

Her favorite photo is dog-eared and small, a 3 × 5 that at first glance appears to be a bunch of people standing around in a truck bed, but she remembers: it's the steak house parade float for Memorial Day. The Cask and Cleaver, that's the restaurant where she met her friends. All five of them were state school girls—they worked their way through the University of Washington and graduated with debts. In the photo, they're holding tennis ball cans, which seems a bit incongruous, but Jean knows the tennis ball cans are filled with tequila sunrises.

Nan is looking closely at Charlotte who stands on the float above a tin foil tide pool; Charlotte is wrapped from the armpits down in green saran wrap—they found the saran at the discount store in the Christmas leftovers. During the parade, Charlotte wore a cardboard salmon head, but in the picture, she's laughing hard—goofy, incredulous—the kind of abandonment Jean rarely sees in any of them anymore. Once they were cooks, barmaids, waitresses, but now fifteen years later, they're all something else: Nan is an obstetric nurse, Virginia is a state college instructor, Tasi is a public relations writer, Charlotte used to be a caterer, but now she's deciding again, and Jean? Until a month ago she was a social worker, and now she's . . . what? An apartment complex manager? A divorcé (in the parlance of her parent's generation) and childless to boot. Jean shakes her head. To think there was a time they all assumed they'd have families when they wanted them.

From the photo, Virginia waves her spatula at Jean. Her job on the float was to flip real steaks on a bright red Weber kettle barbecue while wearing a poofy chef's hat. She was as theatrical then as she is now in front of her classes, and her life as an English instructor and mother involves at least as much multi-tasking as talking, cooking, and gesturing from a moving platform. Charlotte, the sexy salmon, stands dead-center on the float. Nan and Jean wrapped her, handing the saran rolls back and forth around her lovely hips, arse, and thighs. Jean is certain it made Nan feel shorter, rounder, and curvier than ever. They all knew Charlotte was more feminine and photogenic than the rest of them, and there was also something joyful about her that they cherished though at times it seemed a joy too quickly ascendant, risky in its altitude. This drew them to her, made them protective, made her more than their symbolic center. Jean studies herself as the mock waitress wearing the Tyrolean get-up she sewed for the role of Heidi in a play. Ever eager to help, was that the message? Climb any mountain and all that? Meanwhile, Tasi plays the mock maître-d' in tailcoat and vaudevillian moustache. Soon she'll employ that oratorical flair in a male-dominated company. Nan is the only one staring straight into the camera—her shoulders are as wide as a man's and her jaw has clean, strong lines. In her work shirt and baseball cap, she is ruggedly handsome. She watches them, clearly amused, but there is no way she is going to put herself on view for the town. Besides, she has to drive; the rest of them are too drunk.

VIRGINIA

∾

The Costco Debacle

It's a Wednesday night—Finley's night with Milo—and Virginia Alexander is trying to work on her novel, propped up by caffeine and polluted by mundane detail. (Will her son really have goat teeth or is it okay that a canine is protruding from his gum and another tooth has popped up behind one of his baby teeth like a mossy pier piling?) A professor once told her she had a brilliant metaphorical mind. Was she stoned in his class? All she knows is that whatever she had seems to have departed. Sometimes she wonders if she broke up with Finley because it was the only way to get her novel written. Truth is, she envied her divorced friends who had Wednesday and Saturday nights to themselves, or some equivalent, while she had Finley and Milo to feed seven out of seven, or if she was lucky they'd go out for a hamburger and bowling on the weekend and she'd get three hours.

Virginia has quit having an agenda anymore for how to be a writer. Before she and Finley separated, she'd come up with elaborate plans for getting her novel written, but she kept failing at her own program. Get up at 5:00 AM, or write till midnight . . . she always ended up face down on the mattress in her sweat pants on Saturday night. One evening after teaching, she leaned her head back before turning the key in the ignition and passed out in the university parking lot. She woke to the sound of the janitors dropping trash to the bottom of an empty dumpster. Now her classes keep getting larger, without parity in her paycheck. The students can't register for the courses they need, and they're so desperate, they about hang onto her ankles. None of them have any time either. They all work thirty to forty hour weeks, few of them capable of their true grade point average because they're exhausted. When it was time for more budget cuts, some inane association of professors spurred on by the dean held a panel discussion entitled "Doing More With Less." She debated showing up with a tuna noodle casserole recipe. Meatless chili anyone? The college hiked tuition again; the government cut student loans. Not a bad way to get new recruits for the military. She doesn't feel she deserves to complain about her novel.

Now that she has two whole nights a week to work on it, she detests everything she writes. What she is working on isn't the kind of novel she ever envisioned sitting down to write. She imagined a text swept along by an impassioned voice, told by patterns of dream-like images (tra la) that arranged themselves as motifs (la la) till it reached a sort of critical mass that construed plot (yeah, right), and then she could go back to the beginning and craft the whole. Well, there's no time for that. She'd fall asleep first. (She is always short on sleep.)

Still, it's easier than last year when Milo tried to kill himself on the hour. He'd seen some library film called "Preschool Power" and went about the house chanting "I can do it on my own, I can do it once I been shown." He stood on a kitchen chair to get cereal and gashed his head on the stove hood. Things like that. Finley and Virginia stayed up fighting all night. When Virginia taught class the next day, her mind was like one of those cranes with a big steel claw—the signal had to travel a great way up and a great way down before the jaw seized the material. What her students see in her face is grim tenacity. It almost hurts to go the way of another's mind. Her own has been on lease for so long now, it feels like a rental car returned with too much mileage. But she'll run the engine for whatever's left in it.

She stares hard at the screen. Shall she start a new paragraph? Shall she eat more M & M's? She sighs heavily. Writers like to talk about their characters' voices with mystical reverence, as thought they were channeling them telepathically. Virginia feels like she's plugged into a constant conference call: a slew of women characters who won't stop talking. They make her tired, but she is so darn loyal she hangs in there while they complain, though her mind does wander. Forty-six digressions later, she makes it back to the conference call and says "unh hunh." The novel progresses.

She hates to say it, but that's the way she felt today talking to Charlotte. She is mad in a way that she can't admit to Charlotte. Because Charlotte has all the time in the world and she doesn't know what to do with it. She goes on "self-actualization" retreats. She studies Jungian dream therapy or enrolls in a massage school but drops out. She sees a new shrink. She gardens and they eat organic. She's like those people with a live-in nanny who tell you they never let their children watch TV. Charlotte debates what she should do with her life that won't rock the boat with Darius, that will fit in with his travel plans and her hostess duties. Virginia listened today, knowing vaguely that she should feel something more. She has known Charlotte since grade school when they convinced themselves they had supernatural powers, and told their classmates they'd learned astral projection. Charlotte stood on top of a picnic table to demonstrate. She held her breath so long she passed out—smack on the pavement—then off to the hospital with a hairline skull fracture. Virginia will never forget the jagged crevasse that appeared just beside her part, or how she felt peering into the pomegranate red that glistened with depth. No more fantasies of astral projection now, Virginia thinks. At thirty-eight, Charlotte is trying to decide whether or not to have an abortion.

Virginia did suggest that having the baby might be the right thing, the reason (how did she put it?) that Charlotte was in such a contemplative space since she'd quit the catering business, the reason (what New Age vocab did she resort to?) Charlotte hadn't moved onto the next thing. Well, Charlotte had liked that for about five minutes, but then she'd told Virginia she had post-traumatic stress syndrome from her childhood, and that Darius had been abused as a child, and this was bringing up some *really* bad stuff for them and she didn't think they were *meant* (more New Age than ever) to raise a child. Virginia must have sighed then, maybe even groaned, because Charlotte said, "I know you have to go." Yeah, Virginia thought, I've got four other women waiting to complain on their fictitious phone lines, and their lives are even messier than yours. But what Charlotte makes Virginia see scares her: someone who has too much time to feel while she has none. Virginia has got seventy-five papers to grade by Friday, and every morning Milo has a stomachache because he hates school. No wonder she can't seem to focus on her sense of loss, only her impatience with it. By the end of the phone conversation, she wants to shout at Charlotte: "Just do it and get it over with." That's what she's done by kicking Finley out. She used to think she'd lost her feelings for Fin because of their particular problems, but lately Virginia is beginning to think it's more general than that, and she wonders how many women besides herself feel carved by exigency to a ruthless core.

She has had to get very practical since she kicked Finley out a week after Christmas—it would be nicer to say, "since my husband left," but it's simply not true. *I guess I'm serious about my New Year's resolutions,* Virginia thinks, turning her computer off with a vehement flick of the switch. The little window appears to tell her she has not shut down properly.

Speaking of Finley, the next morning she runs into him at Costco, of all places. She doesn't know how it is that she ends up writing checks in there for two and three hundred dollars when she is so busy saving money. But you get inspired by quantity: A year's supply of salsa and a packing crate full of waffles, half of which you'll throw away because of freezer burn a year later when you find them crammed in the back. She isn't buying like that anymore—with the instinct of an ant pulling and pushing a whole wasp's body into the mound. Really, she'd once enjoyed shopping like that—when Finley and Milo were home—everyone's little need satisfied to surfeit and beyond. Now she is in there buying a quantity of Kotex that will last till menopause; that's her mood. And there's Finley, her soon-to-be ex-husband and his sailboat buddy, social climbers with credit cards. He looks *good*, she has to admit, that thinning forelock of his hair still high enough to make him boyish and breezy. There for his econo-booze. She snatches a three-gallon teddy bear jar of animal crackers and throws it on top of the Kotex pads when she sees him coming. She wishes she'd changed out of her Peruvian sweater; it's the same one she was wearing the morning he left, and right now it makes her feel about as attractive as a couch cushion. She wonders why that suddenly seems to matter.

"Hey Ginny," he says pleasantly.

"Hey yourself, Finley," she gives him a smile with her skeptical affection, the only kind she seems to have left.

"Here we are, using up the last of our joint membership at Costco."

"Yeah," she says with some disbelief, both of them clearly thinking what they aren't saying: *Might as well get some good out of it.*

"So, you're living on the boat still?" she asks, a mere whereabouts question.

"Yeah, figured I'd save money till the weather changes."

"Sounds like a plan." *After you spent all my money, you jerk, you figure out how to save some of your own?*

The boat was the debt load that broke the camel's back, though to be fair Virginia had agreed to it. She wanted Finley to be happy. She just didn't know what else he was up to.

"You still sound a little bitter, Ginny."

He laughs quickly and gives her a darting glance, wanting to get the guilt over as fast as possible.

"Why should I be bitter?" she says. "I'm the one who chose to roll over my retirement to consolidate our debt." *Then we cut up the Visa cards and MasterCards one night and made love upon the paid-for mattress of our new life.*

A few months later, Virginia ripped open what she thought were introductory card offers with Sears, and J.C. Penney, only to find he'd already enrolled.

Back at Costco, Finley finds a sudden cuticle on his thumb which he has to attend to while her mind reels through all the crap. Tool charges: compressors, nail guns, weed eaters, sanders. Things you'd need for home and boat improvement. Don't you know how virile a man feels wearing a tool belt and turning the crank on something loud?

It's not that Finley didn't want to pay the bills. Virginia remembers the end. You know, that moment of terrible finality. Gong, it goes, reverberating for about an hour in your head. Finley had put the bills outside on the patio table. It was early fall. Maybe as he was walking up from the mailbox he thought of something else. She could hear him in the shop, hammering on the playhouse he was making for Milo. Her husband, the master builder. If you're Fin, it's easy to lay bills flat on the table and forget about them. Anything one-dimensional is infinitely forgettable.

Virginia couldn't bring herself to tell him, though she knew he was in the garage, nails between his lips, brow furrowed. He was probably thinking—pitch, scale, declension. Or did he think from down to up? Footings, floor joists, girders, walls, rafters, ridgepoles? Truth is, she didn't know how he thought. She sat and watched the bills blow down the driveway, a flock of homing numbers. She remembers thinking: *I can't read any more collection agency notices.* They always wrote, "We look forward to receiving payment," and she used to write back, "We look forward to paying you." She thought about what Fin's expression would be when she told him the bills had blown away—the Big

Gulp. She didn't want to keep administering reality like an unfortunate dose.

At Costco, he can't even look at her. She sighs finally and makes an offering. "With all the remodeling we did, we'd still have had to sell the house to pay the debt."

Poof went my parents' down payment. She listens to herself and wonders how goddamn gracious will she get? Well, she had already peeled him alive, hadn't she? Deveined him like a shrimp . . . when he took up remodeling as his game plan and quit seriously hunting for work. *Who me, bitter? Instead I'm here buying sanitary napkins. Things are looking up.*

Finley picks up a blank videotape, on sale and piled high upon a nearby table. "That reminds me," he says, "I've got some photos." Then he trots off to his abandoned basket to get them. Apparently, his buddy has decided they need chips and peanuts with all that beer. Right then and there, Virginia thinks, thank God Nan and Jean are coming over tonight. Immediately she feels lighter, as though she were merely an observer looking for the choice details that will provide a humorous anecdote that evening.

But when he comes back, she leans into him to see the pictures; together they make a familiar gesture. Their bodies don't know any better. The pictures are from Christmas, a little glary, on the red side, as though all that red foil around the poinsettias created its own light in the wintry rooms. Virginia recalls drinking a lot just to get through the holidays, more likely that accounts for the ruddy hue. But there he was on the living room floor with Milo, putting together a bicycle patiently. Finley has such putting-together patience. The old "what if" rises like a primitive fish from the base of her belly. *What if he could have gotten the money thing under control? Was America's relentless invitation to financial suicide his fault?*

Virginia's eyes are stinging and she can feel her nose itch the way it does when she is about to sneeze her way into serious bawling. The photos shuffle in his hands. A gap on one roll. His trip to California. She sees a woman's midriff slightly blurry, the angle of the gunnels behind her all wrong. Someone leering into the camera, goofing off, holding his beer next to his head in the frame. Then she sees Finley, hand at the tiller, his confident-for-the-camera-smile. "These are just some of the boat," he says, dismissively. Virginia falls back from his shoulder. The person who took the photo of the woman's midriff must have been lying down.

"Well, maybe you could make some doubles of the Christmas ones," she says. "I wouldn't mind having some of those."

"Oh, here," he says, shrugging. "It's no biggie. You can have them right now." And he shuffles through the photos like playing cards, dealing her the last of their togetherness and keeping the beer and bare midriff for himself.

NAN

∾

The Bummer Tent

The camellia next to Virginia's red ranch house has been tightly wrapped in Christmas lights; it looks like a bush that's been taken hostage. Virginia told Nan that Milo was disappointed the eaves of the house weren't decked out, but she'd be damned if she was going to ask Finley to come over and do it. Though all of them were English majors at the University of Washington, Virginia is the only one who stayed in the field—she published a story collection before Milo was born and teaches now at Issaquah State University.

As Nan waits by the front door, steam pours from the dryer vent and the neighborhood smells vaguely of fabric softener and lawn mulch. No one comes to the sound of the bell. The topiary junipers in front look furry and overgrown, and most of the beauty bark has blown away. Now that Finley doesn't live here anymore, Virginia says she's going to leave the Christmas lights up year-round. Her disregard is flagrant. She and Finley used to live in a beautifully restored Victorian with a cupola on the second floor. How Ginny adored that view in her office. But they had to sell the house on an emergency basis. Finley was between jobs and there were too many home improvement loans. Nan doesn't think she's forgiven him. He certainly didn't live in the little prefab ranch for long. She hears laughter from inside, and thumping. She thought she saw Jean's Toyota on the street, but now she is sure of it. She pushes the door open, calling out as she slips from her shoes.

The furnishings in Virginia's house don't exactly reflect her taste. Every time her father remarries (and he is the marrying as well as divorcing kind), he has to get rid of the previous wife's furniture, so he gives it to Virginia. The last wife liked big cabbage chintz prints and wing-backed chairs. But in Virginia's house benign neglect has worn away the pretension, faded the pattern, made for coziness. Where the chair back has gone threadbare, she's thrown an afghan over it. And Virginia has no regard for matching or complementing—her style is haphazard—Milo's art tacked on the backs of doors, prints of Mary Cassat and Frida Kahlo paintings she's had since college splattered with a little egg or waffle batter, and bulletin boards festooned to the edges with paper. You have to be careful not to trip at her house, true of Nan's as well: Little Tyke tables, Tinkertoys, tubs of Lego's on the floor. Nan notices Virginia has put exercise equipment in what used to be Finley's office. In training to forget him, she supposes . . . it does involve a kind of rigor. At least Virginia hasn't added insult to injury by making it into a guest room.

"Oooo, you're here!" Virginia calls as she barrels down the hallway. What Virginia lacks in grace, she's always made up for with effusion. At U.W. (U.Dub as everyone in Seattle pronounces it), she wore yellow tennis shoes and men's flannel shirts—a sort of uniform to disguise the busty body she felt got in the way of being taken seriously. Though she has to dress the part for teaching now, at home she still comes up with personal uniforms and wears them for months on end with little variation. This winter her favorite top is a huge lumpen South American sweater with oddly shaped animals knitted into it in bright colors. For the last three months, as far as Nan can tell, she's only alternated turtlenecks and blue jeans. "I'm an artist," she once said in the kitchen, "I don't have time to mess around with all these stupid details." Her eyes are a snapping blue, and she wears her chestnut hair cropped so short, she doesn't have to brush it. If you'd known her as long as Nan has, you would recognize her little ways of winning the war against time.

Nan pours herself a glass of wine in the galley kitchen, relaxing to the banter and barrage of her friends' conversation. Jean and Virginia have grown closer now that both their marriages have come unglued, though Jean is officially divorced while Virginia's marital status remains murky. In Virginia's own words, "No one knows if the separation will take, not even us."

"Thank God tonight was our night," Jean calls from the living room. "I had to come over and roast Timmy."

"Roast Timmy?" Nan says, "Your apartment doesn't have a fireplace, does it?" Nan steadies herself with Virginia's knee as she sinks into the couch beside her. Because of her short limbs, overstuffed furniture is a bane to Nan; it makes her feel like a munchkin.

Jean laughs, a sound throaty and cooing at the same time. "All I need is a fire *pit*, really." She looks like a flamenco dancer, dramatically, powerfully thin—not enervated model-thin, but ropy and sinewy, and lusciously dark. There is something staccato about her movements, something accented in the way she puts her heels down or waves off a remark. She comes by her thinness honestly, the only one of them who runs the risk of getting too thin. And she really does eat. While the rest of them are trying not to lay into the Oreos, Jean's high metabolism is working overtime.

At U.W., she loved the literature of the mad, Gogol and Dostoevsky. Later she and Nan discovered the madness of the confined in women's studies—*The Yellow Wallpaper, The Awakening, To Room 19*.

Virginia had no patience with the protagonists of early feminist literature; she wanted one of those women to get a gun and turn it on someone other than herself. *Lady Chatterley's Lover* suited her better. But Jean's steady diet of the disaffected led somewhere. In the fall, she entered grad school and pursued a Master's in Social Work. For fifteen years, she was a terrific social worker—the E.R. staff nurses thought her psych-evals among the best—but when she lost Timmy, she dumped her career, too. Nan keeps telling her she'll work through this, it's just burnout, but Jean is not ready yet to consider the future. It's been an unkind concept in her life.

"So why are we roasting Timmy?" Nan asks as casually as she can.

"Well, we tried making a toast to him," Virginia interjects, "but it didn't work."

"Yeah, from toast to roast. It's such an easy segue for me." Jean reaches for her glass.

"What's the occasion?"

"Tim's a dad now. He sent me a birth announcement."

"How considerate of him."

"Yeah, I could steal the baby and become one of those women on the back of a dry cleaning coupon under the caption: 'Have you seen them?'" Jean follows this comment with a long swig of wine. Her laugh is quick and harsh. "To think I used to counsel people."

"I always wonder how many of those women are running from violent men," Virginia offers.

Nan shrugs. "Or how many of them are exacting revenge. Taking the kids is the ultimate way to get even."

"We're lucky to have you, Nan, the only one of us who still manages to be fair-minded," Jean adds.

"That's because she married Clay. We'd be nicer too if we could find a man that good." Virginia's laugh rings in the air.

They're speaking in code now, as old friends will, going around a pain that's too big to go at directly. Jean taps a cigarette out of its case and back in with one finger. In a few minutes, she'll palm her lighter and go smoke on the patio, and Virginia and Nan will have a few words about how she's really doing.

Jean rises from the couch but stands, talking and tapping the cigarette case against her thigh. "I actually felt glad for a few minutes when I got the announcement. I mean, I have to on some level, right? Timmy finally has a baby. But the good feeling evaporated. It'll be the same for me with Charlotte. I'll have so much fun buying a gift for the baby shower and then I'll have to make myself go to it."

"I never buy anything for the baby anymore," Nan says. "I almost always buy a nursing pillow or that foot gel that makes your feet tingle. I'm so pragmatic. All I can think of are aching arms and aching feet."

Around Jean, Nan turns sardonic on the joys of motherhood, continually pointing out the wear and tear of it. It's almost involuntary and though she feels emotionally dishonest, Jean seems to appreciate her tone of hard-bitten martyrdom. But, really, it's not how Nan feels about motherhood. She takes a swig of her drink and looks to Virginia.

Virginia's snappy blue eyes have gone as glassy as cat's eye marbles. She's sitting all tucked into herself, legs pulled up under that oversize sweater.

"What is it?" Jean and Nan say in unison.

"You don't know?" she asks.

"Know what?"

"Well . . . Charlotte called me last night . . . I assumed she'd already spoken to both of you."

"About what?" Jean says, placing one of her long sinewy arms at her hip. But the answer is already clear to Nan.

"Charlotte's not going to keep it after all. I'm sorry to be the one to tell you. I guess Darius came home from Seoul and they had some sort of blowout about it."

Nan notes the transition from the word "baby" to the word "it." Virginia has begun the necessary distancing.

"That shouldn't change her mind," says Jean, plunking her arse down so suddenly on the ottoman, it gives off an audible hiss. "She's thirty-eight years old, for Christ's sake."

"Charlotte called me twice," Virginia says, "last night and this morning." Her words are oddly punctuated and twangy as she alternates speaking with popping peanuts into her mouth.

"Let me guess," says Jean, "Drunk last night and sober this morning."

Virginia allows for a lengthy silence as she wipes the peanut dust from her fingers onto her jeans. She's implying a sympathy Jean obviously can't extend to Charlotte. It's not as though Jean hasn't called up drunk a few times since Timmy left a year ago.

"Listen, Jean," Nan says, breaking the silence, "I know this is hard for you. Still, I think we should be allowed to cry when we want children, and allowed to cry when we don't want them."

Nan really believes this. Either way demands a loss. She is not speaking to spare Jean now. Women are taught not to admit how high the demands of raising children are—the years of relentless drudgery and slop, plus all the promotions and vacations you can't take, conferences you can't attend, hikes you can't go on, books you can't read. And yet if you don't have children, it's a different loss of self, the mother-self who inhales the scent of her baby's neck and is flooded by ferocious love, love as a force of nature. It's good to know you can love like that.

"No way," says Jean, shaking her head. "Charlotte is four months gone, and she's talking about having an abortion."

"I know," says Virginia, "it's late, and the decision seems sudden. But Darius never really wanted the baby. For awhile she thought she could persuade him."

"Why does Charlotte defer to that asshole?" Jean hisses.

Virginia hugs her knees, burrowing further into her sweater. Her tone is tentative, ever the child of a vengeful divorce. "Maybe Charlotte's doing the best she can."

"That's bullshit," Jean practically shouts. "You could say the same of a psychopath or a pedophile. Are we all afraid to say that something is wrong here?"

"Take it easy, Jean," Nan says. "You're among friends."

"I don't understand. Why is Darius acting like this pregnancy is such a big deal? It's not like Charlotte got AIDS or they lost all their money in the stock market. We're talking about a baby."

"Because," Virginia says through clenched teeth, "when they got married, they agreed not to have children."

"So what? When Timmy and I got married we didn't agree to five years of fertility problems. There should be a statute of limitations on the future you agreed to. Because it changes all the time, and most of it is out of your control."

"I guess he doesn't feel it was out of their control," Virginia replies evenly.

"Fucking control freak." Jean snaps her hand back as if she were slapping at a bug.

"Listen," Virginia says in a tone of quiet exasperation, "Charlotte chose Darius. He's her type, authoritarian. Remember that guy in college, Richard? I heard years of talking trash about him. One night my eyeballs were floating in it and I asked point blank, why don't you leave him? 'I don't know,' she says in this little lost voice, the same voice she used last night."

Jean is pacing in front of the couch, pounding her heels down in a staccato rhythm. Virginia is looking down the neck hole of her gigantic sweater. Nan tries to decelerate the conversation by inserting herself back into it.

"What'd you say to her last night, Ginny?"

Virginia raises her head slowly. "I told her we'd support her decision either way. And she said thank you Virginia. I need to know I can count on my friends. She used that fragile voice she puts on. I'm sick of it, too. Get out of the bummer tent, Charlotte." Virginia quaffs half a glass of wine in one slug.

"What do you mean, bummer tent?" Jean asks stiffly.

"You know, like at Woodstock, the place you went to when you were on a bad trip. The bummer tent."

"We're too young for Woodstock," Nan says, fighting the inward sensation of plummeting.

"Don't you feel sad?" Virginia says, instantly putting a name to it. "I feel sad. I remember how Charlotte used to come over to my house after school because her mother was still working the cosmetics counter at Nordstrom's. And her Dad, even in college he'd say the money was coming and then not send it. Charlotte's paying such a high price to be taken care of now."

Virginia is staring at the empty grate in her fireplace, and Nan finds herself staring at it, too, suddenly depleted. She looks at Jean, standing across from them, arms folded, and catches her eye. Jean jerks her head slightly, leading with her chin, a quick acknowledgment and rejection.

"Sad story, all right," Jean says. "Look what happened to our evening."

"Well," Nan says, getting up from the couch, "everybody gets their toughs, I guess."

Virginia leans her head back into the couch pillows and moans: "God, I've got so many papers to grade."

She offers to make them coffee and they move to the kitchen, relieved to go through the motions of something so basic. Jean comments on the crèche next to the fruit bowl.

"Let me guess. Milo put the sheep and cows on the rooftop with the angels."

"It's a statement." Virginia says. "Milo believes firmly that animals get to go to heaven."

They exchange reports on their holiday plans. Jean just returned from a visit to her parents and her brothers.

"You know, the spinster aunt routine, but at least I'm Jewish and didn't have to subject myself to 'a child is born, behold the infant,' and all that torture."

Virginia nods. "Every Christmas, Tasi threatens to become a Jehovah." She is speaking of Anastasia, the absent one tonight, who is firmly single and "child-free," as she likes to say.

The women lean against the kitchen counters, in the old teenage poses of comfort and confidences. When Jean goes to the bathroom, Virginia looks at Nan with her head cocked. "That was a mellow evening."

"Yeah," Nan says, "I'm beat." The kitchen fluorescents are making her see silvery spots.

"In a way, this must be hardest on you . . . because you've seen so much."

Nan smiles wanly at Virginia, grateful for her awareness, but she can't think of anything to say. It seems to her that ambivalence is the only intelligent response to Charlotte's decision. An image coalesces out of the silvery spots, from her residency days, standing by while a doctor performed a late term dilation and extraction—in the tray a tiny, glistening arm, detached and unreal looking, like something that would fall out of a model airplane kit along with a propeller and decals. The urge to put things back together was upon her almost before she recognized it, and then following that, the visceral response, her throat closing with a shudder against the contents of her stomach.

Nothing could have prepared her for it, not even as the daughter of a nurse and a campus minister who'd met in the abortion underground of the 1960s. Nan grew up knowing what OB Infection Ward meant, whole floors in the big urban public hospitals devoted to botched abortions. Her mother worked the ward and volunteered on a suicide hot line on the weekends. Calls kept coming in from pregnant women. Hazel was supposed to say "Call your doctor," but she felt foolish and angry even as she said it. On the state statute book, abortion was described as manslaughter. On the OB infection ward at Tacoma General Hospital, foul-smelling stuff leaked from women's uteruses. Women turned jaundiced from infection, went into shock, sometimes congestive heart failure. They'd die, foaming at the mouth.

Years later when her mother switched from OB to trauma, a resident inquired how she was able to make the transition so smoothly. Nan remembers her mother laughing as she recounted the anecdote to her father: "I told him, if you'd been where I have for the last eleven years, you wouldn't need to ask." The women on the hot line did not want crisis intervention or extended treatment—they wanted abortions. Instead of saying, "Call your doctor," Hazel began conducting extensive interviews, making quiet referrals to specific doctors and midwives.

Nan's father, Sherwin, certainly hadn't intended to become an abortion activist either. He was a United Church of Christ minister on the University of Washington campus in the late 1950s, but a young co-ed he was fond of had gone to do missionary work in Mexico and had bled to death on a bus after an illegal abortion. It was more than he could bear. Nan wondered if people even knew that anymore, that campus ministers became abortion counselors. Her father had had no text to consult in this matter, only his heart to follow. The word "abortion" does not appear in the Old Testament or the New Testament. If a girl felt she had to do it, her father gave practical advice: take someone with you, watch for dirty instruments, and be sure to see a doctor afterward. Soon he grew bold, listed himself in the local telephone directory: Clergy Counseling Service for Problem Pregnancies—and that boldness led him to Nan's mother.

Nan is not sure how to describe what heft and pith her parents' history gives the moment in Virginia's kitchen, only that she is sure of it and at the same time too tired to articulate what it means. Virginia reaches out, strokes Nan's cheek.

"Get some sleep," she says gently.

Nan startles, realizes she hasn't responded in all this time. "Thanks, Virginia," she says, appreciating her friend's acknowledgment of her suddenly vast weariness.

"Roll your windows down," Virginia calls after her.

Out on the driveway, Nan is absurdly grateful for the cheeriness of reindeer on rooftops and big plastic candy canes at jaunty angles and all the bright pinpricks of light through the winter dark.

TASI

∾

Figurines

For years now Charlotte Cline and Tasi Charbonneau have been meeting for lunch, the third Thursday of every month. It's a relief to have a set date, a social occasion you don't have to discuss. In this age of dueling day planners, e-mail, pagers, and cell phones, you can become so irritated by re-scheduling, you resent certain people too much to bother seeing them at all. This way, there are no logistics, sort of the way it was when they met in college.

They've planned to meet at a swanky little bistro behind the fish market, past the shouting and the brass pig where tourists drop their coins, one of those cafés you'd never know was there if someone hadn't told you, like so many others in serpentine Seattle.

As Tasi rides the clogged arterial in a mizzling rain, she gets a call on her cell. At Zeffirelli & Associates, the staff is required to be on twenty-four-hour call. No, it's not a law firm, though she is used to making that correction; Z & A is a public relations company, "strategic marketing and results-oriented communications."

—Tasi at Zeffirelli & Associates—

—Imperial Cruises wants text changes, now.

—Well, we quoted them an hourly rate if they went above and beyond the copy deadline. It's in the contract—

—hen***read***dy***it***on time—

—Yeah, we're breaking up. Stop moving around the office—

—***ey've***re-ead***contract—

—How much time do we have before the trade show?—

—Eight***ing***days—

—Not a problem. We'll send it rush to the printer. If they want to pay up the wazoo for changing the signage this late in the game, that's their prerogative—

—I'll get***new bid.—

—Okay, Chet. I'll be back in an hour, maybe a little more—

At lunch, her mind is drawn to the meaning of other, more personal contractual agreements. Charlotte tells her about the abortion, but Tasi just can't get all that worked up over it. As Charlotte talks, she toys with the candles nestled in a bamboo tray of rock salt.

"It's something I have to go through with," she says matter-of-factly.

"You knew when you married Darius that he didn't want to have kids." Tasi opens her palms in a quintessentially business gesture.

"That was the deal," Charlotte says, "I agreed."

"In my view, what you agree to is binding." Tasi doesn't add that in her experience anything beyond the agreement and you should expect costs.

Charlotte shrugs, raises one shoulder in an infinitely feminine gesture. She's cropped her hair super short and bleached it blonder. It sticks up off her head like dandelion fluff. No matter what she does, she looks like a nineteenth-century children's book illustration—fine-boned, all eyes and pursed mouth.

"Sorry, I don't mean to sound hard." Tasi adds.

"No, no." Charlotte says. "Darius suffered some sort of abuse as a kid; he knows his limitations."

"Don't worry. I'm not going to make Darius into a villain."

Charlotte tears up a little, which surprises Tasi. "Thanks," she says, "I'm relieved. It's too easy an out for everyone."

"Forget about what anyone else thinks. Just get through it."

"Will you drive me if he won't go?"

"He won't go?"

Charlotte makes a little hissing sound and reaches for her Bloody Mary. Tasi rushes in to fill the void.

"Sure, if you need me to."

Later they discuss a business plan for the new catering company Charlotte wants to launch. Weddings only, this time. A good niche for her, Tasi thinks. A clearly targeted market so she won't lose focus.

While they're waiting for the crème caramel, Charlotte keeps staring at the light fixtures, which are geometric shapes covered in rice paper. Tasi doesn't know why, but Charlotte has always been spacey and sensitive; she just doesn't seem to have the fine screen filters. When they were in school at U.W. everything got to her. There was this retarded boy who lived downstairs in the apartment building. "It's so sad," Charlotte would say. Tasi regarded him as a smelly adolescent. The long whiskers on the underside of his jaw made her shiver. In this hollow voice, he would holler all afternoon to his dog and the dog would never come. They all chatted with him cheerfully enough between their comings and goings, but one afternoon Tasi came home from class and found Charlotte frantic. There were muddy footprints across her bed, a ladder propped against the building wall on the alley side.

"The big dufus has probably been rifling through our underwear," Tasi said to Charlotte, who launched into this shrieky sort of laugh.

"Ben?" she said, "Ben?"

"Who else would leave the ladder up? It's the one from the garage."

Tasi pulled Charlotte with her when she went to bang on the neighbor's door. She told Ben's father she'd call the police if it happened again. Charlotte mostly hid behind Tasi's shoulder, occasionally popping out to nod and concur.

At U.W., Charlotte hung out in coffee houses with a group Tasi dubbed the doomsday auctioneers, a scruffy bunch always trying to outbid each other for the most final description of gloom: the slaughter of seals on the Aleutian Islands, the mass killing of whales by the Japanese, the severely stunted deer that survive corrosive rain in the Adirondacks. She tried to credit Charlotte's good intentions. After all, she was a child of the Cold War too; it's not like she didn't worry about humankind decimating itself down to the last atom, but she joined the letter-writing drives because this other stuff seemed pointlessly depressing. Meanwhile, Charlotte dated this guy who wore parachute pants and even slept in his little knitted beanie. "Get real," Tasi said when Charlotte finally broke up with him. "He talked about the court proceedings against Hooker Chemical Corporation and the poisoning of the people in Love Canal for a month straight." Tasi remembered taking huge bong hits with Charlotte after which Charlotte confessed that she'd broken it off with him when she'd found a banana peel in his bed. But afterwards Charlotte continued to hang out with the doomsday auctioneers. Her new strategy was to memorize the megatons that could be accounted for in the U.S. arsenal "at the present date," so she could outdo anyone at any time.

Tasi likes to think of herself as scrutinizing or scrupulous, but not cynical. Today, she reaches across the table and takes Charlotte's hands, remembering a night years ago when she woke to find Charlotte sitting beside her bed, hands open in her lap. Tasi thought she was dreaming, but Charlotte really was sitting in Tasi's typing chair. She'd rolled it over next to the bed.

"Charlotte," Tasi whispered.

"Hmm," she answered as though she were the one still dreaming.

"What are you doing?"

Charlotte had laughed suddenly. "I couldn't sleep. I thought maybe if I watched you sleeping it would help me."

Is it any wonder Tasi will always love her? At lunch, she tells Charlotte, "Don't worry. I'll be there, lunch or no lunch."

Tasi groans when she reads that the expressway lanes are closed. She's got fifteen minutes to make it back to the office. Interstate-5 is more like a flooded river than a highway. Log booms, modular houses, and boats float by on truck beds stories above her Toyota. If Tasi pulls out to pass a truck, she can count on some zippy little car cutting into the fifty-foot space between them just to show her how it's done. Forget it. She'll plug along and think.

Tasi knows other women would expect her to be mortified by the abortion. Certainly, it would fit in with the way the women at work see her. *Poor Tasi, who doesn't have any kids.* As if having kids were the only way to achieve maturity or happiness. Never mind that they're all secretaries and Tasi is the only female executive—well, the only one who has lasted anyway. Her co-workers keep reminding her that there's still time to get married and have a baby if she gets a move on. "Look," she finally said, "maybe I don't want any kids. I wiped my brothers' butts for years and made their macaroni and I'm done." Actually, she only feels that way some of the time, but she is definitely *not* one of these women who falls apart every time she sees some drooling baby. She'll be fine either way. Nan gets it, but not Jean. Some women can't imagine their lives without children. Really, who can account for the varying degrees of desire in that regard? Any more than one can having a sweet tooth?

Tasi knows it's callous of her, but she can't help it. The others are getting all worked up about the age of the fetus. Okay, so it's second trimester; the procedure is still legal. She pictures the fetus as a polliwog. Yes, buggy eyes, but gelatinous, unable to leave the water. She couldn't kill a frog, capable of sitting on a rock and croaking at her, but as a child she caught a polliwog or two and left them to dry in the sun. She doesn't remember any bones. She realizes this may be a lot of hooey, a means of justification. But the world plays upon our sympathies all the time, plays tricks too. Tasi remembers the time a belt in her refrigerator needed replacing, and the big white box emitted diminutive squeaks; it sounded like a batch of baby hamsters. When the repairman came in and opened his toolbox, she had sudden protective urges: to shout, to kick his toolbox away, to wrest the wrench from his hands.

Anyway, polliwogs, that's how she got through her abortion, by picturing them. It wasn't so bad, and the benefits were enormous. Can one talk about that? Tasi wonders. The benefits of an abortion? And she doesn't just mean not having to raise the child. She's not sure how to explain this, but afterwards she felt like she had stepped into the river of time, like she had joined womankind. She thought about every woman before her who had ever wanted a baby or not wanted a baby, or grieved a baby, or wished a baby away, or wished it away and *then* grieved it. She felt, for the first time, that she belonged to women in a special way, as though they were in a place and time where not one of them would compare themselves to her, nor she to them, and not one of them would compare their pain to hers nor hers to theirs. And they would none of them set about the task of ranking pain—least to worst—only nod with knowing looks.

The abortion also helped Tasi get away from Corty. Really, it was her coming-of-age. She can imagine how popular that idea would be with Jean. At least Virginia understood. She was the one who said: "You've got to decide if the fucking you're getting is worth the *fucking*." Corty and Tasi fought all the time. About basic, basic stuff. He'd call her bourgeois and make fun of her magazine subscriptions, but it was always her nice clean house he wanted to spend the night in. She belittled him for splurging when he had money, for living on lentils in between, but she went to him for romance because he could be counted on for the kind of impracticality she needed: making love in an airport utility closet, hoisting her onto the warm dishwasher, faxing her obscenities in Pig Latin. She swore on and off him for months. In between she'd wonder if he was with someone else. She lost fifteen pounds. The desperation diet. The unhappier she was, the more desirable it made her. When she called to tell him she was pregnant, a cool little voice answered the phone. There was only one thing to do.

After the abortion, she felt absolutely still, maybe an awareness of that newly empty place inside her. Sure, she felt loss, but it was good, clean loss—not drama, not experimentation with limits, not how far you'll go to manipulate someone else. Sitting there in that crinkly paper dress, she knew she didn't want to be with Corty ever again. It was apparent to her. Life deals out enough suffering as it is, you don't need to go around making it yourself all the time. That's when she cut it off with Corty, and she realized how much work any kind of satisfaction is. You can always complain about someone else making you miserable, but satisfaction you've got to build. She didn't know that before the abortion. She was waiting for someone to make her happy. Then she realized that happiness had always eluded her, but satisfaction she understood.

If you look at her mother and father's marriage it is no wonder Tasi has resisted coupledom for two decades already. Of course, there were several junctions where she nearly turned left or right, but in the end she drove straight on through. She could have diverged from solitary evenings and the too-professed preference for them. When she fell into the bottle for awhile she heard the voice in the mirror—you've lost your looks, you've waited until it's too late. No doubt that's what some of her acquaintances were thinking. Naturally, this doesn't square with the way women like to see themselves. Yada yada sisterhood, women are supposed to stand in solidarity. Not to is a kind of recidivism we resist. What would it imply for those who have no looks to lose? Is the race still on as it was for our mothers? Transplanted in her old age by her father's retirement, Tasi's mother had a hard time making new friends because the training for competition was so rigorous from such an early age. Tasi is competitive, too, but not about getting a husband. When she puts together a bid, and the client signs with Zefirelli, there's nothing sweeter. That's how she managed to climb back out of the bottle in her thirties. And she found that her friends still loved her, some of those beauties far more ravaged by time than she, while she believes her face has taken on a kind of striking quality it didn't possess when she was a girl. Yet her friends can't seem to shake the question: when will Tasi meet someone?

Well, never. A never-say-never, mind you, but a most emphatic conclusion just the same. You'd only have to spend a weekend with her parents, a special kind of hell with gingersnaps, and Tasi has to visit more and more frequently since her mother had a stroke. Her father employs the biting tone of husbands pointing out ineptitude (her mother can't get the cellophane pouch open). *Here let me do it*, not, *I'll show you how*. Having crouched on his haunches all day, it's a moment he pounces upon. Tasi thinks about the courage these women lacked; they couldn't even turn the TV off during dinner. Courage to endure but not to declare, that's what they had. And the men had anger, so locked alone with fallibility and the responsibility of everything right. Getting it right, making it right, knowing the right thing to do.

Now her mom has had a stroke . . . or is it Alzheimer's? . . . or is it water on the brain? . . . or is it a bunch of those little strokes? None of the doctors seem to know, so any of these causes will do. Mom can't tell the difference between a diaper hamper and a mailbox. Half the time, she doesn't know who Tasi is, but she always knows who he is, and in the olive-drab den when no one's visiting and gingersnaps no longer matter, it comes to fisticuffs between Mom and Dad. She tries to brain him with the porcelain figurine he gave her on their fiftieth wedding anniversary, you know the one, Big Girl in the Dirndl. He smacks Mom against the wall and she dribbles down it. But he won't have a nurse in their house, *not some stranger, not in this house*. There are feces smeared in the bathroom and her bra straps are brown. The whole weekend Tasi is there, she cleans, she washes, she listens to him say, *not in this house.* On the way to the supermarket, he doesn't believe her mother really has to go to the bathroom and drives grimly on, sure of her vindictiveness, until Tasi has to shout "*Dad!*" like that time he didn't believe she was going to be car sick.

He's ready for his drink at 5:00 PM sharp, the old routines, calcified bumps on the day. He still makes Mom a highball, despite the drug precautions on her pill bottles. Tasi resolves to call her brothers and recommend strong-arming these two into convalescent care, assisted living, whatever they want to call it, she'll do it. She goes back home, time for pantyhose and outcomes assessment at the office. Her boss opens the meeting with the usual spiel: *our goal is to create new revenue streams for the client, implement specific marketing tactics, emphasize creative branding, but we should always make the client feel like a family member.* Like hell. Not in her book. She goes to the office because it's distinctly *not* family.

At the end of the week, Tasi calls home and finds out her brothers have pursued nothing. Over the weekend, Tasi visits again and her mother seems better (come back to herself or left, which is it?). She's getting about with an ambulator, her powdered face soft as biscuit dough, ready again to excuse anyone's bad behavior, to trade on it for cheeriness. Mom and Tasi hold hands and she says *sweetie* over and over again. It seems they no longer have to search for topics of conversation that work; they can simply be like this. *Sweetie, sweetie, sweetie.* It's easier than coming home from college. It's sort of a relief. Tasi wonders what her mother did all those years after she left besides play bridge and get her hair done. Not cruelly, she earnestly wonders. Now that Mom can't remember herself, it's possible to ascribe some secret life to her. Tasi always imagined a secret life for her mother, that was the pleasure of reading novels; she could ascribe a secret life to anybody, but Mom only read recipe cards and diets.

Dad's the voracious reader, the one with a mind like a clamp on historical fact. Exigency keeps a tension on his mind. Mom's seems like a string without a balloon, all loopy-loo. She makes him keep track of her medications now. He has to come home from golf in time for her dose, and she doesn't do the things she could do, like the classes at the senior center pool she's supposed to take. She wants him to give up the annual fishing trip. His knuckles are white from the grip on his drink. *Have some ginger-snaps. Have some Scotch.* Tasi feels his fight not to become a shut-in, the severity of his desire. She has it herself. If she could swing a chopping blade down upon the tendon and gristle that binds these two, she would. She *would.*

As Tasi pulls into her designated parking space, she feels a surge of relief, as though she'd escaped a predator. Her mother never got to make wedding plans for her. All those choices she would have made so well: sheets of vellum on the invitations, can-apés, Australian lace, butter-cream frosting, puff sleeves, empress waists, the length of her train, Tasi wanted her to take up some other choices. She took them up herself.

At the office, she's due to meet a client referred to her by the art director. Now that the client's company look has been updated, he wants to discuss pitching a new product. The art director comes to her office carrying a leather satchel, the sort school-teachers carried at the turn of the century, a thick strap and buckle over the top. It distinguishes Peter as someone creative—out of step with modernity—an art director who will become his original self later, after the kids are raised and he has retired, a painter who married his model.

He takes a logo and letterhead out of his satchel—a pet food company launching a form of kitty litter for dogs: Puppy Potty.

"You'll love this one," he says.

"Right, a week contemplating pet poop. Now that's lofty."

"Not to mention the spectacular clumping agents of the product."

His eyes are aquamarine—that gemstone that bounces back so much light.

"I'm going to clump you with this," Tasi says, "if you don't get out of my office," and she holds up her fist.

"Promise?" he says from the doorway, and then he's gone.

The art director is her lover, though no one at the office knows it. Their affair is part-time, twice a year: once at the Public Relations Society of America convention (they call themselves the Private Relations Society), and once at some other convention they manage to obtain travel funds for. At Tasi's age, twice a year is quite sufficient; all that tantalizing innuendo in between is almost as much fun as the sex itself. She likes to stand above the heater vent and feel the warm jet stream between her legs while they sigh into each other over the wire. Her friends say it's a dead-end relationship. They're absolutely right, only it doesn't lead her to the same conclusions. She keeps telling them: Who needs Mr. Right when you've got Mr. Vacation? Charlotte understands. Darius must spend half the year away on business trips. They always laugh about that country & western song: "How Can I Miss You When You Won't Go Away?"

VIRGINIA

❧

Blue Tube

Finley moved out a month ago but sometimes Milo still forgets. Today he asks Virginia as they pull into the drive, "Is Papa home?" It's not that she hasn't tried to talk to Milo, not that she hasn't come home from the library with armloads of books with titles like: *Mommy and Daddy Can't Live Together Anymore.* But she thinks Milo senses her own ambivalence and he's what she'd call emotionally gifted. It's not that he really expects his dad to be home, but that he wishes it, just as she has a wish list for his dad too . . . nine miles long.

At the end of the day, Virginia is homicidally hungry and the rice cakes on the dash don't cut it. She is doing a mental inventory of the kitchen as she drives. Her mind is reeling ahead to fish sticks and French fries and marinara jars. She stomps on the brake pedal at the top of the drive and wrenches on the emergency break and her voice is unduly harsh. "Milo, I've told you over and over, you'll see your papa on Saturday, so don't bug me about it."

"You're an old witch mother," he says, his face ruddy with indignation. He reaches for his lunch box, which is across the seat, and pulls it towards him. A broad white stream of liquid spills from one corner when he yanks his lunchbox upright. It trails behind him and cuts a swath across the seat. He doesn't notice, because he does everything almost at once—grabbing the lunch box, lurching for the door handle, kicking the door open. Virginia watches his angry stomp across the lawn, dribbling milk as he goes, and it's not until he's almost to the front door that she finds herself screaming, "Drop it! Drop your lunchbox!" as though it were a bomb. He spins around and drops it on the grass, just as suddenly bursting into tears. "You scared me!"

"It's leaking milk, honey," she says getting a hold of herself. "Just milk." Then she kneels on the lawn: backpack, purse, Milo's folder, sack of hamster food, down it comes with her, discarded as she takes Milo into her arms. "I'm sorry, sweetie, I'm sorry. I never meant to scare you. It's my fault. Mommy's tired and cranky. She shouldn't have shouted."

"That's right." He pulls back and looks at her sternly. "You shouldn't shout. That's against our rules." Virginia nods, gravely admonished. Bad Mommy.

She hopes it helps that she apologizes, that she fumbles to explain what she can. Her parents never felt they had to apologize or explain. Virginia tells herself it must be better.

While she is assessing the ingredients in her kitchen, Charlotte calls to see if Virginia can come to dinner while Darius is out of town. Virginia double-checks the stove clock. 5:12. Right, some people eat at 7:30 or 8:00, but she still feels annoyed. Did Charlotte forget she had a kid? Virginia's mother used to say, "People who don't have kids are the most selfish."

Even if she knocked herself out to get Finley or her mom or the student sitter, and figured out a meal to leave at home for them, Charlotte was prone to canceling plans at the last minute. Virginia remembers when Milo was a baby. Charlotte would always say: "Oh, bring him! Dinner won't start until seven-thirty and he can snuggle up and sleep in our room."

"But Charlotte—" Virginia would say.

"Oh c'mon. Babies his age are so portable and you need to get out."

In Virginia's experience, babies are not at all flexible. They are as attached to their schedules as eighty-year-old men. How did Charlotte suddenly know so much about babies?—and at the same time she bristled because Charlotte made her feel like such a boring old barnacle, and really, maybe she *was* no fun at all anymore. But they'd tried a weekend with friends when he was six months old—he was wiggled and jiggled and cooed at by everyone and he smiled so rewardingly, then when he got home, he screamed for three days. With a stab of pain, Virginia remembers joking with Finley that the only fantasy she had anymore was of a mattress, *unoccupied*, extra-firm, and Fin had laughed with her so sweetly.

Over the phone, Virginia begs off, saying she has papers to correct. "We all missed you the other night," she adds. The words feel greasy in her mouth, as she pictures Jean's angry face.

"Me, too," Charlotte says, sounding uncertain. "Darius and I are going to have to cancel a trip to Tahoe now. It was part of my Christmas present."

"Bummer," says Virginia, afterwards remembering last night's bummer tent remarks. She feels flushed, prickly with heat. Was this any way to acknowledge an abortion? It meant a missed trip to Lake Tahoe?

"When do you go in?" she asks, dropping her voice.

"A week. I've got a week in limbo."

"Just give me a few days to catch up and I'll call."

Virginia opens a jar of mango chutney, then slathers chicken breasts with it. The truth is she already knows about the Lake Tahoe trip, and she feels a twinge of guilt about it. Last week, she'd gone to the mall for a few hours, seizing up in those twinkly lights and getting panicky because all the corridors are designed to intersect at oblique angles; the developers figure you'll get lost and fall into some store and buy something, which she never did. Instead, she'd go home with nothing but a stomach ache and have to come back, having strategically planned her attack.

Virginia was standing at one of those octopus-arm intersections trying to figure out which way to J.C. Penney when Darius caught her by the arm in his charming way. He and Charlotte were going to Tahoe for New Year's—some business with the

Silicon Valley crowd, mostly pleasure. "Yes," he said laughing when she coined his own phrase for him, "that's how I like it, part business, mostly pleasure." He asked her to come with him for a moment; he wanted to get Charlotte after-ski boots and it was difficult to decide. Virginia allowed herself to be steered there, a relief to be with someone whose sense of direction was definitive. But she could feel herself smelling his cologne for the heat beneath the spice and looking at his glistening ears to where they turned like whirlpools and she had the impulse to dart her tongue. She told herself she was trying out his charm—all the better to be pleased for her friend when next she saw her. But it wasn't true.

The truth is, Virginia looked down on Charlotte for not having "taken hold," as her grandmother would say. A year had gone by since Charlotte dissolved her company, and since then she mostly redecorated the apartment or tried new therapies—herbal, aroma, REM, hypnotic, colonic—Virginia lost track in irritation. She tried to force herself towards generous conclusions. They must be trying to have a baby. "No," said Charlotte. "Darius doesn't want children." And she didn't seem any too unhappy about it. "It would get in the way of our plans to travel."

That afternoon at the mall, Virginia saw herself in Darius' eyes—busy, professional, bemused but not reserved, like him, granting attention in the world to those eager to have it—all of which made her attractive to him, and like a nasty sister, she wanted to compete with Charlotte and win. It wasn't about him. If he was the prize, really, it was an afterthought; Virginia didn't imagine what having him meant. But competing with Charlotte to prove she could have chosen a life like hers, could have won a man like hers, now that was something she wanted. Or was that her point? Nothing so articulate at the time. Inchoate. But now? Some getback at women like Charlotte who have time and don't know what to do with it. Virginia wanted to stay home and write and here Charlotte was, on a chaise lounge with foam rubber between her toes while her pedicure dried. Virginia admitted to some fury with the Charlottes of the world for always drawing protection from men, for staying home with cramps while Virginia had a miscarriage at the podium and lectured on—thinking she'd hit the mother lode of all menstruation. So this moment felt good, jostling through the crowds with a handsome man at the hour when working people shop.

The walls of the store were a pale, celadon green; black boots on clear pedestals and mirrors making it as three dimensional as a sculpture gallery. Darius and Virginia walked round and round the boots and round and round each other. The saleslady assumed they were a couple. Virginia protested and Darius didn't. They discussed lasts and crepe soles. He bent boots back and forth in his long hands. She walked to the back wall where the after-ski boots were. "Would you mind trying a couple on?" Darius had asked. "It's the only way to detect a pinch." The salesgirl with licorice black hair, that color so in style, slapped some boxes on the floor. Virginia leaned down to take hold of the first box, when suddenly Darius knelt before her, like the salesman used to when she was a child, and when he took her slender bony foot in his hands and slipped it into the shoe resting on his upper thigh, she had to admit she'd wanted him to. A little tug and ah, the heel in so snugly, his hand, resting warmly on her calf. She walked to the other side of the store in the creaky boots, collecting herself. By the time she returned, he was standing, watching her intently.

"Not these. Her toes will go numb." Virginia tossed the boots in the box with a kind of brusqueness that would discourage Prince Charming behavior. She made sure to put the next pair on herself.

After her next lap around the store, she stood with him deliberating. "You know," Virginia said, "Maybe she'd rather have these slip-ons. All that lacing is a bother when your hands are cold. These are so much easier to get into."

"Yeah," he said, cracking a dry laugh, "but Charlotte needs something to do."

Virginia's face was warm as she absorbed his derision and unlaced the boots. The irony of being in Charlotte's shoes suddenly shamed her and she understood certain things in the ugliness of epiphany. Darius had worked hard to bring Charlotte to this; to make her a person he no longer had to admire. And she'd colluded in it. The more Charlotte had given up in order to become his dependent, the more license she had given him to be a brute. The trade-off for her? She was his moral superior. Neither of them wanted what they seemed to want.

The smell of the chutney on her hands is piquant; it holds heat. A swell of longing takes her by surprise. She couldn't name it at first . . . longing not for youth itself, but for the longing of youthfulness, all that projecting onto possibility, all the things she might yet live or become. Fast rides, syrupy drinks, coastline lights, always the brink of broken hearts, and best yet the poetry, the whole night world rustling with romantic potential. Joni Mitchell on the jukebox: "Oh, I hate you some, I hate you some, I love you some, I love you when I forget about me." Always trying to write her best break-up poem ever. Cigarettes, joints, smoke switchbacks on the air. The illusion of philosophical insight. Of soul searching. Of getting down to meaning. Meaning what? Just meaning itself. Back then, she wrote in bars and she always left with international travel plans.

Milo watches a *Thomas the Tank Engine* video and she reads the paper while they eat. 'We don't do this every night,' she tells herself.

She gets out a pack of cigarettes she keeps hidden in a vase atop the armoire and steps outside to sneak one. Smoking feels ludicrous, damn near makes her sick when she's this tired, and it's obviously no substitute for travel. She thinks about Charlotte, who gets to travel when Darius is on business trips—Singapore, Malaysia, Bali. Computers in Asia and venture capital are his specialty. Charlotte looks lackluster these days, not simply thin as she's always been, but anemic. Charlotte had a triumphant sort of vitality in her twenties. After finishing culinary arts school and realizing she was still stuck with the misogynistic banter of restaurant kitchens, Charlotte had found a way to call the shots with her own catering business.

Virginia looks through billows of smoke at the plastic Payless patio furniture, and thinks about Charlotte's husband Darius with all that Asian computer money. At first, Charlotte house-sat while he went on trips, trying out his life without him in it—martini glasses and leather couches and plaque remover machines. Maybe that was the problem. He wasn't home when she fell in love with his lifestyle. He said it was ideal that the catering was inconsistent, and took Charlotte on mini-honeymoons to Bali. Evidently, she was ready to step into the postcard—a bright cloth knotted against her hip bone as she sashayed onto the beach, and those little saucy breasts that would never sag, pointing gaily away from each other. When she moved in with him she gave up the big Victorian kitchen in the rental, she gave up the catering company. "Listen," she told her friends, "this is a great time for me to figure out what I'm going to do next. If I keep up all the chopping and rolling and hauling, I'm going to get carpal tunnel. You should see these old chefs. I already tore a rotator cuff. Darius is giving me an opportunity to heal." That's lovely they all said, not sure if they had misgivings only because they were envious: no one in their lives was saying quit your job and take it easy for awhile.

After she gets Milo to bed, she feels rotten and hateful and alone. The fat lady at home with her chocolates. She knows damn well her spirit simply needs a field trip—to walk a new beach, to find a piece of driftwood that looks like . . . yes, that's just it, not knowing. But when she's in the bottom of herself, she weeps to think she'll never travel, that romantic possibility is going away from her forever, that everything from now on will be money-worry and work and Milo's needs.

On Saturday mornings, she and Milo go to the pool. Virginia has to make herself do it. She stands Milo up on a bench in the woman's room and tells him not to get down, then she puts on her suit. She smells what she imagines is a combination of dry rot, mildewed calking, and strawberry shampoo. There are little curliques of hair on the cement floor and a pink plastic comb discarded in one corner. Milo wraps his arms around her neck and she holds the leg-holes of his suit open, and he steps carefully. Meantime, the bag stuffed full of their clothes and snacks rolls gently onto the wet floor. Virginia plucks it up right away, repressing the urge to swear mightily, but the damage is minimal. Her tennis shoes were at the bottom, sparing the rest.

Once they're in the pool, that warm little bath for youngsters, everything is fine. In fact, they're amazed by how much they love each other. Milo bobs about in a little yellow life jacket, no urge yet to play with the rings, balls, and foam objects; his body affords him so much pleasure in a state of pure floating. "Here, try it on your back," Virginia says.

He lets her support him, a hand on his neck, a hand on the small of his back. He keeps his eyes ferociously squinted, as though something terrible were about to happen. He lets her hold him, even believing the terrible thing might happen. With his slippery boy body in her hands, she knows for a moment how it feels not to be able to protect one's child from harm. Not the harm of divorce, the harm of sniper fire, of detonation, of hunger. The extremes seem to help her think when she starts blaming herself for Milo's pain. Tell that to Milo, she says to herself, and dunks her head under.

When he's done on his back, they bob up and down together. He hugs her so tight that his shoulder puts pressure on her trachea and she has to reposition him. Then he's off on a dog paddle.

"I love you, Mommy," he says when he comes back.

"I love you too, Boo." And they bask in their well-being, the opaline light at the bottom of the pool shifting in patches and the brightness of the voices bouncing off the walls. Virginia can relax in all the noise, words she is not obligated to discern.

She runs into another mother from kindergarten who tells Virginia, go ahead, go to the hot tub if you like. Virginia looks at Milo who is pouring from a plastic watering can into the other child's hands and decides to go for it, but when she gets out of the pool, it's not the hot tub she heads for.

She lines up with the rest of the goose-bottomed butts on the stair for the big slide. At the top she looks down at Milo who in the same second looks up, his face a suspended portrait of dependence. What will his mother do? She waves at him and smiles emphatically even as she feels something like bent metal twist in her chest.

At the mouth of the tube, she sits for a moment, the water pushing at her thighs, her vision narrowing to just this blue tube and the turn ahead of her, then she lets go. How lovely. How warm, to feel her body swing into the curves and twists, to feel that she too is a container whose liquid sloshes and she can let it slosh, she can hoot in there if she wants to, she can let her ears fill with water and her hair spring out behind her. She can make a decision to go on with small joyous things, she can laugh and be shot out feet-first.

Until she took that ride, Virginia didn't realize how her energy reserves had been tapped by practicing detachment with Finley, by tamping down on comments and questions to Fin about his job hunt: "Have you read the classifieds yet, dear? Or can I recycle the paper?" The ruses were so silly, he saw through them, but it was better than full-scale fury, or so she thought. As she makes her way back to the kiddie pool, she sees a former student with a ring in his eyebrows and barbells in his lips whose pallor resembled pimento paste. To think you could raise a boy who'd look like that after all the healthy lunches you packed.

"Go, Mom," Milo says admiringly as he wraps his arms around her waist.

"I did," she answers. "Whoosh!" But beneath her cheer, she can already feel how tired she'll be by early afternoon, the cumulative effect of slighted sleep on too many nights making her feel as though she has jet lag, as though every morning she were in the wrong time zone. See what happens, she thinks, when I stop being angry—the exhaustion catches up with me. Finley has a decent job now, working for a company that recycles construction materials—he does their demo and salvage—not great money but decent, something he can stay with because it doesn't go against his politics. Nothing had prodded Finely into action quite like telling him to leave. Now, in the pool where not even Milo will notice, Virginia cries.

When she and Milo light the candles on the dinner table Tuesday night, she lets Milo blow the match out and take it to the garbage, except that instead of throwing it in the garbage, he throws the kitchen match down the garbage grinder, where it jams lengthwise. The garbage grinder now sounds like a chain saw hitting a nail. On Wednesday morning, the plumbing place won't give her an estimate other than to say it will cost her $38.00 for the plumber to turn the key in his ignition and drive over there, and possibly $300 if she has to buy a new one as this isn't the sort of thing covered by the warranty. She can't stand to call Finley so she waits until he comes over to pick up Milo that afternoon.

"Fin," Virginia says, trying to sound sweet but not saccharine, "the garbage grinder is acting up, and the plumber will charge an arm and a leg to come over here."

"An arm and a leg?" chirps Milo.

"That's just a way of saying it could cost a lot, Milo," Fin says, resting his hand on Milo's shoulder. "Sure, I'll take a look at it."

Virginia does feel a twinge of guilt as she leads Fin into the kitchen. Really it was a set-up to ask him in front of Milo, who, she notices, isn't volunteering the crucial information.

Finley turns the thing on for about one second, then turns it off. He reaches down inside, grimacing as he shoves his hand through the too-tight drain ring.

"Ginny, what the hell is wedged in here?"

"I dropped a matchstick down it," Milo volunteers instantly.

"Well," Finley says, lightening his tone, "I'm going to have to floss the garbage grinder."

"Really?" Milo is impressed.

"Yeah, like old dragon teeth." Finley is already going through the kitchen drawers until he finds what he needs: two chopsticks. When he asks, "You got some floss, Ginny?" she knows he's serious. He then winds the dental floss from stick to stick and goes at it, flossing the garbage grinder until he's gotten the pieces of splintered wood loose. Watching him, she has to ask herself: "Is there anything really so wrong with this man?"

JEAN

ભ

Threats and Imprecations

Jean has her eye on a troublemaker in the complex, a scrappy kid who ducks away just in time. She has her eye on this kid because his favorite pastime after school is throwing pine cones senselessly and relentlessly against his neighbors' walls.

The first time she came close to him was quite by accident. She was taking the weed eater back to the shed when she heard the steady *thwonk, thwonk, thwonk* of his ambitious arm. She doubled back to the upper parking lot and came up behind him, a rangy kid, slightly pigeon-toed in his throwing stance. Jean stood still for a minute or two, watching. He pulled his arm back way behind him and threw so hard, he grunted. Then he turned and saw her, which neither of them expected. His sixth sense was finely honed, Jean thought, that or he was really keyed up all the time, but with the tool shed on his right and the dumpsters at the bottom of the cul-de-sac, he'd put himself in the proverbial box canyon.

"Hey," she yelled and he took off, nearly spinning on the balls of his feet as he banked left and into the parking garages. It was fairly predictable where he'd be, crouched down behind the car in the last stall. The apartments are built above their garages on timber pilings; they're cedar shingled and brown, all very North-westy. The architect staggered them so that each one is set back from the next, ostensibly to preserve privacy and view, though all anybody stares into is Douglas fir and the poolhouse roof. But because they're staggered, it's very easy for a kid to disappear from view. Jean stood a few feet back from the garage of the last unit, listening to the boy's breath echo against the cement walls.

"Hey," she said. "You need to quit chucking pine cones at people's condos."

Nothing doing. Just the little squeegee sound of a tennis shoe, the scruff of denim seam against seam.

"I know you're probably bored, but there's gotta be something else you can do."

"Like you care," he hissed savagely, not rising.

"Well," she said dryly, "you certainly don't have to listen to me, but one of these days instead of calling me, the neighbors are going to call the cops."

Jean didn't stand around waiting for a reply. She slung the weed eater over her shoulder and did her best to swagger away.

The phone starts ringing early. At 8:30, it's Mrs. Saffian in B-7. Her toilet isn't working, but it's only the chain to the stopper that's broken, so Jean uses a paper clip to reconnect it and *presto*. Jean has figured out that the property management company likes her in direct proportion to how little they hear from her. She hasn't been a renter in so long, she'd forgotten how that worked.

In the afternoon, the pool man with tinted hair will arrive (he always wears shorts, even in January), and so will the man who comes to change the locks when someone moves out. The lock man wears Carhart overalls and doesn't seem to realize that he' s shouting when he tells Jean about taking care of his aging mother and his mentally ill sister—Jean gets updates every week—and she honestly tries to think he is the nicest guy in the world though there is something about him she finds vaguely scary. He seems to lurch at her from around the corners of the complex—behind the laundry room door when she is putting coins in—but his smile is sincere when she startles and he always apologizes, so she tells herself it's her own paranoia, though she is not sure she believes that. Other than these guys, she has a list of plumbers and plasterers she is evidently not supposed to call if she wants to keep the job. When she gets home from Mrs. Saffian's, Jean pours another cup of coffee and pulls out the rent ledgers to have a look, but her mind refuses to obey.

She woke up thinking about Charlotte, and she knows she'll go to bed thinking about Charlotte. Jean knows she must be off-base in some way because none of the others seem as angry with Charlotte as she is. Virginia is disgusted, frustrated with Charlotte, but Jean doesn't imagine Virginia's interior monologue to be anything like hers. Jean calls Charlotte a cunt. She says: you cunt, you rotten cunt, you mildewed cunt. She sounds like an abusive husband in a case study. She knows she is "masking pain"—to use the old mental health parlance. Certainly she doesn't sound like someone fit to be a mother, which is why she asked Nan to make the call to Charlotte. Really, it's not so far-fetched; she could raise Charlotte's baby. Lesbian couples do that sort of thing all the time—make babies with the sperm of their gay men friends who then watch over as loving uncles. Why couldn't Charlotte and Darius be extended family of sorts? They've all known each other for years. The bonds were already proven. Hadn't she read in *People* magazine at the doctor's office about a younger sister who'd given her older sister a few embryos? Maybe it wasn't so strange; maybe it was flexible and tribal in a way that people should be, children as children, not private property. Then again, maybe she'd been reading too many *People* magazines in doctor's offices. She'd kill if she thought someone else was raising her kid and doing a rotten job of it.

By mid-morning Jean wants to call Charlotte. She wants to call Charlotte and apologize for all the nasty things that Charlotte hasn't even heard. She wants to call her so bad it makes her joints ache, but she also can't stand the thought of Charlotte saying no. It makes her want to burn down whole forests; it makes her want to roar dragon flames. Jean is, distinctly, unsafe with herself and has the good sense to know it.

In this state, a memory surfaces, unbidden. Fire to water, maybe that's the association. She once watched Charlotte crossing a log over a swollen river, a heavy pack on her back. Charlotte faltered, the pack shifted, she slipped, went down on her hands and pubic bone, her legs straddling the log. It must have hurt terribly. Jean shudders, remembering that she laughed. Reflexively, she thinks now, because she was frightened and it was her turn next. Charlotte wouldn't speak to her for the rest of the afternoon and Jean didn't blame her, wouldn't have blamed her if she'd quit being her friend altogether. That night the mosquitoes were fierce, biting them as they cooked pasta, but Charlotte eschewed the bug repellent, smashing them to her forehead one after another. Not long after they had to dash for the tent, pelted by a sudden storm. Charlotte turned her back to Jean, and Jean lay there watching the fat droplets as they fell toward her open eyes but landed on the clear tarp and slid away. In the morning, Charlotte caught a view of herself in the kettle lid—black insect spindle and dried blood— and turned to Jean.

"How can you stand me?" she said, smiling at last.

"How can you stand me?" Jean answered.

They apologized; they embraced. They vowed to open their peppermint schnapps once they'd crested the next pass. *Charlotte,* Jean wants to say now, *you're stronger than you think.*

Well, strength has many uses. Jean should know. She is trying to learn how to stop suffering. After all, Tim has figured out how to be happy. In her kinder moments, Jean thinks he probably had to leave after a decade of depression by association.

If she were to call Charlotte, Jean knows what Charlotte would say. "Don't get self-righteous with me. You had an abortion when you were twenty." The very reason Charlotte finds to discredit her is the reason Jean thinks she should listen. Children are easy to have when you don't want them. That's what Jean has learned. Back in college, they all had illusions of control. The very term, "birth control," implied that if you took away the "control," *bammo*, birth would be the result. Jean had an abortion in her sophomore year—pregnant after a kegger party and a boy who sealed his mouth to hers like a space shuttle O-ring. There was no question in her mind then, but she thinks now about that child who would have been. Charlotte doesn't know about the phantom children you accrue, the child's voice that rises above the others, the voice at the lake that makes you startle from your dozing amidst the din of children calling Mama and Mommy—vigilant for your own. Then the adrenalin subsides; you realize—not your own, never your own—and sink back down.

Jean suddenly wishes the phantom children upon Charlotte, as though she could will their visitation upon her before she has the abortion . . . but like ghosts they don't come till after. Yet if Jean could send her one, just one, perhaps Charlotte would change her mind. Jean knows she can't call with threats and imprecations. But Nan can convey Jean's offer with good will and accept Charlotte's answer with grace. Jean can do neither.

Her period comes that morning and she cries, then washes her face. It's almost habit. Still, she is glad to have some justification for her lassitude this morning. When she gets herself back to normal, she has a gander at the paper—who's been blown up, who's been kidnapped, who's lying now—it's a perverse way to begin the day when you think of it. Just then, Jean spots one of her neighbors coming up the walkway and makes towards the front door; it must be another renter problem. She opens the door just as the neighbor is about to stuff a toys pamphlet behind the doorknob. Jean can't remember the woman's name, only that her yard is full of cute signs—Trespassers Welcome, Moles You Dig. The renter looks at Jean—obviously she can't remember her name either—and something seems to register. "You don't have little ones anyway," she says, stuffing the toys pamphlet back under her arm. "No, I don't," Jean says in this tone that sounds oddly blank, even to her. She stands at the door and watches her. The woman feels Jean's eyes, casts a glance back over her shoulder. Jean wants to shout: "Just because I'm not a parent doesn't mean I don't have kids in my life." But she makes herself close the door.

Jean is more than a doting aunt. She wants to bury her nose in her nephew's hair and inhale him. Tim and Jean had Stevie over for a week their last summer together. She was aware of Tim watching her and her watching Tim and both of them thinking, "So this is what you'd be like if we had kids." They were fighting about adoption by then. Sometimes it seemed to Jean one and the same: talking about the child they could adopt instead of the child they couldn't have. Phantom Child. They'd spent so many years talking about this child, sometimes Jean had the odd sensation that she and Tim weren't two people trying to have a child but two people who'd lost a child. To some awful mishap: a fire or a fever or a fall. Two people whose pain compelled them to blame each other, two people who would have to leave each other to get away from the endless spread of sorrow. Stevie was their joyful respite, their week of playing happy house.

It was clear that Jean's sister had sat Stevie down and coached him about what he could and couldn't say, which of course just made Stevie blurt out awkward comments. Jean tried to be charitable. Maybe Stevie had questions of his own about why his aunt and uncle had no children, or perhaps he'd overheard something. Anyway, on his last Sunday with them, Tim and she took him to the water slides. Afterwards, they lay down for a few minutes before dinner while Stevie watched some television. Or so they thought. It was only minutes before Stevie's choirboy voice came through the door: "Are you mating?" That's the Discovery channel for you.

Tim and Jean had made an agreement. If the in vitro fertilization didn't take, they'd investigate adoption. When the time came, they decided not to use an adoption agency. There was no need; Jean knew so many social workers who could make the contacts. The I.V.F. procedure had nearly wiped out their savings, and she'd heard about lawyers who kept inventing fees and couples who went right on paying. She knew how that worked already—the more money you invested, the more emotional stake you had, the more you needed to have a result. It was so easy to be preyed upon. The lawyer, the doctor, they kept saying, "We're almost there."

It's amazing the things you find out about your spouse that you don't want to know. No one takes marriage vows that say: "Here's what we'll do if we're infertile." When Tim had to go back for the advanced sperm count, he said, "I don't think it's me. I mean, I think my fertility is a given. I got a couple women pregnant before I met you." He saw the look on Jean's face and added: "I didn't want to tell you."

Maybe he shouldn't have. She wanted to know if he'd supported these women when they'd had their abortions. Had he gone with them for the procedure? She wanted to know how he could have let it happen the second time. Didn't he put himself in charge of the birth control? Did he break up with them afterward? Did he think of these women now? She was suddenly so prepared not to like him.

What about Darius? That's the kind of thing she might yell if she called Charlotte. *Have you ever asked him? How many unmade children on his roster?* Men don't count abortions. Not in Jean's experience. Not the way women do. An unbirthday a woman silently marks. Abortions don't happen to men, it seems. . . .

Another MSW from the Birth to Three Program contacted Jean. Twin two-year-old boys were available for adoption. Both parents had been drug users, the mom on methadone during the pregnancy, somewhere along the way the parents contracted HIV. The mom got full-blown AIDS right away and died. The grandmother told the social worker that the mother's dying wish was to see these boys adopted. So Tim and Jean did it all, the paper work, the background checks, then at the last minute the father changed his mind. He wanted to keep those benefit checks coming in. It was perverse and painful, but Jean kept up with the case. A year later the father was dead and both kids had been put into foster care.

Then there was the seventeen-year-old mother they courted, her floor covered in newspaper and puppy shit, her bookcase filled with bongs and Cabbage Patch Dolls. "I have goals you know," she told Jean, flipping back her winged bangs. Jean knew she made the girl defensive without trying, but social workers are used to that.

"Really," she said. "What would you like to do?"

"There's a nail sculpturing school. You can make a lot of money at nail sculpturing." When she said the word "sculpturing," she seemed to slurp the sound down.

"Sounds great. Though you're smart. You could go to junior college." Jean saw her reflection shine in the hardness of the girl's eyes as she spoke, heard the rote phrases of her training protecting her. "I mean later, if you want something more long term."

They paid for the nail sculpting course, for prenatal care too. The day Jean's friend brought the papers to be signed, the girl changed her mind, told the office that her aunt from out of state had called and offered to help raise the baby. Could Jean be angry? This girl had hoped her twenty-two-year-old mechanic boyfriend would marry her and take care of them all, something to compensate for tough beginnings. Whatever motives were at work when she got pregnant might not have anything to do with how she would eventually feel about her baby. Sometimes we grow into love, Jean thought. Charlotte should consider that. Tasi insists that Charlotte is right to honor her agreement with Darius not to have children. Jean wonders: Should we agree when we marry that we won't be transformed by forces larger than ourselves? Charlotte doesn't know that she's going to be changed; that either way, there is no going back. Jean is wholly willing to raise Charlotte's baby. She is ready and willing. When she is not cursing Charlotte, she is praying to her, praying she will let Jean be the mother she wants to be. There isn't any part of Jean's history that Charlotte doesn't know.

The nail sculpturer's baby was born with a serious heart defect, irreparable. A month later, she told the social worker they could have the baby now . . . if they wanted it. *Here, have my dying baby.* Jean thought about it. But she wasn't sure she and Tim had love to give anymore. Evenings at home were excruciating. The bare bones of their commitment lay upon a plate like a picked-over fish, one dulled blue eye fixed upon nothing, its rainbow tail a fried brown. The sound of glassware and ice were gratingly loud.

What does Charlotte think she'll have with Darius after-wards? Jean wonders. Will she cherish her resentment? Nurture it? Raise it through the years? She pictures Charlotte on the sur-gery table, and thinks of all she went through to get what Char-lotte is giving up.

In an effort not to cry anymore, Jean opens the paper to the classifieds. She, too, needs to think long term, and managing an apartment complex for the rest of her life is not it. Nan had asked recently if this thing with Charlotte had opened up all the old wounds. Jean didn't say that the wounds had never healed. She nodded instead.

She finds herself doing it now as she scans the columns, con-senting to what will come next without believing it will be better. When Tim left, hadn't her grandmother sighed and said, "Next one will be worse." She didn't mean anything by it; fatalism was the Eastern European way of cheering a person up. Jean shakes the paper to make herself focus on the tiny font, then she hears a thwonk against the roof, then another. Thwonk, thwonk, thwonk. It takes her a minute to remember the kid with the pine cones. She decides she's not going to give him the satisfaction of a response. He may be persistent, but Jean has learned how to do relentless silence.

∾

Size Twelve Regal

Tasi stands in front of the mirror in the bathroom at Zeffirelli & Associates, readying herself to go from work straight to a company dinner. She has just had a bad run-in with the mascara wand, having side-swiped her eye. Runnels of black are streaming from the eye, which has turned red and bleary. She presses toilet paper to it, then studies herself—one eye emphatic with blackened lashes, the iris a beady dark blue, the sort of eye one could imagine sighting down a gun. The other eye rheumy as an old washerwoman's, like her mother's staring up from the steam and bleach.

She imagines Peter's wife, Trisha, laying out her clothes on the bed, trimming her cuticles, getting ready for this company dinner all afternoon. A trip to the stall reveals that Tasi's stockings have ripped at the thigh where a pocket of cellulite bulges out like sausage from a casing. The spare pair of stockings in her desk are gone so this is how she will arrive at dinner. Now that the eye has calmed down somewhat, she reaches into her makeup bag to resume the task of facial symmetry. She makes a small noncommittal smile at the mirror; this is the one she will offer Trisha.

Tasi met Peter when she first started at Zeffirelli & Associates six years ago. She was thirty-one, an uncomfortable single at the summer party amidst scads of children and wives wearing espadrilles. He wasn't art director yet, and they hadn't been introduced because he was sick the day she did the office walk-through. So Tasi met him at the party, over everyone's heads, because she was tall, and she was looking out the skylight. When they happened upon each other's gaze, it was quizzical, bemused, unrushed. No one can explain presence . . . why it is you know there's only one person in the room you want to talk to and you wade in, armpit deep, to cross a swarm of loud people . . . but it is presence you feel keenly when eyes meet yours above the rim of a glass.

When Peter caught up to her, he said, "You're like a gerbil in a box, aren't you? Jumping about with a waving tail."

"Yes," Tasi said, motioning toward the patio door, "and if you open this, I'll leap out."

She was attracted to Peter because he talked nonsense to her nonsense, because his hands were so expressive. His fingers were long and bony like the hands of a cellist or bass player, someone who could span notes on the neck of an instrument. She was attracted to him because of the timbre of his voice; it had a low rumble in it, the sort of rumble the center of the earth must emit before a quake, a rumble gathering itself and traveling along fault lines through stone. She didn't care what he talked about so long as he kept talking.

Peter was a relaxing man, if a little inconvenient. He never tried to wrest confessions from her. Not the way women did. Sometimes it seemsed to Tasi that women's conversations were a contest about who could have the most emotions. Peter chose to have his emotions in a universal way. "I see," he'd say, "Sadness." Or simply, "Terrible, terrible." Peter didn't bring up his wife to Tasi, and Trisha seemed to exist in the abstract—in the same way a fairy tale must have a woodcutter or a step-mother, or at least Tasi rarely ever thought about Trisha, only now before these ghastly dinners when she knew she'd have to see her.

Tasi stands back from the mirror and composes herself. She is a big woman with big features, an oversized mouth; hers is a strikingly theatrical face, one that would project well to the back row of a theater. With a little Julie Andrews jut of her chin, she concludes her inspection and girds her loins, if that's possible, she thinks, while wearing a shredded pantyhose crotch.

Imperial Cruises is taking them to dinner tonight—Peter and his family, the boss and his wife. *Me and my purse,* Tasi thinks grimly, locating a lipstick. Occasionally, she has considered taking a man to one of these client dinners, just to give Peter a start. Her girlfriends may be right about Peter, but he is a treasure to her, and she is determined to keep him. Tasi has always been good at finding things—needles gone missing, the baby's pacifier, her grandmother's reading glasses—and she is also good at fitting keys in locks, good at jarring loose bowls that are stuck inside each other, good at easing corks so the champagne won't spill. As a girl she loved the hidden pictures games in her activity workbooks: *Find an egg, a mushroom, a haystack, a leprechaun, and the letter m.* That first office party was her hidden picture game, and Peter was her prize.

They meet at La Fiamma, which, despite its name, has a cool little decor, wallpaper in stripes of lime green and silver so that you see vague blurry strips of yourself everywhere. Tonight Peter wears a light gray suit, which makes him appear more dashing than Tasi is used to. Though he has no gray on his head elsewhere, he has, by some fluke, two swaths of it from temple to nape, brilliantined silver. His wife Trisha is strappy all over tonight—strappy back dress with a velvet evening jacket and strappy kid suede pumps. Tasi studies the Victorian carriage boot shape of Trisha's shoes and thinks: foot lingerie. She is, of course, wearing the clothes she put on at 7:30 AM—a blue gabardine skirt and a wool challis blouse printed in pheasant feathers. Does she feel dumpy next to Trisha who must eat a tablespoon at each meal? No, she is size twelve regal.

Pers, the Norwegian president of the cruise line, does not stumble all over her name like most American men do. Her name is Anastasie Charbonneau to those who have not yet been given permission to use the diminutive. Her French Canadian grand-mother always called her Tasi. She has to admit she likes the way her full name throws most clients off balance. Certain facial tics and contortions let her know they're debating whether to risk the last name instead of the first, which is what most opt for since you can get the first syllable right if you know how to say Chardonnay. Tasi has met a few men who thought it might be cute to call her Annie; they ended up having to say the whole mouthful of her name for the duration of the acquaintance.

While they wait for wine and hors d'oeuvres, Peter is intent on his own conversation. He's a regular conversation turbine, always talking about books and movies and plays and articles and the meanings he has culled from them, but as he knows his own conclusions already, Tasi tunes him out half the time. The other half, she puts questions to him and he evades them by making her laugh, watching her all the time for signs of acknowledgment—he wants to be sure she is aware of the evasion—and she finds ways to nail him on it. The others must think Tasi and Peter are playful, combative work pals, but it's not one-upmanship. It's the badinage of love. She likes him best when he is close upon himself and uncomfortable with her, when his voice shifts to that lower tone.

Peter's wife has a crafted girliness about her. You can see it in the little way Trisha folds and unfolds things, the way she wraps and tucks and containers everything in the baby bag.

"My mother was supposed to take the kids, but she called sick at the last minute. Wouldn't you know?"

"That's no fair," Tasi chimes in. "I bet you and Peter rarely get a night to yourselves."

Trisha exhales a long sigh and blows her bangs off her fore-head. "Birthdays and holidays only."

"I function as the family pressure valve," Tasi says warmly. "My brothers have five children between them, and I am the auntie who arrives with kites and stuffed animals. They've dubbed me the Minister of Out-to-Dinner."

"Lucky them. My siblings all live on the East Coast."

"Yeah, it takes all my brothers' control not to lay down rubber on the driveway as they leave for the weekend. Really, every family should have one unmarried, unencumbered member."

"You're right. Last year when Peter had to have back surgery, his sister came to stay with us. It was heaven."

As Trisha and Tasi chat along, she is aware that the conversation around them has drifted toward business—stock market trends and discretionary income. Tasi catches Peter's eye several times by mistake as it travels across the table towards his wife. Trisha once modeled for clothes catalogs and is used to being very beautiful. Peter watches her intermittently, watches her as she poses for an off-stage camera ever present in her mind. Trisha watches others watching her, even the waiters. Sometimes she catches Tasi at it, too, and she laughs quickly as though covering some gaffe on Tasi's part, as though she were extending sympathy. Peter translates the Italian entrees for her, and when the waiter comes, he says, "My wife will have the Capretto Alla Romano."

He would never order for Tasi, of that she is sure. She seems to inspire admiration in men, but rarely the devotion that makes for domestic arrangements. She doesn't do dependence well though she realizes that's not the only alternative. But even when she is in a relationship, she has a hard time remembering there's someone she has to confer with before making a decision. For women like Charlotte and Trisha, it's the old trade-off—your autonomy for his protection. Tasi doesn't condemn it; in this day and age, it's an arrangement between consenting parties, just not one that has ever looked attractive to her. It is true that she has never quite felt feminine. Even in sixth grade, her role was to be the brash one. She was always picked to start spin-the-bottle because the boys knew she was daring. They couldn't be so sure of the others. But boys don't want to kiss girls who are taller than they are, whose foot size is nearly the same. It was years before she met the Italian who told her that a statue must have a strong pedestal. Tasi polishes off the last melon and prosciutto appetizer with a relish that Trisha seems to observe closely.

She is proud of the fact that she has never displayed an iota of jealousy about Trisha, but she knows that the reason she detests her and admires her springs from the unquenchable longing of grammar school. She can't be some other way, but she is supposed to want to be. There are signs of her jealousy. If you were to see her with Trisha you might notice how she leans in a little too close, so she can inhale the combined scent of her shampoo, her deodorant, her perfume, and the body heat beneath.

Tasi does know the careful steps to the chess game at the office. Like the Knight, it's up two spaces and then one sideways, or some days like the Queen, diagonals only. She started as an administrative assistant to the Vice President and learned quickly that you're admired for your brains so long as they serve to make your boss shine. Criticism is best when oblique or put in question form: "Did you mean to. . . ? Was it your intention to. . . ? But it's a tricky maneuver to last at Zeffirelli because if you kowtow too much, the men of the inner ring are irritated by your fawning. The less they respect you, the more martyrdom they demand of you, until you find yourself working late Friday nights, and on Saturday morning picking up your boss's cleaning, and there's still the day Human Resources has a memo for you. Goodbye, you made some important man feel guilty. But if you don't placate them at all, if you show genuine irritation when the CEO forwards all his calls to your line (without so much as asking) because his assistant is sick, then they tell you plain to your face, you're not Zeffirelli material—you seem to lack the speed, the versatility, the savoir faire, the acumen, the ability to look ahead. Or was that the ability to look behind? Tasi was determined to last, which meant she had to understand the fine art of flirting.

Tasi learned that she could make almost any observation she wanted if she used the bad boy tone and smiled with a question mark afterwards. Her eyebrows seem to say, "Really you can't mean that, Mr. Cranky," and her refusal to take nastiness seriously had the effect of making these men safe with themselves. In her presence, the id of the powerful was chided. It made Tasi popular, popular enough to rise from administrative assistant to senior copy writer. And because the secretaries like her, root for her really as the only female executive, she knows much more about the men of the inner ring than they know about her—the little extra items on the travel expenditures sheet, the request for an insurance policy on the valuables at home, the afternoon appointment for marriage counseling.

Peter has never required Tasi to employ these tactics. In fact, he's always been rather self-effacing. If she comes up with a particularly shiny idea, he'll say to her: "You're brilliant, you know, not that you need me to say so."

By the time the dinners have arrived, Trisha seems to be virtually soaking up the elegant Norwegian who has launched into a discourse on the Italian wines they feature aboard their cruise ships. She can't seem to hear enough about what a cruise has to offer and clearly is taking a vicarious cruise while the children reach an unbearable din at Tasi's end of the table. Peter gives her an imploring look from his end though her boss and Pers are entirely oblivious. Apparently this task falls to Tasi. The baby is pooching out his lips and making the sounds of a rubber stopper half-jammed in a bath drain. Really, she has to laugh. He's already chucked his Healthy-Time biscuit twice so she hands him a spoon and he's instantly entranced sizing himself up in the ladle. Peter's older daughter isn't playing with the baby at all. No, she's preoccupied with her own orthodonture and keeps telling Tasi how many of her teeth have been pulled and which ones have yet to be. "It's terrible," she says in a voice overly arch, one that imitates parental concern. "My mouth is so overcrowded."

"Why you can't tell at all," Tasi says loudly, and the girl's face turns suddenly sullen.

Tasi takes up again with her brother. "Can baby say duck, yet? All babies have rubber duckies." The baby reaches suddenly for the topaz beads around her neck and grasps them with surprising tenacity. His winsome eyes are the same light green as Peter's and there's a familiar cast to his wet smiling mouth. Just as she pries the fingers on one hand free, he latches onto her hair with the other, then both, and is pulling her, pulling her towards his familiar glistening mouth. Tasi pushes him away roughly, but still he clings to her hair, and she has to unpeel his fat fingers one by one. "Goddamnit, you little shit," she says under her breath, but Peter's daughter has heard her, and she accuses Tasi with a flat metal stare.

NAN

∾

Wistful

On the drive home, Nan catches glimpses of the Snoqualmie River as it meanders across the broad flood plain. Today, she is gladder than ever that she lives north of Seattle, forty-five minutes from the city but a world away. The house is a 1940s style craftsman bungalow in a birch grove by the river, with lintels and floor trim the span of your hand, floors that resound with reassuring solidity beneath your feet. She and Clay sanded the oak floors themselves, reclaimed every inch of the house as well as the outbuildings, one of which became Clay's office, set up with his drafting table. The house is too small, especially with Irene's teenaged friends constantly banging themselves on the china hutch or the refrigerator as they get up from the dining room table. But Nan relies on the drive to decompress after work, and at night, she and Clay can hear the river; the sound of coursing water textures the first layer of their slumbers.

A red-winged blackbird rises from a bush brown-tipped with rotting rosehips. Nan sees that Clay is in the shed, his computer terminal on, his designer's brain intent on three-dimensional modeling. As a couple, they tell people that the shed is his office when in reality he spends the night in it a couple times a week. Clay is a man who ought to have a bumper sticker that reads: "I survived Catholic boarding school." Someone whose pet names were numbskull and dumbbell, whose father's edict, "if you can't do it right, don't do it at all," had left him diminished and defiant. Clay is one of those men who rarely had the chance to try anything for the first time without his father's critical eye upon him.

He was taught to analyze how to throw a football, how to cast a line, before he could ever *feel* how to do it. There's a legacy for sure. Woe to the woman who asks such a man to feel first, though initially she's what he wanted. Then the day comes when the exact quality he was attracted to becomes an expectation upon him.

Nan has always known that Clay's emotional timetable is glacial compared to hers, so when there are emotional issues to be faced, she sets out her grievances matter-of-factly and gives him a few days to respond. Typically, he retreats to the shed, which has allowed them to stay married because he can make good on his need to leave, just not very far. Men like Clay fear the loss of their autonomy almost as much as they fear becoming old and untouched. They are reassured by the woman who won't defer and placate, but pleas for negotiation often register as complaint. He says, I'm always the bad guy, he feels that he can't do it right. So, it's safest to do marriage partially, not to risk the total failure. Because Clay is loyal, the long-term and committed works for him, but it has to be a limited arrangement. Nan doesn't mind; she spent ten years as a single mom, and after a few days in the shed, Clay is like the ideal ex-husband, who does all the things you wanted him to when you were married: cleans the bathroom, takes the kids to dinner. He even demonstrates his loyalty by fixing the garage door opener and wiring new outlets. He is marvelous, truly, but he can only be successful in increments. Nan knows how to keep it light. When they kiss goodnight he either says, "See you in bed," or "Going to the shed." And the truth is, sometimes Nan likes to sleep alone, because she can read as late as she likes and feel her girl-self restored to her.

From the kitchen window, Nan sees clumps of Oregon Grape climbing up a blackened stump and the huckleberry bush whose berries her son likes to snack on in the summer. She is not much for planting unless it's a hardy native that can revive itself; gardening is not on her triage list. Her daughter, Irene, appears wearing hip hugger jeans and a shimmery silver belt. Her face is broad, like her mother's. She has a ranch woman's handsome ruggedness, wide-set blue eyes ablaze beneath a cap of sandy hair, but she doesn't appreciate that at sixteen, longing instead for the slender oval face of some Disney heroine.

"Mom, who ate the last of the Honeycomb?"

In the background, Luke's Hot Wheels hit the loop-the-loop and he shrieks an appreciative "Yes!"

"I don't know, Irene. I'm sure 'it wasn't personal." She gives Irene her exasperated look.

"Guess I'll have some cardboard flakes instead." Irene takes down the box of Special K. "You don't have to worry about portion control with the way these things taste."

"You don't have to worry about portion control anyway."

"Mom, what do you think of my new eye make-up?"

Nan puts down the paper and looks closely at her daughter. These moments of requested intimacy are rare or maybe it's just that they're not alone together much on the weekends.

"Very mermaid," she answers approvingly. Irene's eyelids are shellacked silver with speckles, and her fingernail paint is the silvery green of abalone shells.

"Cool."

She's loved mermaids since she was a toddler, when Nan read to her about the monkey's rescue by the winsome mermaids in *Babar and Zephir.* Nan has been absolutely candid with Irene about everything that goes on between a woman's legs, so she tries not to think what it means that Irene's beloved icon has no legs at all. The possibility that she hammered home too much responsibility about sex makes her a bit wistful. Perhaps Irene had to resort to the mermaid—a seductress who never seduces. At any rate, the mermaid has persisted into adolescence and Irene seeks out make-up and accessories to match her persona. She's working part-time at Value Village, the Mecca of thrift stores, and was ecstatic when she found a floor-length silver lamé skirt that could be converted into a tail in time for Halloween.

"Mom, I put this leather jacket on layaway for Jason. You should see it. Black leather, like it was made for him."

Nan shakes her head and Irene jumps to the worst immediately.

"What? It's my own money!"

"I know you want to get him something nice for his birthday, I just wish it didn't have to be something so spendy." Irene's penchant for lavishing gifts on this latest boyfriend pains Nan. There's too much desperation in it, as though Irene could indebt him to her, as though she weren't reason enough to stick around. Of course Nan reads her absent father into everything. What choice does she have?

"How do you know it's spendy?" She shoves her cereal bowl away and stands.

"Well, leather is always high-priced. I don't imagine that's changed too much."

"This is used, Mom. Used. It's not that much."

"Fine. But don't complain to me about riding the bus."

"I won't. It's my decision. If it takes a little longer to save up for the car, so what? I don't care."

Nan and Clay have told Irene that they'll pay for half a car when she has the matching funds. She's relatively cheerful about it most of the time considering many of her classmates' parents presented them with twenty thousand dollar death rides on their sixteenth birthdays.

The door to the garage opens and Clay pokes his head in. "Time to go," he says.

Irene swings a huge black book bag up from the floor and answers without looking at him. "I'm coming." Her tone pierces Nan. Clay looks at his wife and makes a little kiss noise. He refuses to take Irene's resentment to heart. God love him for it, Nan thinks, because she wants to kill Irene every time.

"Do I qualify for a kiss?" she asks Irene, emphasis on the "I."

"Yes," she says with a slight hiss at the end. "But you're still an M.O.M." Irene smiles warmly, her face open like a sudden vista.

"That's my job." Nan answers as she pecks her daughter on the lips. "Mean Old Mother."

"Back in a few," Clay calls.

Irene stops at the last moment, dramatically, one hand on the jamb.

"I forgot. You owe me one, Mom."

"What for?"

"Luke lost a tooth yesterday. Remember?"

"Oh, Jesus." She sinks into her seat.

"Don't worry, Mom. I covered you, but you can't run a tab with the tooth fairy, you know?"

"How much?" Nan wads up her napkin and throws it at her.

"I'll tell you after I get done calculating interest."

"Ireeeene," Clay calls in a falsetto singsong, and then they're gone.

Nan feels a pause in the day, standing above the kitchen sink where the brushed patina of stainless steel makes a tranquil surface for her mind. So does the collection of antique bottles on the windowsill, especially the gleaming blue milk of magnesia bottle. That blue, lapis lazuli, it's the color of wistfulness, the wistfulness she feels for Charlotte and Jean, her two friends who overnight became catalyzing chemicals in a reaction. Nan has agreed to call Charlotte, but she's avoiding it. Instead, she's searching through a portfolio of images from the past for clues about how they arrived here. Back in college, she could always tell when the checks from Charlotte's father's hadn't come in, when it was emergency loan time again. Charlotte would be sitting on the living room floor in the morning wearing a man's apricot-colored silk shirt, with a shoebox lid between her knees, which she tilted so the pot seeds would roll to the bottom while she scooped the shake with a matchbook. Certainly she wasn't going to class. She'd play that Roche Sisters song over and over: *I work at the circus and I sleep with the clown. When I took off my dress the sky fell down and if the sky falls down we play on the ground, cause I'm pretty and high and only partly a lie, pretty and high and only partly a lie. . . .*

Charlotte's mother worked hard as one of those ladies behind the cosmetic counter at Macy's, and Charlotte saw the tired face before her mother got glamorous each morning. Lilly simply couldn't help. She would have told Charlotte to get the money from her father. That had been the family dynamic all of Charlotte's life: her mother would ask first, her father would deny, then Charlotte would get put up to asking. Occasionally, he was the Disneyland Dad: ski trips, summer camps, slippers from Chinatown. But most of the time he said no, and Lilly was vindicated again. Charlotte's father, the bastard.

When Charlotte would look up from the floor, Nan always felt startled. Charlotte's face was like a celestial map, freckles denser at the center and spreading outwards proportionately: a suspended explosion. She laughed more than other people, in gales, determined to stay amused. They'd go to the House of Pancakes and swallow spongy globs of buttermilk pancakes. Comfort food. Charlotte compressed several layers at a time beneath her fork. "Squash, squash," she said smiling, "life won't do this to me."

In the midst of Nan's reverie, the phone rings. Almost on cue. She stares at the receiver, with all her concentration as if she could apply telepathy to it: good ring, answer, bad ring, no. She picks it up anyway.

"Hello . . . Nan?"

"Yeah, hi Charlotte. I've been thinking about you."

"Good or bad thoughts?" Her voice guarded, no pretense of cheerfulness.

"A friend's thoughts. Are you free to talk right now?"

"Yeah, it's fine. Darius left for Singapore this morning."

Nan knows that if he's home, Charlotte won't do anything but chitchat. Darius is paranoid she'll talk about him. He hovers. More than that. Charlotte has to keep herself a secret. There's some code she has to abide by to go on living with him. "Leave him," her friends have urged. She's always considering it, from the couch. Depression. Nan told her years ago. Now Charlotte takes Zoloft and drinks, too.

"So, I guess you're feeling pretty awful."

"Yeah, achy all over. Full body cast." Sparse laugh.

"I wish I could help. I'm not going to judge you, you know."

"Thanks, Nan. Thanks a lot." Slight pause, scritch of a lighter, dramatic exhale. "This one's a bitch. There's no way around it. . . . If I have the kid, I lose Darius. He can't handle it. I knew that when I married him."

"What's the deal with him? Things change."

"You really want to know?" Laughter—acrid, short.

"Yeah, I really want to know."

"Why? The only one of you who likes him is Virginia. Tasi thinks he's a necessary evil. She thinks if I were to choose again, I might do worse. Besides, with her an agreement is an agreement. All contracts are binding unless there's a contingency clause. Shit."

On a different day and in a different mood, Tasi would be the woman Charlotte wanted to talk to—her businesslike confidence and her been-there-done-that attitude.

Another smoky exhalation, a soft crunch, ice shifting in a glass. Nan notes the time on the oven clock: 11.07 AM.

"I don't hate Darius, but I've never thought he was good for you. And mostly it's because of stuff you've told me over the years."

"I know. But you don't see his tender side. He had a terrible childhood, and he's so scared of this, he's like a crazy man right now. We had a big blowout last night. He threatened to pitch my stuff on the curb and me with it."

"I'm sorry to hear that. Really, I am."

Nan is careful to keep the frustration out of her voice. She told Charlotte two years that the riskiest thing a woman could do in a relationship was give up all sources of independent income. Charlotte agreed. Nothing came of it.

Luke calls to her from the other room.

"Yes," Nan answers.

He shouts again, "Can I watch another show?"

"*Yes, you may!*" she shouts back. She hears a staticky click and then the cranked up glockenspiel music of Looney Tunes.

"Charlotte, I just want to be sure this decision is coming from you, not him. I want you to think about how *you* feel."

"I have. Believe me." Her tone is pleading. Nan moves on.

"Do you feel okay about your medical care? Has someone explained the procedure? It takes a couple days."

"Yes. Shit, I knew you'd start asking me all these questions." Whap! Nan jerks away from the phone receiver. She pictures Charlotte smacking it against the glass table. She hears background clanging . . . weeping. Nan wonders if Charlotte is coming back. Then there's a sudden screeching in her ear.

"I'm a fucking alcoholic! Nan. Get a clue."

"We all have bad stretches, Charlotte." Keep it even, she tells herself.

"This isn't a stretch, Nan, this is the highway. Remember the Cask & Cleaver? Fucking place. What did we call it?"

"Bask in Cleavage." Nan remembers the rusted saws on the walls, the washboards; the 16-ounce steak called Yukon Jack's Slab.

"Yeah, you looked cute in those lace-up blouses. I drank all the mispours and barkeep's rejects, that's when I learned how much I liked drinking in the afternoon."

"We were only in our twenties, Charlotte. Everyone partied then."

"Yeah, where did that verb go? Let's party. WooHoo! Now we're all bingeing and addicted and shit."

Partying. It was once innocent, idealistic even, homage to the sixties they had missed. Fragments of the music that played in their childhood broadcasts itself in Nan's mind. "Why don't we do it in the road. . . ?" "Lord you know it makes me high when you turn your love my way . . ." Ice chests in state parks, Tequila

Sunrises in tennis ball cans. She remembers. Love was a high, feeling high was love. No difference. Not until she had Irene.

"You can get off the booze. You've got lots of support."

"That's what I'm going to do, after the procedure." She spits the P-word out in scathing syllables. "Darius has found a place, a recovery place he thinks I can stand. He's more supportive than you think."

"If you want the baby, Charlotte, you don't have to wait. You can be pregnant and in recovery." This time she keeps the phone away from her ear.

"The baby will come out green! The baby will be a fucking Martian!" Her crying sounds jagged, hoisted over a rusty saw.

"Not necessarily, Charlotte. There are mediating factors like dose levels, chronicity, gestational age, duration of exposure. If you stopped drinking right now, there's a good chance the fetus would be all right."

"Don't tell me. Don't even start. You shift into nurse-speak and I can't stand it. The point is if I have this baby, my marriage is over, and I'm on my own. I can't face that. I don't want to be alone."

"You're not. Your friends love you. Your child would love you."

"How can I take care of a baby when I can't even take care of myself?"

Nan has no answer to this. She pushes away the distancing medical language in her mind . . . *ethanol and its metabolites cross the placenta and disrupt cell differentiation and growth.* Instead she sees the intensive neonatal unit—preemies shaking in incubators as though dreaming a dream of being dropped over and over again.

"Maybe you're right. Maybe all your strength has to go to battling alcohol. But there are a couple of things I need to let you know."

There's no intelligible response from the other end . . . globbering sounds. Nan might as well tell her now.

"Last night, Jean offered to raise the baby. She wanted me to ask you."

"Wait. I need Kleenex." Nan hears clambering, a thud. "Is Jean serious?" Charlotte's tone is abruptly controlled.

"Yes, she said she'd take all the responsibility of mothering and you could be . . . sort of the aunt."

"Wow."

Nan hears the soft crunch of ice again, the scritch of the lighter. Silence, then Charlotte's voice rigid. "No. I couldn't handle it. Darius couldn't handle it. It'd be like a permanent reproach to him, to us."

"Wait a sec." Nan peers into the living room. Luke is using the back of the leather couch like a pommel horse to vault off. "Cut it out, Luke! You know better than that." She draws a blank for moment before remembering her place in the conversation. "Is that the only way you can picture it, Charlotte? There are all kinds of family arrangements these days."

"I'm not that New Age, okay? I like being taken care of and I'm not going to rock the boat. I don't have big ambitions like you guys. I understood that a long time ago. If Jean wants to prove she can be a single mom to get even with Tim, that's not my problem."

Nan takes a huge breath, down into the gorge of her belly. She feels the ease that indifference would be, the temptation to cast Charlotte off like a bad fish on the line, and she resists it, speaking slowly.

"I don't think this is about Tim." Then she feels something rising up inside her, a widening bubble, the thing she told herself she wouldn't say. It breaks. "Charlotte, if you didn't feel strong ambivalence, you wouldn't have waited this long."

A long silence follows. Nan washes her hands and in her head sings "Yankee Doodle Dandy." Two times all the way through the way she was taught to scrub for surgery.

"Get off it, Nan," Charlotte says finally. "Tell me you didn't feel ambivalence about having a kid alone. You were working your ass off and living in a converted chicken coop."

Nan turns the water on hard, loud. She tries to wash the remark away. Charlotte goes on talking.

"That doesn't look good to me. And watching Jean do it with my kid, that doesn't look good either."

Nan figures it's her turn to be silent now. She is not going to say anything trite—how love makes it all worthwhile. Sometimes, love makes it hell. She was the first to get serious. Pregnancy has a way of doing that. Her daughter, Irene, was born six months after graduation, the father long gone to Alaska. Nan was getting up every four hours and putting hot compresses on her swollen breasts while her friends were ducking into the bathrooms to snort a line, or flopping on a mattress with some cute guy to make out.

Nan understands now that Charlotte's catering company made the "partying" fancy and formal. The party grown-up. Ice swans and roses and floating candles. Still, there was drinking. The crew in their twenties eager for afterward. The party Charlotte never wanted to give up. Party of one now.

"Nan?" Charlotte's voice sounds tremulous, frightened.

"Yeah, I'm here."

"Will you still be, when it's over?"

"Yes, Charlotte, I will. You don't get new old friends. Be strong."

"I'm not, not like you are."

"Be strong like you. Learn to take care of yourself."

"I'm not doing this to spare Darius. Honest to God, Nan, I'm not."

"I hope not . . . but I understand part of it. Believe me, I've seen a lot of couples who didn't think long and hard about becoming parents."

"Thanks for saying that."

"I'm saying it because it's true."

"Listen, I'm exhausted by now."

"Me, too. We'll talk later."

"About boring mundane shit, okay?"

"All right. Only boring mundane shit."

"Love you.

"Love you, too."

Nan makes Luke a piece of toast and watches him wipe his mouth on the shoulder of his robot pajamas. He has drawn a picture of three fish looking down inside the mouth of a volcano and he wants to be sure she understands the perspective. "See, this is the top of the ocean and this is the ocean floor." Nan pays close attention.

Charlotte's remark about Irene's early years stings. Irene didn't get to stay home in her pajamas like Luke. Nan's parents did what they could, but they both still worked, and Irene's father was only around long enough to complain about what a heavy trip Nan had laid on him. There was a hard place in Nan about that time, a hardness that wouldn't dissolve. She worked clerical jobs and later went to nursing school when her parents offered to take a loan against their house. Irene went to day care—the nine to five grind as a toddler, worse even because her day started earlier so Nan could get to work on time. She remembers Irene's rages by the front door, over putting on her shoes and coat. *Irene don't like school! Irene think it yucky!* And the clogged weeping of her submission. There are real reasons to be afraid of raising a child alone. Nan still feels Irene's every ache like a blow to the belly, but she has Clay now to help her keep things in perspective.

Nan has nearly unloaded the dishwasher when the phone rings again. Mornings like this are the reason all her plates are chipped.

"So what did she say?" Jean asks without preamble.

"She said no."

"Let me guess. Darius wouldn't like it."

"Right, but I think it's more complicated than that."

"It's as complicated as she wants to make it."

"Jean," Nan says, "you've always been a very secure person. Charlotte isn't."

"No, I've always been mouthy and gregarious. That's not the same as being secure." Nan hears Jean take a dramatic drag off her cigarette before she lunges ahead. "Darius is a dick so Charlotte is guaranteed perpetual wounding, and we're all supposed to sympathize until Kingdom come. I'm sick of it."

"Look, I wish she'd leave him, too."

"Yeah, it's not a question of whether she loves him. Loving him is against better judgment. But Charlotte could choose to make a whole new story with her child. I don't get it. She's almost five months pregnant for God's sake."

"Seventeen weeks."

"Okay. Eighteen by the time she goes in."

"I don't think we should talk about this anymore, Jean. I know what you'd give to have a baby."

"I think we have to talk about it. Men don't talk about abortions unless we make them. Are we going to be the same way?"

"I've had an abortion, Jean. And we've talked about it. But you're not judging me. How come?"

"Because," says Jean. "You're not self-destructive. You wouldn't wait this long. You wouldn't wait on a guy's opinion, especially a guy like Darius. I'm tired of everybody debating when life begins instead of when the woman could have and should have known. And it's not like Charlotte and Darius can't afford to raise this baby. Even if they divorced, she'd still be in pretty good shape."

"I agree with you, Jean. In France, abortion is illegal after ten weeks. But the commitment to an infant human is eighteen years, at least. If Charlotte says she doesn't feel capable of it, I think we should listen to her—"

"Will she feel it? Nan." Jean's voice cuts me off. "Will she feel the baby dying when she does it?"

"I doubt it. Twilight sleep is provided for all patients undergoing a second trimester abortion."

"So it'll just be another blackout for her."

"Jean, I don't think pursuing this is good for you."

"I don't care if it's good for me or not. Charlotte and I have
been friends for twenty years. I have to know."

Nan pictures Jean's face, splotchy from crying.

"Jesus Christ," Jean mutters. "How can Charlotte do this?"

"Because," Nan says grimly, "her assessment of herself is
realistic, even if her deliberations took too long. She's not cut
out to be a mother. Don't think she isn't going to feel dreadful
about this."

"Am I supposed to give a shit if Charlotte feels bad about it?
Am I supposed to make it okay to abort a five-month-old fetus
because she's got a self-esteem problem? Maybe Charlotte could
feel good about herself for doing something selfless. That'd be
a change."

"I did my best, Jean. I asked."

"Sorry, Nan. I don't mean to be so bitchy. Really, thanks a
lot. Bye."

Nan stands listening to the even growl of the dial tone; the
conversation ended as abruptly as it began. It's only noon, but she
feels like going back to bed. Instead she builds a swooping, inter-
secting maze of marble chutes with Luke, and something about
the clatter of marbles turning stiles and dropping down funnels
is pleasing.

Nan is convinced that there would have been another little
boy playing with them, if she hadn't had an abortion right after
nursing school. When the Diazepam hit her bloodstream, she
floated above herself, and saw him, running along an angle of
the prismatic ceiling light—curly-haired, his glance a quick jab—
running away from her. Though she felt sorrow, she can't say she
regretted the abortion. There was no reason to fool herself. She'd
been celibate for so long, she practically assaulted her date. She
got drunk; she got laid. In retrospect, she saw that her attitudes

still bore the legacy of high school sex ed, which had taught her not to admit to herself she was going to have sex: to abstain was holy, to plan was harlotry—the median between these two was total inebriation. In reality, she had carried her diaphragm in her purse that night, but in the morning, to her horror, she found that the diaphragm was wedged sideways. Whether she'd put it in wrong or it had became dislodged during the calisthenics, she'd never know. Irene was six years old, and Nan wasn't kidding herself about having a baby. Fetus aborted at seven weeks. She hardly felt it. What Charlotte may feel is another story.

Years later, Nan saw an ultrasound of Luke at seven weeks, the heart pulsating like a flare amidst the dark fluid. Clay, of course, was thrilled beyond belief; he even asked the doctor if they could take home a printout of the image. But for Nan, it was the beginning of a long period of dread. Against all reason, she feared she would be punished for the abortion, and she wondered if all women felt this. She knew it was positively draconian. Her father told her, "Honey, Puritan women were blamed for the deaths of their own babies, told they had displeased God. There's a lot of that attitude still floating around, but don't you take it on." Nan's dread increased anyway, especially when she underwent the amniocentesis. It took no small amount of pressure to puncture her uterine wall, like putting a nail through a basketball. Clay was there to hold her hand through the amniocentesis, but she lay in bed the rest of the day praying the hole in the amniotic sac would mend. She napped that afternoon and when she woke to the sound of the river, to the sound of Clay and Irene chatting in the kitchen, she found that the dread had lifted, and in its place an implacable joy. By the time the results of the amniocentesis arrived, she was no longer concerned if they were normal or not. She knew she would love her baby no matter what, if his brain were an open bloom, or his heart had three chambers. She knew she would love him even if she had to watch him die. And though in the end, Luke was born totally healthy, Nan understands why Charlotte is unwilling to subject herself to this kind of love.

VIRGINIA

ॐ

Fool Star

This spring Finley started dating. Virginia knows because she wanted to trade one of Milo's Saturdays for a Sunday and Fin couldn't.

"I'm going on a date," he said, sounding slightly chagrined.

She tried to play her part lightly. "Oh, really. Where did you meet her?"

Whenever he needs a date, it seems he just goes on a hike and there she is, some twenty-three-year-old enacting the Diana-archetype that Virginia abandoned a decade ago. She can just hear her. *Yeah, I often hike by myself. Me and my dog Justy, that is.* Nature Girl has a hole in her jeans and her hair smells strongly of herbal cream rinse. Pow, they're dating.

"I don't think Milo is ready to meet anyone else right now, Fin."

"I'm not sure I am either, Ginny. So don't worry about it. If I get into something hot and heavy I'll be sure to let you know."

His sarcasm was defensive, a reminder of Virginia's rejection. She didn't rise to meet it. She couldn't. Her throat felt like pine bark. "Ginny?" he said into the silence.

"Yeah, Fin. I'm just trying to be a grown-up about this. It's going to take me awhile to adjust."

There it was. The admission that she still cared about him that way. Now he'd probably be totally messed up for his date. Well, good, Virginia thought, though she wondered how she could be so sincere and pained one moment, and wicked the next. The guilt wore her out.

The truth is, Virginia is still recovering from a full-blown crush on one of her students. It has never happened to her before; she can honestly say that, not in ten years of teaching . . . but suddenly she feels a profound attraction. She isn't scooping babies out of cradles (this fellow is thirty-five if he's a day) though certainly she has had some opportunities with the downy-cheeked ones. No, this guy is your typical atypical cowboy of the sea who strides into her office trailing a whole interesting life—fisherman, charter captain, bartender, legal assistant, corrections officer. If he'd been born in Jack London's day, his résumé would have included stevedore, hod carrier, drover, longshoreman, and the like. Jack is what she calls him, and to herself, Jack of Hearts. While everyone around him seems to get through the days on little Bunsen burners, Jack stokes a bonfire day *and* night. He's got three part-time jobs or something ridiculous but still manages to read the homework five times before class and make searingly astute comments. He's also irreverent in a way that few of the twenty-year-olds understand, and Virginia has to keep herself from falling into private jokes with him in front of the class. The man lets her know she's alive.

Their little flirtation goes on for some months. Jack comes to her office regularly; she loans him books. At the end of the quarter, he writes her a thank-you note for the class. Nice. Complimentary. Full of well-placed innuendo. "I completely enjoy you and your class." Which she disagrees with of course. Virginia's idea of his "completely enjoying" her is a variety of positions none of which have to do with the rank and file of faculty. He's taken to greeting her with the words "Hey, lady," which is, she knows, hopelessly seventies, but it also says something sweet about romantic notions she still responds to, when Led Zeppelin could write lyrics that began, "Hey, lady, you got the love I need." How many times did she drop the needle back at the beginning of that song when she was twelve? Rock'n'roll meets courtly love.

Briefly, Virginia is foolish enough to believe she has some sort of hold on Jack—a charismatic combination of age, intellectual prowess, beauty, and vitality. Until she runs into him in the hallway two weeks into the winter quarter. He hasn't been to visit her yet and she finds herself making cloying comments about books of hers in his possession and the discussion about graduate school they need to have and any other shameless entanglement she can remind him of. He says, "Maybe I'll come by later." Maybe. Has she ever heard him use the word before? She goes back to her office and sits.

She has never known what it felt like to be an older person nursing an infatuation for a younger one (only three years, for criminey's sake!). But it's not chronological age alone; it's the shift to family life and all its attendant worry. Scraps of a Carl Sandburg poem come to her like bits of far off music. *I could love you as branches in the wind brandish petals, as dry roots love rain. Love is a fool star.* The overbearing steam heat of her office brings out the smell of cleaning fluid in her jacket; the red message light on her phone blinks like the Cyclops' eye. She waits the whole hour, her heart yanked open each time she hears the hall door and brought to a shuddering close with it. Jack does not appear.

Virginia fishes around in the back of her desk drawer and finds the picture of her husband she threw back there amid the stray tea bags and tacks and busted-up chalk. He is standing on the beach in Oregon, Milo on one hip and a pastel baby bag knocking against the other—there's a nacre sheen to Finley's skin, a roundness to his jaw that's no longer there, in his expression the unabashed desire to be a good father. Virginia's sigh is a substitution for words she can no longer find. . . . Was it only four years ago that they took that trip? *Dear battered Fin*, she thinks, *You've been my scapegoat. Because when I look into your face I can' t reject my own aging.*

She doesn't know what to do with the photo now that she has it out. She told her office mates she was separated from her husband. That's their status. He's dating Miss Hole in Her Jeans. But it doesn't feel right to stick him back in with the stray staples. Virginia climbs up on the desk and puts him behind a stack of books up high, and it gives her some satisfaction that only she knows where he is. Then she draws her shoulders back and ties the sash of her coat briskly, trying out the new formality she intends to adopt with her former student. Fuck you, Jack, as the proverbial saying goes.

As it turns out, Virginia gets to test her new sentiments toward Finley that afternoon. They're to meet at Powell Elementary at four o'clock. She is glad Finley can make it; he's the type who wants to go to his kid's conferences and means it. Milo has had a very rough start with school. His kindergarten teacher is big on routines, and the first few days of class have been all about when to do what and how. Virginia is working hard at reserving judgment. How could a teacher manage without routines? When people gripe about teachers taking summers off, Virginia asks them: Could you spend your day with twenty-five six-year-olds? Only she wishes Mrs. Melveny had tried harder to make the first few days fun. Milo told her he was sick of sitting in a circle and listening to that lady yabber. His words exactly. But the crux was when he was asked to color. Finley and Virginia have had an easel set up in the kitchen since he could stand, and Milo loves to draw. To say that he doesn't like school would be an understatement. *I'm not ever going back and you can't make me.*

Virginia seems to take Milo's side rather readily . . . because she doesn't want to teach him to override his own judgment about what's best for him. That morning, she told him they'd find a solution or send him to a new school.

"What?" said Finley on the phone, "Like we can afford to send him to a private school?"

Virginia had to lock herself in the bathroom to talk because she'd let Milo take the day off from school while she corrected papers at home.

"You let him stay home?" Finley said, in the sort of measured rhetorical way meant to call her parental judgment into question without direct confrontation.

"Just until we can meet with his teacher and straighten this out. Listen, Fin, we'll do what we have to. I'm not going to have his creativity squelched in kindergarten. We've got twelve more years of this."

"Yeah Ginny, but you don't want to teach Milo to bail at the first sign of a problem."

Virginia knows there's some balance between listening and being an advocate for your child, and teaching him to persevere and find solutions. She is just not sure what it is and she has no intention of admitting it to her estranged husband. Not now.

"Four o'clock, Fin, just be there at four o'clock."

Milo's new school is the usual institutional brick and stucco, though because it's one story and small, it doesn't seem too imposing. Finley meets Virginia in the parking lot, still wearing his steel-toed boots and workshirt. The man has a master's in cartography of all useful things, and she suddenly wishes he didn't look so working class. Yes, that from Virginia who is always berating the women of her generation for griping about a lack of nice men when they won't date guys in the trades.

They walk by the school office and down the corridor together. Virginia steals a few glances at Finley. She is scrutinizing his face for signs of age. Ever since he told her about the twenty-three-year-old she can't help it. Today, he looks harried; he swipes his face with his palm, then scrubs at his forehead. Virginia thinks he is more handsome than he has a right to be.

Mrs. Melveny's room is covered with those prints you can make by pressing leaves in paint, very veiny and bright. Virginia notices that the turkeys have been taken down and the snowmen stapled up. She and Finley sit in the tiny chairs with their knees right up to the edge of the table. Mrs. Melveny is wearing ice pink lipstick and a little pin on her collar—a heart-shaped chalkboard replete with miniature writing that says 2+2=4. She has one of those haircuts that makes you look like you've been hit in the back of the head with a snow shovel, this great whacked off shelf that tapers down to a little rat tail. "Call me Susan," she says to them. Virginia is trying very hard to like her.

Mrs. Melveny's pellucid blue eyes are sincere and Virginia thinks how nerve-wracking it must be to meet twenty-five sets of parents. She tells the teacher how excited they are about the field trip to the hatchery and the upcoming focus on the developmental stages of salmon: egg, alevin, fingerling, fry, adult. Is that right or is she adding an extra? Finley gives her a look, and Virginia knows she's laughing too much. She wants to make Mrs. Melveny feel appreciated so she'll know they were not a pair of gripers. It's Fin who brings things down to business.

"We have some concerns," he says carefully. The moment stretches out oddly for Virginia. There's no hesitation in Fin's use of the pronoun "we," and she can feel Mrs. Melveny regarding them as an intact couple. It occurs to Virginia that in this room where they belong to Milo, they are intact, his basic story—the Ur-story of their child's life.

"Of course," Mrs. Melveny says, "And that's what I'm here for, and I want to assure you that I'm always available to hear parental concerns."

It sounds very nice. It also sounds very canned. That's the part that Virginia doesn't find reassuring, how well-modulated her voice is.

"You know Milo really loves to draw," begins Finley, "beehives and beaver dams, and the insides of the body. That's his thing. He's really depressed about having to color."

Mrs. Melveny continues smiling, the sort of held-onto smile a person makes for a camera when the photo opportunity is taking too long. "We all have to do things we don't necessarily like," she says. "That's what I tell my kids when it's time to vacuum."

Finley looks up from his hands; his gaze on her unwavering. "Mrs. Melveny, learning is not vacuuming. Milo *is* doing things he doesn't necessarily like, most of the day, and he's doing a good job." A rueful smile plays over his lips.

Mrs. Melveny's eyes widen, then water perceptibly. Inwardly Virginia is cheering Finley. He not only bears discomfort well, he knows when to create it. Virginia knows she's the sort of idiot who'd jump up and pass the cookies by now.

"He'll still have to color on the worksheets," Mrs. Melveny says guardedly. "That's part of identifying the sounds or numbers."

"We understand that," says Finley, again making them a united front. "But we can't see any benefit to coloring between the lines rather than free-drawing."

"Well, it does improve manual dexterity, focus, and control." Her intake of breath is sharp.

"Susan," Finley says pointedly, in a way that utterly dismisses her previous comment, as though she had lost consciousness and he were saying her name while waving smelling salts under her nose. "Susan, is there some reason Milo can't have a blank sheet of paper when the activity is coloring? Drawing is what he loves. Being able to do that could turn his attitude around."

"No, no, certainly not," Her voice is brittle cheery. "I just wanted you to understand that there would still be some coloring in the curriculum."

Virginia quickly brings out his first painting assignment, a sky with a moon and a star already drawn, and tries to soften the discussion. "I realize that for some children the forms will be comforting, if they haven't had the kind of encouragement that our son has. But for other children, the implicit message is 'I can't draw the stars or a moon.'"

She can see Mrs. Melveny's chest fall as she lets out a huge breath. "Well," she says, "I have had some MonArt training. You know, getting the kids to work with the shapes and forms that make up, say a lion or a steamboat. I could include some of those lessons this year. I certainly do want Milo to be happy here."

"Thank you, Susan," says Finley, firmly sticking to the first-name basis. "We appreciate that."

Outside, Virginia thanks Finley, profusely, and he tells her "Don't sweat it, Ginny. Milo's my kid." The fact that he says it, feels he *must* say it, seems to stun them both. The wind is warmer than Virginia expects for January; the cherry trees in the parking lot have leapt into false spring. They shed blossoms onto the wind, and the pavement turns glittery when a cloud is torn by sun. Virginia suddenly feels trapped in some sad little haiku, seventeen syllables of poignancy in a parking lot. Unbearable.

"Fin, let's pick up Milo together and get a cheeseburger. Just for fun. Just to show him we still can."

Finley drags his palm back over his face and one corner of his mouth goes tight. "I can't, Ginny, I've got to be somewhere."

"Oh," she echoes, "somewhere." He doesn't elaborate. She steps back and holds up her hand; it's a cross between a wave goodbye and a gesture that says, "Stop, too much." Too much innuendo for Virginia in one day, and none of it the kind she likes.

ॐ

The Next Station

This week Tasi is going in for a body tune-up. On Tuesday she has a doctor's appointment and on Thursday another, then on Friday she plans to pick up Charlotte after the abortion and drive her home. First, there's the mammogram and then the gastroenterologist to discuss the return of her ulcer. Tasi prefers to schedule these kinds of appointments back to back. She and Peter have a pact about not discussing middle-age medical problems. They mention things in passing. When she learned at the office he was going in for back surgery, she allowed herself to ask, "Are you all right?"

"Of course I'm all right," he answered jovially "I'll be whiny and miserable, one more for the Boring Ward."

Ever after, this has been their short hand, and occasionally when one of them has been absent from the office, the other is permitted the question and the piercing look: Are you all right? And the answer is invariably "One more for the Boring Ward" with some eye rolling. Tasi feels this is one consolation of growing old alone; she won't have to listen to some old man discourse on his ailments as though he'd become the project manager of his own bodily breakdown.

On Tuesday, she goes to the Northwest Radiology Center about a lump, not her first. Tasi has fibrocystic breasts (which means hard and lumpy), though she sometimes gets the term mixed up with cystic fibrosis and alarms the nurses. Anyway, with her chest it's difficult for anyone to tell what's a scary lump from a regular lump. So they smash her boobs flat in the tortilla press and then the nice ultrasound technician gouges around with her wand while narrating the event in a high 1950s falsetto voice. The tech keeps finding this little grainy mountain. "There it is again!" She leaves Tasi in a cubicle the color of graham crackers and goes to find the booby-doctor while Tasi wonders what she would put at the top of her wish list if she really were dying. First to come to mind is a naughty weekend with Peter at the Four Seasons Hotel, one in which she laughs a lot but hints at bad medical news, relegating everything to the "Boring Ward" if pressed further. And then of course she wishes for an incredibly speedy demise, like the following Monday, which would make Peter realize . . . what would it make Peter realize? That he should have married her? That she was his incomparable soul mate but he'd been too caught up in a script of social obligation to notice?

She tries to imagine herself as a bride, but all she can think about is how much fatter white makes you look and her mind runs like a home video of a gi-normous bride holding hands across from a groom the size of the wedding cake prop, except all he can hold onto are her pinkies, and then the camera moves too close and there ensues a catastrophic, blurry, white-out interrupted by the doctor's entrance in a lab coat. While she blinks at his face and tries to remember his name, Dr. So & So props her up with pillows for a better grinding and gouging angle. Then he explains: "The up-shot is the hard tissue is close to the chest wall so it's pushing up into the fat layer, but it's all healthy tissue."

Tasi's body floods with almost orgasmic warmth and she momentarily considers that this is what it feels like to be attracted to yourself and too bad it took near death to induce it. When Charlotte calls later that evening, she tells her "Yeah, I'm okay, just getting lumpy like an old couch. In fact, when the doctor asked me to find the lump one more time, I couldn't even find it . . . guess they'd smashed my lump to smithereens."

"You'll be fine so long as no one hugs you for the rest of the week."

"No danger of that."

"Is Peter playing distant?"

"No, no. His kids are sick."

"How can you stand to play second fiddle? There's another reason not to have kids."

"I don't feel like second fiddle, Charlotte. I'm the tuba or something, essential but in a class of its own. How are you feeling about Friday?"

"It can't get here fast enough, Tasi. That's how I feel. My boobs hurt. The drop of a pin makes me cry. I fought with Darius about artichokes last night, if you can believe that."

"Why artichokes?"

"Because he wouldn't spend three dollars on one. I decided to hang the fate of our whole marriage on that fact."

"You could always buy yourself an artichoke."

"True, Tasi, but I wanted him to buy me one."

"What you really want is for him to come with you on Friday, but—"

"I know he won't. That's it, Tasi. He doesn't do pain well. What can I say."

"But he'll be helpful when I bring you home?"

"Oh, yeah. By then he'll be fine. He's already stocked the freezer and organized the take-out menus. He's not afraid of recovery. And he's talking about taking me on that Cayman Islands cruise because he knows I've always wanted to go—not business either, just vacation."

"Well, you take him up on the grand gesture, honey. It'll even out the scales."

"Oh, I will. You better believe it."

At the office on Wednesday, Peter puts his head in Tasi's office. Beneath his beard, his cheeks are ruddy; his rosecia flares up when he's stressed.

"Yeeesssssss?" she says, making it a glissando from low note to high.

"I'm about to be an absolute boor. Are you up for it?"

"What are you dumping on me?" she asks, squinting at him.

"I can't finish the British Petroleum account before five, but I've got to pick up Annie from day care because Trish will be at the orthodontist's with Haley."

"So overtime for me and undertime for you. Is that it, darling?"

"I'll make it up to you. I'll overtime you until you squeal for me to stop."

"I never squeal."

"We'll see about that."

"Go," she says, waving him out of her office. "Just go."

But her face goes absolutely glum as the door shuts. She'd wanted to stop by Hendrickson's, her favorite used bookstore, and buy herself some paperbacks, then indulge in tea and a marzipan cookie at the European bakery next door. Now it would have to wait. At the base of her sternum, she feels the acids of her stomach begin to boil like soup in a rusty pot on a cook stove. The faint taste of aluminum and tomato come up the back of her throat. She pulls out her purse to see if she can take another pill—Protonix, Prilosec, Prevacid—she can't remember which one she is on.

There has been too much extra work recently, and it isn't all from Peter. The notion that single people have no lives is embedded in countless workplace decisions. Tasi gets the out-of-town assignments more frequently, and once when she was late for work, her manager pointed out, "You have no family."

"And if I did, would that be an acceptable excuse for tardiness?" she'd shot back.

The truth is, she does have family, just not immediate family, though she can't imagine what could be more immediate than a mother who spits her medicines out and a father who fires the home-health-care nurses. It has been peaceful for awhile though, because of her brother, Bayard. Of her three brothers, she would have nominated Bay "Least Likely to Help Out," but now he is living in their folk's camper in the driveway and managing the marketing and the cleaning with an almost saintly forbearance, as though he'd waited his whole life for this opportunity to prove his usefulness. And he is earnest about it. On the phone, he told Tasi, "I'm finally able to do something for the folks. And that feels really good to me." Bay is nothing if not earnest.

"Shall I leave on my bottoms?" Tasi asks the nurse on Thursday.

"Oh, yes," he answers, cheerfully. "You don't want us to do the wrong end."

The very thought of a colonoscopy makes her shudder. "God, no. It's bad enough to be plumbed from the mouth down."

The nurse giggles. His name tag says Wyatt and he has red highlights in his hair. He undoes the clasp of her opal necklace very gently.

Dr. Ackley, the gastroenterologist, who looks a bit like Kris Kristofferson if you added fifty pounds, stops by to see if they're ready. He hands her a color chart entitled, "Diseases of the Digestive System," pointing out gastric ulcers as well as acute and chronic gastritis. The whole thing—with its bulbs and ducts and valves—reminds her of a gigantic mollusk, something that should definitely stay inside the shell.

Tasi shakes the doctor's hand before he leaves to change into scrubs, and he looks mildly surprised. She always makes a point of shaking a doctor's hand before he does anything to her. It makes the moment more like a business deal in which he has to make good on his end of the bargain. Then Wyatt pushes the clear liquid of the syringe into the clear liquid of the I.V. bag and the darkened room begins to warp, bend, and buckle as the anesthesia takes hold. The nurse checks on a machine across the room, then places his hand soothingly on her forearm.

"How are you?" he asks.

"I'm having an affair with a married man," she hears herself answer, except it sounds like "I'm making muffins with the muffin man."

"Oooo," he says, swishy in his disapproval. "You know he won't be there when the wind blows."

"The wind is blowing now," she hears herself say, except it sounds like, "I'm going to be going now."

"Open your mouth," the doctor says. He seems to be stuffing something down her throat. She can feel her windpipe, like the plastic ring around a milk bottle. Down, down, down, the tube goes, bringing with it remarkable awareness that her stomach is indeed a cavity. The doctor pulls it out with a whipsaw sound, like a sword vibrating. "I'm a sword swallower," she says cheerfully to the gastroenterologist, "And you're the magician."

"She shouldn't be saying anything," the doctor says sharply.

"I'll up her two cc's," replies the anesthesiologist.

Nan arrives on her lunch break to take Tasi home and finds her in the recovery room with her head resting on her chest, drooping slightly to one side; she looks like a child passed out in a car seat—her carefully lightened hair so shot through with silver it gleams. All of Tasi's features are large—a broad mouth and distinctly Gallic nose, long and snubbed with that almond shape at the end that a psychic once told her portended intuitive power. Nan touches her friend's face.

"Hey, honey, how're you holding up?"

Tasi snaps to attention like a bird dog pointing. "Jesus," she says, wiping at some slobber on her cheek, "I don't want to keep you. I'll be just a minute."

Nan holds her hand firmly. "Not until the doc okays you to leave."

As though on cue, Dr. Ackley appears. His eyes are too blue, contact lens blue, the color of lakes in menthol cigarette commercials. He immediately takes in Nan's uniform, and after the exchange of formalities, falls into discussion with her of the photos he holds in his hand. One of them appears to be a straight black tube descending into a pit of pink wriggling worms. Though he holds the photos where Tasi can see them, it is clearly Nan he is speaking to as he points at an orange blob that looks like a vinyl beanbag chair.

"We won't know what to make of this lesion until the biopsy results come back in a few days."

"Could it be merely an irritation of the stomach lining?" asks Nan.

Tasi can feel her mind like quaking protoplasm trying to unstick itself from the drugs and consolidate, but like the word "lesion," it seems too firmly adhered to budge. What does lesion mean anyway?

"Nan," she croaks when he has gone away, "what's a lesion?"

"It's one of those catch-all words, Tasi, when they don't know what to say yet."

"It looked nasty. It looked like a big ugly tumor."

"When you look inside the body, you see all kinds of funky things," Nan says, helping her rise. "Most of them you just live with without knowing it."

"But he did use the word biopsy."

"Yes, but your stomach lining could also be so irritated the tissue looks bubbled."

"I'd be insane if you weren't here. What did they give me?"

"Hmm. Let me look at the discharge sheet. Says here they gave you Versed and Fentanyl. You should be able to take a nice long nap. You're going to be sore for a few days. Here, I'll just come in with you while you get dressed."

"Don't worry. I'm not going to fall down."

"Oh, I'm not worried. I know you too well. Someone would have to knock you over the head first."

On the car ride home, Nan asks, "How are your parents?"

"Not good. Mom has got gout in one leg, so it swells. She never did do the knee surgery, so she drags it everywhere. They've got her arteries dilated, but she still keeps having these mini-strokes that no one can seem to stop."

Tasi's seat is reclined and she's looking out the window. For a moment, Nan thinks she's drifted off, but she speaks, seems to want to keep on talking.

"Mom's batty as hell basically. She'll ask if anyone wants coffee. We all say no. And then my dad catches her making coffee, and wigs out because he doesn't want her getting burned, but she won't let go of the coffee pot so they both end up burned."

"Not good. Sorry, I'm laughing."

"You have to laugh."

"Is your Dad still firing the home health care workers?"

"Yeah, they won't even send them anymore. Not since he locked the Romanian woman out. But my brother Bay came last week. He quit his job at the organic market or whatever and moved home to take care of them."

"God love him for that. Now you won't have to be driving to Bellingham every weekend. You've got to decrease your stress if you're going to heal your stomach."

"Yeah, I know. I realized the other night that I ate a whole bottle of Canadian aspirin this fall."

"The stuff with the codeine in it?"

"Yeah, what else. I'm an idiot, I know."

"Well, that will tear up your stomach pretty good."

"Hey, did you know that Charlotte is going in tomorrow for the procedure?'

"You mean the abortion?"

"Yeah."

"I knew it was sometime this week."

"Darius won't go in with her so I'm going."

Nan smacks the steering wheel with one hand. "I know teen-aged boys who can do better than that." She sighs audibly. "But some men can't face it, I guess. You shouldn't be going anywhere tomorrow."

"Well, I am. I don't have to do anything but walk and sit, and I've got the day off already."

"I brought you some ginger ale and saltines. Jean says she'll stop by in the evening with tapioca."

"Thanks. Thanks a bunch. Do you think Charlotte is wrong to be getting this abortion?"

"Tasi, I'm a nurse. My job is to help people get to the next station in life, whatever that may be. Charlotte may or may not regret it, but wrong? That's not my language."

At home, Tasi stands in front of her answering machine swaying on her feet, one hand on the desk. "First new message received at 8:34 AM. "Hello . . . Hattie? It's Winnie. Don't forget our lunch date . . . at the . . . at the . . . you know the place . . . the Coffee Break. We'll go to bridge after . . . [Beep, Message deleted]."

"Who was that? A wrong number?" asks Nan, popping her head out of the kitchen.

"No, it's my mother, who thinks I am her sister."

Nan nods, then does the tactful thing. "I have to go now. Promise me you'll put your feet up for the afternoon."

"Promise," Tasi says as they hug. Nan's head nearly fits under her chin. When she hears the front door click into place, she punches the button again.

"Next message at 8:42 AM. Hello . . . Hattie? It's Winnie. I miss you so much. I hope you'll come to see me soon. Leonard just gave me the most beautiful string of pearls and I want to show them to you . . . [Beep, Message deleted]."

"Next message at 8:46 AM. Hello . . . Hattie? I've got a bone to pick with you. When Aunt Esther gave you that silver tea service, she told me expressly that Mama had said I should have the serving platters . . . *Give me the phone, Winnie . . . Give me the phone, Winifred* . . . Ouch, Leonard. You don't have to do that . . . *Who were you calling? Who were you calling?* Hattie . . . *Hattie? Oh, for the love of God* . . . clatter . . . dial tone . . . [Beep, Message deleted]."

"Next message at 9:06 AM. "This is Doctor Ackley's office calling to confirm that your prescription has been filled and you may [Beep, Message deleted]."

"Next message at 9:22 AM. "Hey, Tasi. This is Peter. I know you're taking a sick day, but if there's any chance you finished proofing the copy for that B.P. project and could give me a [Beep, Message deleted.]"

"Next message at 2:02 PM. "Hey Tasi, it's your brother, Bay. Just wanted to let you know I'm here, trying to keep the scene copacetic. Dad is going golfing this afternoon, which is good 'cause he looked like he was going to blow a gasket, and I'm driving Mom to the hairdresser's. Now that should be fun. Give me a call if you want an update. I love you. I'll see you next weekend [Beep, Message saved]."

Oh, thank God for Bay, Tasi thinks as she veers toward her plump and welcoming bed. She curls around her hot water bottle and sighs. Behind her eyes appears a web of blue. There seem to be bubbles coming up all around her and she is trying to see through chlorine which hurts her eyes while light plays off the pool walls in bright and shifting oblongs. Isn't that Willie Moses from sixth grade kissing her best friend Denise? She tries harder to see. Willie's hair is lifting off his face. At the same time, he is trying to sink Denise with his weight so he can keep kissing her. Tasi kicks to stay down. Denise's hair washes over her face. Denise is hanging onto Willie and pulling the strands away. The veins under Tasi's eyelids are starting to hurt. She pivots: all around her are the other underwater entanglements of her classmates. Her 360 complete, Tasi watches Denise break away from Willie's kiss, releasing bubbles. When the wake of Denise's kicking clears, Tasi suddenly sees Peter on the other side of the pool, coming at her in bloated slow motion, making poochy lips. She spurts to the surface for air and hangs onto the side of the pool. She wakes up panting; she wakes up remembering.

In real life, when Tasi got home from Willie Moses's birthday party, she discovered her bathing suit was on inside out so that the white crotch patch was showing. No one had told her. All were treacherous, even her supposed best friend, Denise, who had Willie Moses after all. He was the sixth grade model for masculinity. Moz, as the boys on the swim team called him. After that experience, Tasi knew what was the matter, why the boys used to call her to the back of the bus to start spin the bottle, but no one ever wanted to go in the closet with her for truth or dare. She was too forward, which was sometimes convenient. But she didn't cultivate the popular wan femininity. Femininity—a word that sounded like it had ninny in it. And though she was mortified to think of her appearance poolside in a navy blue-one piece with white crotch patch showing, she thereafter took a stance of defiance.

JEAN

∽

In Flames

Jean rings from the lobby to Tasi's cell phone before coming up. She comes in carrying a bowl, which she balances against one hip while closing the door, a maneuver a person of shorter limbs or less grace could never have managed. Jean's movements are eloquent precisely because they are entirely unself-conscious.

Jean kisses Tasi on the forehead then perches on the bed, her arms extended, elbows appearing to flex slightly in the wrong direction. The two friends smile at each other, taking their time, basking in a certain likemindedness they have always enjoyed. Neither of them is the gushing type.

"I brought you chicken soup and tapioca."

"Wow," says Tasi. "Thanks."

"There's no wow about it. The chicken soup is Progresso in a can, but I did make the tapioca."

"Hey, Progresso's the best. We're not make-it-from-scratch types." Jean stokes Tasi's hand on the coverlet. Tasi's cut-and-dry assessments always soothe her. They are both women of unlikely alliances, who forge coalitions from unlikely factions: Tasi can get developers to donate land to greenways coalitions and land conservation trusts while Jean used to negotiate daily between the Department of Social and Health Services, service providers, and clients. When Tasi and Jean first met each other, they'd both been bristly, given each other the once-over, even as potential roommates highly recommended by others. It's a memory they like to share frequently. *We weren't taking anyone else's word for it, were we?*

"How're you doing?" Tasi asks, heaving herself up. Without a word Jean pushes a few pillows behind her back. "I heard from Nan that Timmy and what's-her-face had a baby boy."

"They did, and that's all the news I can handle this week."

"Just remember, babies drool, spit, and shit."

Jean laughs. "I've always appreciated your attitude. Tough luck, too bad, move on."

"Well, that's me. I can be counted on for a sentimental response."

"How are *you* feeling?" Jean asks, nodding towards her friend. "Nan said they did some biopsies."

"Pretty sore. The way I felt after someone gave me acid cut with strychnine. Jesus." Tasi grunts and reaches for the bottle of Percocet. She surrenders it to Jean who twists the top off.

"And now you'll be happy if you can drink a cup of coffee a day." What Jean doesn't say is *now we'll be happy if you don't have stomach cancer.* "When will you know the test results?"

"In about three days. There won't be anything the matter with me, but it's a hell of a way to shrink things back into perspective."

"Like what things?"

"Oh, projects I was worried about at work." Tasi pauses and shrugs. "Whether or not Peter really loves me. I had to have dinner with his wife last week."

"Ugh," says Jean, pondering Tasi's rare admission of need, patting her hand again.

"Funny, he was all I could talk about going under anesthesia." Tasi ducks her head back and swallows the pill she has been holding. Jean takes the glass. "I know we'll never ride into the sunset together. That's the wrong advertisement. He pulls into suburbia every night in his mini-van. Home to Trish and the kids."

"Your separate time together isn't enough anymore?"

"I guess. I thought I'd eradicated the princess dream, but I guess I still want to be The One."

"You're in bed, Tasi. You're not well. That's when we all want to know who we can count on."

Tasi looks out the window for a moment and smiles. "I can count on my friends."

Jean takes a breath and speaks tentatively as though merely offering a reflection of Tasi's thoughts. "It'd be nice to have a man you could count on. That doesn't mean you have to do marriage and go the whole conventional route. Maybe it's time to move on?"

Tasi squints at Jean, her old assessing look, and draws her hand back. "Maybe moving on is something we should both be thinking about, hmm?"

Jean runs her finger along a seam of the bedspread. "You mean Charlotte?"

"Yeah, Charlotte, Timmy, the works."

"Easier said than done. Is Charlotte really going to do this thing?"

"Yeah, she really is," Tasi's look is direct and fervent. "I don't understand why you'd think otherwise. I know Nan can make anything sound reasonable, but Charlotte isn't mother material and she's not magnanimous either, not the way you want her to be."

Jean crosses her arms, pulls her limbs in toward herself. "She's grossly irresponsible and destructive. I can't help it. That's what I think."

Tasi stares hard at Jean, who is swinging her foot and watching it. "You've got to find some way to forgive her."

"I don't have to anything, Tasi," says Jean, the turn of her head punctuated by her beautifully elongated neck.

Tasi sighs, and Jean notes with a pang how pasty she looks.

"Charlotte is a beauty who suffers," says Tasi slowly. "That's all there is to it. Beauty in distress. I leave the diagnosing to you and Nan. I know we're all supposed to believe in woman's empowerment, but in Charlotte's case you can't separate the beauty from the sorrow."

"That used to move me, Tasi, when we were young and thought we were tragic, before we'd seen the real shit this world can deal out. Now I just think she's unbelievably self-destructive. What self is there to be friends with? Everything beautiful about her is being swallowed."

"Forget it," says Tasi. "We're not going to talk about it, Jean. We're just not."

Jean stares hard at the heater vent, little barred window that it is. "You want some tapioca?" she asks, standing up to get it anyway.

When she comes back, Tasi is out of bed, standing at the sink and filling a hot water bottle. Punishing me, thinks Jean, by doing it herself. As if in answer, Tasi speaks. "I had to get up and pee anyway." But when Jean makes motions to take the water bottle so Tasi can pull the covers back, Tasi waves her away irritably. Jean leans against the wall, hugging herself.

"I'm sorry," Jean says, to the center of the room. Tasi is still harrumphing around in the covers and pillows trying to get comfortable, so she says it again. "I'm sorry. I know you love us both."

Tasi puts a spoonful of tapioca in her mouth and closes her eyes. Jean waits, wondering if she had been heard.

"You know what I most want for you?" Tasi says slowly.

"No . . . what?"

"I want this to be your last desperate measure. I want you to be released from this ruthless desire. That's what I want for you, more than anything."

Jean registers the stinging sensation brought on by Tasi's word choice—"last desperate measure"—but she closes her eyes and waits for it to pass, and then she finds herself crying.

"Me, too," she says to Tasi, collapsing on the bed beside her. "Me, too."

Jean slows the car in front of Unit 72; she thinks that's where the troublemaker lives. She hears his father calling him sometimes . . . Tor, that's his name. His dad was at the last "neighborhood" meeting. A hefty man with a cookie duster mustache and the body of a soccer player: thick-chested, bandy-legged. She remembers him because the discussion of satellite dishes had become ridiculously hung-up on some regulation about size when he raised his hand and said: "If I don't see it, what's it gonna bother me?" Then he laughed, not cynically, but this disarming robust laugh, and sighed audibly as though they had all just come to the end of a long joke. Shaking his head, he sat down. The head of the property management company nodded as if to say that plain good sense was just what the situation called for, and they voted quite rapidly to review applications for satellite dishes on a case-by-case basis.

Back in her apartment, Jean gets a call from Velma Vinegar in Unit 21. A retired state employee and a lonely woman who sometimes calls to make horticultural suggestions: why not plant *arborvitae* to hide the brown back wall of the compound or put aluminum phosphate on the hydrangeas by the Birnam Wood Sign? If Jean would only sprinkle aluminum nails around the base of the hydrangeas, they would bloom blue instead of pink.

Today, Velma says she sees smoke coming from the lower parking lot, where the dumpsters are. "Probably someone burning leaves," Jean answers.

"They shouldn't be. You know that. We have a covenant against it."

"I'll go check, Mrs. Vinegar. I'm on my way now."

The roads inside the complex are quiet—most folks are at work. That's what Jean likes about this job . . . the illusion that she is not really at work because everyone else is away. She hears the high hum of the pool house as she walks. Soon, she can see the kid, crouched by the recycling bins over a fire of cardboard and sticks. Again he looks up, long before he could have heard her. He has that hungry, defensive look that women will later find attractive, and Jean muses that he'll probably learn to use it, but now he only looks desperate.

"Nice little fire you got there."

"Yeah," he says, giving her a quick glint." Yeah." He goes back to the work of his hands, feeding sticks in, tearing the cardboard.

The last leaves of a vine maple skitter over the pavement in a gust. Otherwise, it is an unrelievedly gray afternoon. The leaves and the little fire. Mesmeritic. The boy looks comfortable in crouch position, knees against his chest, and crab-walks left or right when he wants more fuel. She studies him in the moment, the flame in the fluid of his eyes, the serious and deliberate movements he makes. He doesn't seem overstimulated by the fire. Now there's assessment language for you. She is looking at this boy and thinking the old thoughts: Should he be evaluated for a mood disorder? Serial murderers usually have had well-documented histories of fire setting before they moved on to murder. Young offenders include New York's "Son of Sam" killer David Berkowitz, who set more than two thousand fires before he turned to murder. On the other hand, her own brother melted her baby dolls when he got done exploding his army men and he didn't turn out to be a criminal. She doesn't want to ask these questions anymore, to walk around with the entire DSM in her head—the American Psychiatric Association's *Diagnostic and Statistical Manual*. That's what happens when you pathologize behavior for a living. She looks at this boy now and hears that old camp song "I'm going to let my little light shine." How is she supposed to know who is an angry teen and who will become a murderer?

A year before she left practice, a sixteen-year-old lured an eight-year-old to a vacant lot, made the game so much fun that the eight-year-old volunteered to be tied up and then the sixteen-year-old shot his victim up with a lethal injection of his own insulin. The teenager was described by his high school counselor as "not exhibiting predatory behavior."

As she stands there thinking these thoughts, the boy's concentration on the fire seems a bit artificial. He stares at it hard, then flicks a glance her way and right back to it. She studies him openly, glad he's not a part of her caseload. She will not have to fill out an incident report, deal with a stalled referral, try to find temporary shelter for a fire starter, or record a mileage and expense report. He is intent on ignoring her, but every time he looks her way, there's an earnest curiosity in his face. She likes the shape of his head, the red sheen in his dark hair. She is sure he gets teased about the fullness of his mouth but he's lucky; when he is an old man, he will still have lips. The boy doesn't know what to make of her presence, and she doesn't either. All she knows is that this little bit of defiance feels right. The gray, the silence, the flames.

"So what's your trip?" he says to her. "Isn't this against the rules?"

"Sometimes the rules should be against the rules."

Disbelief blooms in his face. He smiles, fast and pure. "That's what my Dad thinks. When he gets the updated rules he yells, 'They want covenants; they should read the Bible.'"

"Where's your Dad now?"

"Out of town on business, as usual."

"And your mom?"

"Drunk in a hole somewhere." He looks up at her briefly to see that one register, then he's back at the arduous task of tearing cardboard.

"Sorry to hear that."

"That's why I hang around here in the afternoons. My dad doesn't want me downtown after school." He shrugs. "I don't like the Y after-school program. Lame-o."

"You're on your own then? Till he gets back?"

"Naw. My aunt'll come get me when she's done at work. Then I gotta deal with my bratty cousins. Aren't you the manager or something?"

"Yeah, I am."

"So, like, don't you have work to do?"

"Yeah, I'm doing it. I'm supposed to come down here and tell you that there's a fire ban and it's against city ordinance blah blah blah and if you don't put that fire out, I'll blah blah blah."

The kid looks at her like it's not quite safe to laugh around anyone her age who is this weird, but he does anyway, more of a snort, really.

"So do me a favor so I can keep my stupid job. Put it out in a few minutes, okay?"

"Yeah, all right," he says, looking at the fire and not at her, so she turns on her heel and walks away like she trusts him.

Jean really doesn't want to rat on this kid, but he's back at it again on Monday, only this time, he is jumping from his balcony onto a tree branch and swinging onto the pool house roof—his own private commando raid. She watches him the first time from her own unit and is making her way down to the pool when he loses his footing and slides down the prefab roof—scrabbling uphill with his arms as he comes down in slow motion and lands on some patio chairs, the kind made of vinyl bands. He has his butt on the cement and a chair stuck on his leg when she finds him. He struggles to his feet before she comes near.

"Are you all right?" she asks, reaching out to steady him.

"Fuck yeah," he shrieks, flailing her hand off him and trying to kick his foot free of the chair. It crashes against the cement several times before he reaches down and yanks the bands back. When he stands up, his head seems to tremble on his neck and he reminds Jean of a wild animal quaking at the end of a tether. What is he . . . eleven . . . twelve?

"That was totally unsafe. I'm going to have to contact your father now."

"Good luck finding him. He's never home."

"Number 72," she says, nodding his direction. "See you there." She stands her ground, knowing he will have to go by her to get to the gate.

"What are you waiting for?" he snarls, but it ends on an abraded note, close to a cry.

"I'm waiting to watch you walk. I want to see how you're moving."

"I'm moving fine." He ducks his head and the rest of his body follows around her and out the gate.

The afternoon mail brings a card from Charlotte. The inside of the envelope is a gold foil paisley in royal reds and blues, the card a heavy cream with matching borders. Jean stays outside while reading it; somehow she feels safer than being enclosed with its contents indoors.

Dear Jean:

I have to say Nan's message from you took me by surprise.

I'm really trying to understand. I guess I can understand why you wouldn't call me yourself, but I'm hurt, too. It feels like a disconnect, and I hope you don't intend to make it permanent.

We've been friends for so long and I've seen you go through a lot trying to have a baby. I realize recent events may have made you feel this absence in your life keenly, but I must ask you to respect my privacy and not judge me. I have my own reasons for choosing to terminate this pregnancy. For one thing, I've finally admitted that I'm an alcoholic, and I'm seeing a counselor. These are big steps for me, Jean, though I realize they may not seem like much to you.

Believe me, I've thought long and hard about this. I'm sorry if my choice causes you grief, but you're the last person who should judge me. I remember when you and Tim were trying IVF, and I always wondered what you'd do if there were excess embryos, but I didn't ask and I didn't judge you. I'd appreciate the same consideration from you now.

With love,
Charlotte

Jean swiftly drops the letter back into the mailbox and shakes her hands as though she'd been stung by nettles. The rant in her head resumes. *You cunt. You rotten cunt.* But she makes herself stand stock-still and stops it. *Hurt,* she says to herself. *Go ahead and hurt.* Immediately she feels her chest wall like something tangled with vines of muscle, a shoot seeming to burst through her throat. *How could you?* she gasps. *How could you compare my experience with yours, choices no one should have to make . . . All so I could have a child, Charlotte, so I could have one.* Jean is mumbling to herself as she walks toward the maintenance shed where she picks the largest pair of shears from the hook and heads toward the ornamental fruit trees that don't need pruning but that will, nonetheless, be pruned.

In the early evening, Jean walks over to Unit 72 and knocks. She is wearing her favorite navy blue hoody, and a purple down vest, which means she has two sets of pockets, double assurance against the kind of wide gesturing she is prone to. The Christmas wreath attached to the door is made of Texas Willow wrapped in ribbon and there are little bears with drums marching around it. Like a craft project laid out step by step in *Redbook* magazine. The door swings open vigorously and Jean squares her shoulders to face the boy's father. But it is the boy himself who answers, looking younger wet-haired and in airplane pajamas. He gives her a serious, open-eyed stare and shouts "It's that manager lady," then takes the stairs in bounds. She is left standing in front of a gaping door. She can hear the clink of metal on metal and running water from inside. The man with the cookie duster mustache appears before her, wiping his hands on a dishtowel and smiling. His hair is as silver white as the flash of a fish out of water, but his face is robust, cheery.

"So what offense have I committed now?" he says.

"No offense. I'm just concerned about your son."

"I'm Reio Hansen," he says, extending his hand, scrutinizing her for a moment, his smile extinguished.

"Jean Brovak. I'm the complex manager."

"Yeah?" he says, "I'm pretty complex too."

"I'm sorry," Jean says, taking a step back off the landing. "I don't mean to interrupt your family life."

"You're looking at it," he says, pushing the door open with his fingertips. "It's just me and Tor." The boy is sitting on the landing, glowering at them.

"Hey," his father says, "don't you have homework to do?" and Tor scrambles up the rest of the stairs and out of sight. Reio rolls his eyes and recovers from his momentary gruffness, "Why not come in?"

Later, Jean will think back on it, realizing that if he'd said "Would you like to come in?" she could have maneuvered her way around the question but "Why not?" seems to require an impossibly deep response.

She follows Reio into the kitchen, catches a glimpse of a huge, round-backed wicker chair, like Morticia's of *The Addams Family*, and pine bookshelves stuffed with paperbacks. The kitchen is a replica of hers except the ugly brown cabinets have been painted brick red. There's a loaf of bread sitting on a cutting board—good bread with a tough crust—and a black wire basket full of oranges next to it.

"Is this conversation going to require coffee or wine?" he says, opening a cabinet. "Should I let down my defenses or brace for the worst?"

"I always brace for the worst," Jean replies, "But coffee just makes me overreact to it."

"That settles it then," he says, pouring her a glass from the bottle of red next to the bread and the oranges. The wine seems to dissolve the muscle that's been bunched in her throat all afternoon. She takes a second sip quickly.

Jean is looking into the sunken living room, at the burnt orange Oriental rug with its black, cream, and sienna filigree that seems to have incorporated the rust-colored wall-to-wall carpet she loathes in her place. She sees now that there are two wicker chairs and a black enamel table between them. He's managed to transform the hideous seventies color scheme into an earth-toned tent of Araby.

"Brought to you by Pier One Imports," he says, catching her looking.

"At least you knew what to do with it. I haven't gotten beyond wanting to rip everything out and start over. You've done a nice job."

"We've been here two years," he says, shrugging. "You've hardly had time to settle in."

Jean perches on one of the black bistro chairs at the kitchen table and sips from her wine. Reio puts his arms on the table; they're ropey with muscle, the hands calm. He leans forward intently. "So, what's Tor been up to?"

Jean points to the balcony over the half wall that partitions the kitchen. "He swung from the balcony, onto that branch, then climbed up the next few, near as I can tell, and swung himself onto the pool house roof. I saw him fall off of it into the patio furniture."

"Yeah, I can believe that. He's a testosterone idiot right now." Reio strokes his mustache down with thumb and forefinger. The look he gives her is beleaguered, an appeal. "I don't know what to do with him anymore. He hates the teen program at the Y. My sister tries to help, but she's got kids of her own, and he teases them. I'm not home till six. He's off the bus by 3:30."

"His mom's not on the scene?" Jean feels suddenly comfortable in her old role as the asker of questions.

Reio shakes his head slowly. "That's part of the problem."

"I'm sorry."

"It's okay. My feelings were finished off in that department a long time ago. She's a drug addict. I've got full custody." He shrugs as if to shake off the past "What about you, you got kids?"

"No. I couldn't have them." She puts this out there flatly, examines how it feels to say it with such finality. The heat of the wine is in her throat. She will be an answerer of questions from now on. "My ex-husband remarried last year and had a baby."

"Ouch," Reio says. His gaze on her is direct, kind but not pitying. His eyes are green with flecks of brown, eyes full of tree canopy and filtered sunlight.

"Well," he says with a little twist of his mouth, "If you haven't hit some disappointment by our age, you're kidding yourself." He nods as he looks at her over the rim of his glass, and she picks up her glass reflexively and drinks with him to it, but without comment.

"What did you do before you came here?" he asks.

"I was a social worker." Jean's grandmother used to tell her she should state her profession with pride, and she tries to now. She pictures Grandma Sophie saying, "You should be proud you descended from serfs," but at the same time remembers her pulling a pickled herring tail from between her teeth.

"Whoa. You crossed the fire line every day." His admiration is open, and she feels her face flush in response.

"Yep. Fourteen years. I did youth welfare services, mother/baby home care, and visiting nurses. I heard a lot of life stories."

"The rough ones I bet."

"Yep. Lots of those."

"Man. I could never do social work. I'd be too directive. That's what my ex-wife told me after I put her through two rounds of rehab. That I was too directive."

"I never did abuse and addiction, not directly. Some of the moms I worked with were pretty unstable when it came to staying sober, but they were making an effort."

Reio is gazing out the little window over the kitchen sink, the one that looks a onto gravel clearing in the trees, but he looks like he is seeing five hundred miles. He turns back to Jean abruptly.

"Why do you think some people seem to be on this endless trajectory down and others are able to pull out of it? You know, what makes that difference?" His voice sounds husky and Jean recognizes their conversation is hurtling in unanticipated directions. "My ex couldn't clean up. Not even for her kid."

Jean watches her fingers play over the stem of her glass, aware of the intensity of Reio's eyes waiting on her, but determined to resist the idea that she can comfort him. "I don't know really," she says, looking right back at him. "Some combination of luck or grace. We used to find my father on the front lawn in the morning, in his suit. Nothing changed it for him. Not even his kids asking. Maybe it's karma. Maybe they have to come back for some reason we can't fathom."

Reio looked down, splayed his hands on the table and stared at them. "I just hate the hurt of it. For Tor. At the lowest point, I used to think that if she weren't so busy killing herself, I'd do it for her. Quicker and cleaner."

"She still around?" Jean wonders why she is emboldened to ask.

"We don't hear from her, haven't since Tor was nine."

"What about you? What do you do?"

"I'm a CPA."

"CPA? Don't you guys make a lot of money?" She blurts this out before she can stop herself.

"Ye-ah," he says slowly. "But if your not-yet-ex-wife stops paying the mortgage while you're undergoing a 'trial separation,' and you don't find out until the bank is repossessing the house, you got a problem. Same goes for the credit cards if she goes on a charge-o-rama while you're not paying attention. You got a problem. But, hey, I signed up for it."

"Testosterone idiot?"

"Yeah," he says, blowing out a breath, "I grew up a caretaker. My mom was frail . . . asthma, diabetes. . . . Anyway, it's not like you think. I'm not doing corporate taxes or anything like that. I'm a CPA with the state gaming agency. I work on regulations and taxes with the casinos."

"You work with the tribes then."

"Yeah, I like that part. I like being on Indian time. With the commercial casinos, it's all pretty straightforward. But with the tribes, there're no taxes, we're in the world of what they call commissions, and with each tribe it's a different deal."

"You like to gamble?" she asks, smiling, but really wanting to know.

"Only socially," Reio remarks, raising his glass again, this time with a bemused smile as much to say *so you're interested, too.* "I stick with small stakes. I like to hear the nickels when the bars, bells, and fruit align."

"Tor started a fire, you know," Jean says decisively.

"You're shittin' me." All the flirtatiousness drains out of his face, and he smoothes his mustache down.

"Nothing big, a little leaf fire he was feeding. Don't worry. He didn't set anything on fire. But it's something to consider."

Reio has made a fist of one hand and is pressing it to his forehead.

"Is there an after-school club? Or something where he could do what he likes?" Jean inquires, aware that this sounds all too easy. Pro-social activity, she would have written in her notes if she were still a social worker.

"He likes to be with animals. He likes to be in nature. There's no school club that covers that." Reio's voice is gruff again. "When Tor was three, he put beetles in his marble chutes. We gave him crickets for Christmas and he could have watched them all day. I guarantee you right now he's upstairs doing his homework with his snake in his lap and his cockatiel on his shoulder."

"How about Big Brothers, Big Sisters? Maybe you'd find someone who could take him to do something a couple times a week?"

"We're on the eligibility list, have been since last year . . . tried Boys and Girls Club, but it's mostly sports and he's not a jock. What we really need doesn't exist." He looks at Jean, who has to stop herself from biting her lips.

"Hey, Dad. Has that lady left yet?" Tor yells down the stair.

Reio maintains eye contact with Jean, gestures with his chin toward the stairwell. "We'll figure something out. We always do."

"Tor," he yells back affably, "Come down here and meet Jean. She likes snakes."

"You do like snakes, don't you?" he whispers, bemused again.

"Yeah, I can do snakes," she shrugs.

"Get ready," he says. "You're going to meet Onion."

NAN

ᴏᴠ

Cape of Stars

As she drives out into the county, Nan scans the riverbank for a sighting of a heron or a kingfisher. Instead, still as a fence post and standing squarely atop one, a red-tailed hawk watches the world. Nan can find none of this stillness in herself this afternoon; she is riled up, aware that she spilled over the container of professionalism like a foaming beer. She is thinking of the woman in her early twenties who came into the Birth Center this morning, heavy-set and heavily made-up, probably one of those women who has heard a thousand times, "but you have such a pretty face." Her hair was that fried orange color of hair too dark to go blonde, gold at the scalp, urine tipped at the ends. Sheryl was her name, real quiet, meek quiet when Nan took her blood pressure, pulse, and temp.

The boyfriend was with her, arms like ham hocks, the splotchy complexion of a redhead. He was on the phone, with his free hand twiddling a lighter back and forth over his knuckles. Sheryl was looking out the window, holding herself by her arms, wiping at her eyes with the length of a finger. Nan registered the tension between them instantly, as always prepared to offer support to every family in her care. But today was one of those days when support did not take a conventional course.

"Yeah right," he was saying into the phone as Nan came in to check the bathroom for a urine sample kit. He cut his eyes towards her and away dismissively. His laugh was marled by phlegm and seemed to exude smoke.

"Yeah, if I'm lucky the baby will be born retarded and then the state will have to take care of it."

Nan looked at Sheryl who hid her face in her hands. She went quietly to the wall phone and requested hospital security. Sheryl's tear-stained face came up out of her hands, and a vacant look of curiosity took over. Nan walked decisively over to where the boyfriend was sitting, leaned down behind him, and unplugged the phone.

"What the fuck?" he yelled.

Nan stood in front of him, her stocky, athletic body grounded firmly in her thick-soled shoes. "If you want to talk like that, there's a pay phone by the gift shop."

"I'm the father. You can't fuckin make me leave." He stood up and threw the phone receiver at the cradle.

Nan turned sideways, motioning toward the security guards at the door. "We have a code of behavior here at the birth center. You just violated it."

"Fuck it," he said standing. "I'm outta here." And at the door, where they took him by the elbows, he shouted again, "I'm outta here, you bitch." It was not clear to whom he was referring: Sheryl, Nan, or both.

To Nan, each newborn child is holy, trailing behind it a cape of stars the way children's books sometimes depict infants. She did not judge Sheryl's decision to give her baby up for adoption; what mattered to her was honoring that child's presence in the world. Yet when the social worker came to talk to the mother about adoption, it did trigger some sadness in Nan for Jean, who had only called once since she'd heard the news of Charlotte's abortion. Jean needed her indignation right now, to protect herself. Evidently, Charlotte had written Jean a note saying that she'd been drinking heavily throughout the pregnancy and planned on going into recovery, but Jean had not replied.

"She wants to elicit sympathy," Jean had said wearily to Nan. "I just don't feel any. She tells Virginia she's doing it because

Darius was abused as a child and can't handle it. She tells Tasi she doesn't want to be some strapped single mom begging for child support. She tells each of us something different."

Nan had shrugged. "Alcoholics let themselves be defined by whomever they're with. They operate to avoid pain, even though they're in untold degrees of pain all the time."

"I'm glad one of us can be non-judgmental." Jean said, her tone sincere.

"Maybe I'm not judgmental, but I make judgment calls all the time. You know that." Nan felt compelled to resist.

"Yeah, so did I, every day as a social worker. I mean I know, on an intellectual level, that *Roe v. Wade* was a medical decision, not a moral one."

"Right. To save lives."

"Yeah, it was never meant to resolve the unresolvable dilemmas. And I used to have that kind of detachment, professional distance, whatever. But now it's close to me, really close to me, and I can't help it. I do condemn Charlotte on a moral level."

"I wish I could change it for you both," Nan had said, before signing off.

Now she sighs loudly in the car, pulling into the drive and allowing herself to sit for a moment while the engine ticks. This friendship she can't fix. Given that she has seen preemies at twenty-two weeks who lived a few days or few hours, it isn't hard for her to picture clinically what Charlotte has chosen. She doesn't imagine that Charlottte thinks of the fetus much. Charlotte is focused on the drama of the act, on releasing pain that is already there and which will surely build back up in some other form. The abortion is like an act of self-injury. Nan isn't unsympathetic. Self-injury is a coping mechanism to release or manage overwhelming pain. She doesn't villainize Darius or make scathing assessments of Charlotte's marriage. She believes that Charlotte has chosen an exterior life that matches the interior one. For all that psychiatry has to say about depression, it's like an artesian well, a dribbling steady source from beneath the ground, unchartable. Charlotte has found reasons at the surface to describe the pain that comes from beneath. There is a whole pharmacopoeia devoted to making people like Charlotte happier, only they have to want to try it, and even then it sometimes doesn't work.

From the car window Nan sees Clay's head bent over the drafting table and briefly considers taking the path to the shed, but she can feel a post-menstrual headache slamming into her left temple and this is her time to sleep before Clay picks up Luke from day care. Irene has spent the night at a girlfriend's, trading clothes and watching movies. In the house, Nan heads straight for the medicine chest, debates taking an Extra Strength Tylenol but decides on a Tylenol Three with codeine instead. She shakes one out of the bottle and is about to gulp it down when something makes her hesitate.

She flips the white tablet over in her palm: no number three imprinted on the backside. Regular Tylenol tablets are slimmer, a hairsbreadth smaller in diameter. The pill vial appears to be full of them. There in the bottom she finds a couple with the big three on them, and takes one. Then she scrutinizes the cabinet before her. Like a quaint shadow box full of knick-knacks, its shapes are impressed on her memory. Up in the left-hand corner, something is missing; the calamine lotion and wart remover have been shifted to fill the space. Suddenly, she knows: the ancient box of Trojans that have been in there since before Clay had his vasectomy. She begins opening the vials on Clay's side of the cabinet; the Endocet and Percocet he uses when his bulging disks act up are seriously depleted. The Diazepam is gone altogether. Nan turns on her heel and walks through the kitchen, about to beat a fast track to the shed when the blinking eye of the phone machine calls her back. She hits the Play button.

"Hi Nan and Clay? This is Annette's mom? Annette called a few minutes ago to say the kids were going to be late getting back from Tacoma. I guess the traffic was real bad after the concert so they decided to stay in a motel. I just didn't want you to worry. Okay? Talk to you later?" [Beep. Message saved].

Nan stands stock still, staring out the window at the tangle of red willow and the stone path that leads to the river. The boldness of Irene's lie leaves her breathless. She reaches into the drawer and locates her little red address book beneath the county phone book. The phone rings three times before the answering machine picks up—"Hello, you have reached the Hurlburt family." Nan lays the receiver quietly down. She is dialing Irene's cell when she hears the Volkswagon Rabbit pull up and sees its blue reflection in the French doors.

Irene gets out of the car, her tawny hair pulled up high in a ponytail, about where you'd put a baby doll's. She is wearing black hip huggers with a silver studded belt, a tight black top with a shimmery silver panel across her breasts. She slings her volleyball satchel over her shoulder, calls "here kitty, kitty" as she makes her way to the door unawares.

Mad as she is, Nan can't help but admire Irene's loveliness, which only makes her more livid . . . all that could happen to destroy this shiny mermaid girl.

"Hiya, Mom," she says, dumping the satchel on the counter. "How's the workaday world?" Irene slides a cake plate towards herself and begins picking at the exposed ring of frosting.

"About as expected. How was your night out?"

"Fun. You know, girl power at Annette's house. We watched *Mona Lisa Smile.*

"Really?"

"Yeah. Why are you looking at me like that?"

"I'm waiting to see if you're going to tell me the truth."

"I just did, Mom. Jeez, get off it."

"I got a call from Annette's mom. She said you were in Tacoma at a rock concert with some other kids."

Irene puts her hand to her mouth and looks stonily at the floor.

"You're busted," Nan says wryly, determined to keep her calm.

Irene's response is meteoric. "Like you would have let me go if I'd asked. If I'd said, 'Mom, Annette and Danny's parents are going to let them go the Dave Matthews concert, can I go?' you would have said 'No way.' You treat me like a twelve-year-old."

"Danny? Does he even have parents?" Nan's mind is lurching and staggering. Wasn't he the eighteen-year-old with a beard? "Where did you stay last night?"

"We stayed in a Motel 8, Mom. You should be proud of me, for not getting on the road late with a bunch of concert stoners."

"Proud of you? Who took the painkillers out of the medicine chest? Irene. You want to talk about stoners."

"I can't believe this. I can't believe you're accusing me of stealing. You treat me like a total fuck-up."

"Don't duck it, Irene." Nan is yelling now, waving her futile finger in Irene's face. "I know what you did. That box of rubbers you stole was about a hundred years old. Not a safe bet."

"Oh, well," says Irene, flipping her ponytail with her hand. "If I get pregnant, I can always have an abortion. That's what you should have done with me."

Like the spark released by steel drawn across flint, Nan's hand lashes out, finds its mark, and burns.

Irene is holding her cheek and screaming when Clay opens the front door. "You abused me! Abused me!" she shrieks as she grabs her bag and runs down the hall. Nan lets her knees go and slides down the cabinets to the floor where she puts her hot and smarting hand to the side of her face.

"Hey," Clay says, leaning against the counter. "What is going on here?"

Nan stands up and bashes some dishes into the sink. "I shouldn't have struck her. Goddamnit, I totally lost it. Someone should call CPS on me."

"Nan," Clay says, picking his words carefully. "One slap does not constitute abuse."

She looks at him in his rumpled grey sweats, the paunch, the hunch, the grey stubble on his chin, and feels unspeakably grateful that he can be discerning at a time like this. When she finishes with her narrative, which could have been titled, "Why My Thursday Afternoon Went to Hell," he surprises her.

"I'll go see if I can talk to her."

She watches him saunter down the hall, dishrag hanging in her hands.

Clay and Irene have a relationship which most of the time can be described as cordial, merry at its best when the jokes are flying. By the time Clay came into their lives, Irene was no longer the father-hungry waif who befriended every man at the beach or in the park. She had entombed that part of herself.

About the time she turned ten, Irene's paternal grandparent's had written asking to see her. They were getting old and no longer wanted to abide by their son's request that they stay away from Nan and Irene. Nan had told Irene, left it up to her really, and they went. It was a hot three-hour drive east and an awkward visit. Nan suspected that Irene had secretly hoped her father would be there. How could he not come when he heard she would be there? Nan had no such illusions and tried for damage control: "Irene, he chose not to make a family with us. I don't think that has changed."

"Well, I love him anyway," Irene said.

The grandparents had set up a formal tea tray in the living room and set about asking Irene the kinds of questions only a much younger child wouldn't feel were contrived—What is your favorite subject in school? Do you have any pets? Who is your best friend? It was very clear they wanted to leave no space for Irene to ask the hard questions of her own, and when she told them she wished she could have the picture of her father on the bureau, they took it out of the frame before giving it to her.

On the car ride home, Irene had asked: "Do we have to do this again, Mommy?"

Now at Christmas and on Irene's birthday, cards come, pink ink and maudlin verses, always containing odd amounts of money: a five-dollar bill and two ones, or a ten dollar bill and four ones. Nan sends them Irene's school picture once a year. But that's the extent of it and never, in all this time, have they heard from Irene's father.

It hurts Nan that Irene has kept at a remove from Clay. It's not that she only tolerates him—there is affection and Clay has wisely left the discipline issues to Nan—but Irene treats him as part of her mother's life and never as part of her own. On good days, Nan feels that Clay is right to take Irene's cues and not force the relationship; on bad days, she wants some backing up and finds Clay passive, an observer because it's easier. Now she walks back to the bedroom, ostensibly to lie down, but really she wants to hear what will happen.

Irene's sobbing has not diminished. Clay has to knock on the door twice.

"Leave me alone," she screams.

"It's Clay," he says simply, in case Irene thinks it's her mother.

"Go away," she yells, "You're not my father."

"I know I'm not your father," Clay says neutrally.

It's quiet for a moment after that. Apparently, Irene is stumped. Clay surprises Nan again. "I don't want to go away," he says resolutely. "It hurts me to hear you cry."

It makes Nan weep to see Clay stand there, with his head bent solicitously toward the door. There's more muffled sobbing from Irene. Nan wonders if it is all her fault, it she has tried too hard to protect Clay from Irene and Irene from Clay and control just about everyone and maybe they all should have gone to counseling a long time ago and maybe that's her fault too because she buys into this image people have of her being so steady and balanced because she's a nurse. Then Nan hears the doorknob click, that little sound the button makes when it pops out, signaling that Irene is letting Clay come in.

Irene looks up from the bed, raccoon-masked from all the eyeliner and mascara rubbed around her eyes. He leans back against the door after shutting it. There is nowhere to sit down really. The bedrooms are small. Irene's contains a dresser with a vanity top and a captain's bed for maximum storage. Clay isn't sure he should sit down on the bed next to her.

"She slapped me, Clay," she says, her lips puffy, but she sounds more plaintive than caustic.

"I know. She lost it, and she shouldn't have," he says slowly.

"That's abuse, you know. Hitting your kid."

"Abuse involves a pattern of behavior. Has your mother ever slapped you before?" he asks calmly.

"No," Irene says, eyes cast down upon the fringed pillow she has been fiddling with.

"Then I would be very careful how you use that word, Irene, because I don't think you want to wind up in foster care."

"Foster care?" Irene ceases crying long enough to look quizzical.

"Yeah, schools are obligated to call Child Protective Services if abuse is alleged, and while they decide whether or not your home is a safe place, they often put you in foster care."

Irene looks around the room and hugs the fringed pillow. She sighs the equivalent of a landslide.

"I really pushed it," she says, dropping her head between her arms and letting loose a sob. "I did steal you guys' drugs and the condoms, too. Danny wanted me to. He wanted to get wasted with his buddies at the concert. I only like drank a few beers. Honest.

I'm the one who drove to the motel." Irene pauses and looks up at Clay, who is merely nodding, waiting for the rest. "I mean, okay, I did take a Valium at the hotel, but that's because Annette and Luis were going for it in the next bed and I just wanted to sleep."

"What about you and Danny? What about the condoms?"

"Well, Danny got so fucked up we never had the chance to use the condoms . . . Oh God . . . Oh shit." Irene breaks out crying anew.

Clay settles himself gently on the bed next to her and strokes her back.

"I'm still a virgin. I still am! But he was so fucked up he wanted a blowjob in the car after the concert. In the parking lot. He was all like, 'c'mon baby,' and I felt like I had to do it. The other girls think he's the ultimate, you know, upper-classman and everything."

Clay's hand stops on her back. "Irene, what it looks like on the outside is one thing, how it feels on the inside is another."

"How do you know anything about what I feel?" She twitches away from his touch.

Clay searches his memory for a moment. "I once went with a girl who was pretty addicted to cocaine. I'd buy it so she'd want to be with me. Then I figured out it wasn't me she really wanted to be with."

"Well, Danny can be so sweet. He really can. But in the parking lot he was all like 'you gotta do it.' It was gross."

Clay briefly entertains the idea of explaining mutually consensual sex, or emphasizing respect in a relationship, but it all sounds too canned to him, like something in a health insurance pamphlet.

"Do you want him to be your first lover?" he asks simply. "Because that's a memory that is going to stay with you forever, Irene. I guarantee it."

Irene seems to be doing a great deal of snuffling on her shirt sleeve, and Clay considers getting up and going to the bathroom for a Kleenex, then decides against that, too. She turns so that her back is no longer to him, both of them now staring at the floor. As though readying herself, Irene wipes her face with her hands, then tucks her hair behind her ears.

In a small voice, she says, "I don't know how to break up with him."

"Where do you feel safest?"

"Here. But he doesn't like to come over. Anyway, if I saw him he'd like be all sweet to me and then I couldn't handle it."

"Do you think it was sweet of him to ask you to steal drugs?" Clay pauses. "Do you think he's sweet when he's messed up on them?"

"No," Irene wails, flinging the fringed pillow into the corner. Then she puts her head down so that her hair swings forward and creates a curtain around her face. Clay glances at his watch: Harmony School gives parents a fifteen-minute window in which to pick up their children before they are escorted to aftercare. Clay is just going to make it to pick up Luke. He puts his hands on his thighs and is about to get up when Irene speaks.

"I could write down everything I want to say, and then call him."

"That's a good idea, Irene. But what will you do if Danny starts sweet-talking?"

"I'll tell him I have to go."

"You may have to tell him you don't want to talk to him anymore. . . . Anyway, I'd be happy to be here when you do it, Irene. Right here in the house with you."

"What should I do about Mom? Is she going to like ground me forever?"

"It was a pretty serious breach of trust, Irene. You'll have to earn that trust back."

"Is she sleeping?"

"I doubt it. She may be lying down, but I doubt she's sleeping." He stands up. "I've got to go get Luke."

Irene stands up, too. Clay is just turning to go out when he hears her whisper, "Hey? Can I have a hug?" and swiftly he envelops her in his arms.

Nan wakes alone the next morning and makes tea. She feels like she has molasses running through her veins.

On the table she finds a note from Irene, written on the back of the utilities bill.

> *Mom,*
> *Milk is sour.*
> *Bagels is moldy.*
> *Daughter is nasty.*
> *Lawd hep us.*
> *(I'm sorry.)*
> *Love, Irene*

Nan sinks into her chair, exasperated, smiling, the hurt of last night lifting from the day. She remembers Irene as twenty-eight pounds of thrashing toddler. Stuffing her into her car seat was like landing a twenty-eight-pound tuna. Those guys who love trophy fishing should try it, Nan mused. Their wives are home wrestling the toddler into the stroller, into the high chair, into the market basket. Christ, someone should have taken their picture. Nan would have held Irene up by her ankles. She was her trophy child, the one she had held onto for all she was worth, despite the father's pleas for an abortion, despite the specter of loneliness and economic hardship. Nan wonders what made her so stubborn back then, as stubborn as Irene is now.

∞

Tippy Pedestal

Finley calls Virginia at the office to tell her that Milo doesn't look well.

"Really. Is he running a fever?" she asks though she knows damn well what Finley means.

"He's got bags under his eyes, Gin, and purple circles too."

"I'll get him to bed earlier, Finley, I promise."

"I could cut out early on Fridays, then he wouldn't have such a long day."

"Finley, if one of us is going to work less, it ought to be me."

"Okay, Ginny," he says in measured tones, "we're right back there. I can hear it in your voice."

It's true. She can even acknowledge to herself how true it is, but it doesn't change her behavior one bit. She feels like a carnival game: swing the hammer down hard enough and the needle rises toward the bell. No stopping till she has hit that shrill pitch.

"I'm not the one who put us in debt, Finley. And next time you get so worried about Milo, tell your date he doesn't like being tickled."

"She wasn't my date, Ginny."

"Like I care who she is, Finley." Clearly, she does.

"She's my next-door neighbor. And it happened before I could do much about it."

"Just like everything else, huh? You haven't got a clue."

"You should get a dog, Virginia, something you can kick around the house."

"Well I know one thing for sure. . . ."
"Goodbye Virginia, I'm hanging up now."

Civil to the end, that's Finley. She was about to finish her sentence, "old dogs can't learn new tricks," and is left with its brassy taste in her mouth instead. She's mad of course because Finley is right. Milo has creases across his cheeks and charcoal-hued shadows beneath his eyes. In the new year, she increased her course load so that she could nail down the mortgage by herself and it means Milo is in after-school care now five days a week. Often when she picks him up he is standing by himself at the bunny cages, feeding grass stems through the chicken wire. She knows how he feels—tired of human exchange. It wasn't always like this.

Finley and Virginia had been determined that the bulk of Milo's time be at home, and it was. She was lucky that way too: afternoon and evening classes meant she could spend her mornings with Milo, and Fridays she had off. So she was there for the crucial conversations. Like why some children don't have enough to eat. Her mother, when she came for a visit, had used that old line on Milo, "Eat your dinner. Think of the starving children in China." Of course Milo had never thought about children going hungry at all, and the comment punctured him. He cried in earnest, long and hard; that night her mother sat in the living room and actually read one of her books on the new child-rearing methods. Virginia settled Milo onto her lap and they had a heart-to-heart about the workings of the world . . . how it is that some people take so much more and have so much more than they need and then other people can't have what they do need. Then Virginia proposed a plan, and they went to the cupboard and took down cans of pumpkin and cranberry and tomato soup, and put the cans in a bag for the food bank barrel at the market. The minute they had a plan for helping, Milo felt better. She wants to be with Milo when it's time for these conversations, as much as she can, and Finley feels the same way. And now neither of them is with him very much at all.

Virginia shakes out the student newspaper to read while she munches on a granola bar. There's an interview with a writer who recently came for a campus visit. The man says he jogs five or six miles, then writes ten to twelve hours a day. "The discipline of running and writing are very much alike. You get caught up in a rhythm. You can't stop." Virginia almost spits her coffee out onto the newspaper. She knows for a fact that the man has two children under the age of three. That's how it is, she thinks. If you want to be an artist, you want to have a wife, not be one, and then you never have to mention her.

The male writer, it seems, sets out rules. No one is to disturb him at the office before two when he's writing. He tells the proverbial Her to live with it or don't. He is rigid, fastidious, productive, admired. He gets divorced. He only sees the children on weekends now. He is separate, volatile, consumed. He gets more work done now than ever.

What does the woman writer do? When the newborn finally sleeps through the night or at least long enough for her to connect two sentences, it is time to return to work, yet she stalls, reads instead, joins a mother/baby group. Starting again means first admitting how long she's been gone from the novel, how dead the material is to her now. She reads her characters, but she doesn't know who these people are anymore. What are they talking about? It's like walking into a third-year language immersion class.

Virginia finally made some headway last weekend when Milo was at Finley's. She had hoped the old feelings about writing would come back to her and revive her from a state of domestic depletion. *Hoping for that old feeling*, the words in her head were as bad as AM radio lyrics. She had forgotten that the act of writing was for her self-care, regardless of what she actually produced.

She had forgotten that the act of writing could create the quiet, could create the stillness, could banish the odd internal blips and hisses at the end of the day.

Before Finley moved out, the interruptions were incessant. Virginia would remind herself that Harriet Beecher Stowe had written *Uncle Tom's Cabin* at the kitchen table while her six children squabbled about—after her husband had denied her use of the parlor. So, Virginia would get the novel in the box out from under the desk and find a place she could start, any old place really, and just as her pen careened from the bottom of one page to the top of another, Milo would wake. It wasn't that Finley didn't support her writing; he just never seemed to hear Milo, always seemed to be in the wrong part of the house, and as he said, "Milo prefers you at night," which Virginia thought was damn convenient for Fin.

"Mama," Milo called, in that drifty tone, "count the trains with me." Milo seemed to possess extrasensory hearing, and almost every night when the freight trains passed down by the harbor, he would sit bolt upright, though the sound came from so far off the volume was the equivalent of a mouse squeaking.

"Yes, sweetest, yes," she would murmur, and eventually some breaths later she was back for a sentence or two. But what had she established in the last chapter? Where was the last chapter? It was under the day-care calendar, which cheerfully announced: "Our goal this month is to gain knowledge of change and comparison through direct experience. We will be weighing and measuring ourselves and other things, too."

During a recent job hire, a candidate had confessed that he could only generate original material when he was at a writer's retreat or colony. How precious, thought Virginia: once again, the male writer exploring his break from society, his need for separateness, the threat of connection. The woman writer stands at the antipode, not like an explorer with a flag at the South Pole, but as one in a crowd scarcely discernable for the barrage of noise and chatter that surrounds her. It is the thread of connection which is barely recognizable amidst the fracas that she wouldn't want to miss, the thread of connection which she must explore.

"Virginia?" someone calls. Juanita is at her door, her spiky orange-tipped hair making her look like a pixie or carnie character. Virginia is sure that's not the intended effect. "Hey, can you come to the Women's Studies meeting on Thursday? It's a breakfast thing," Juanita asks.

Juanita is the cat-woman type who can successfully wear short black skirts even though she's in her forties . . . none of those baby-doll dresses and empress waists favored by academic women. Unlike Virginia, who is a lecturer, Juanita is a tenured professor.

"I don't know, Juanita. I have to decide if it's more feminist to raise my son in the morning or go to the Women's Studies meeting. You know, I don't have Finley around anymore to fill in."

"If we lived in a kibbutzim like we should, you'd come to the Women's Studies meeting." Juanita leans against the doorframe, one hand dramatically on her hip.

"Right. Wasn't the feminist movement supposed to change the system instead of guaranteeing our entrance into the 9-5 grind?"

Juanita's laugh is a husky bark. "That and a career arc that peaks just as women's eggs go defective."

This kind of banter is always safe with Juanita, who also has kids. Virginia used to sense some friction from her, but now that Virginia is teaching a full load, Juanita has become unexpectedly chummy. There seem to be two scales by which women judge each other, Virginia thinks: the stay-at-home moms use the sacrifice scale as in have-you-sacrificed-enough-for-your-kid? while the professional women use the martyrdom model as in have-you-martyred-enough-for-your-career? Virginia finds the similarity pretty scary.

"Well," Juanita says, "I'll let you off the hook this time. But we'll expect you at the next meeting."

"I'll be there," says Virginia, trying to muster loyalty.

After Juanita has ducked back down the hall, Virginia remembers a conversation they had at this time a year ago, back when Virginia taught part-time and could pick Milo up from day care in the early afternoons.

In the hallway they'd ended up comparing childcare schedules.

"My kids are at All Saints every day from 9:00 to 4:00," said Juanita.

"And your youngest is the same age as Milo, right? Five?" Age always seemed a neutral subject.

"Uh-huh, same age. But I've got all these curriculum committee meetings, and faculty senate meetings, and search committee meetings. God, it never ends. You were so smart not to make that choice. And you're such a good mother."

Virginia was not sure what to say. She had mumbled some thanks. It wasn't the first time Juanita had seemed jealous of her position as a lecturer. Of course, Virginia made about fifteen thousand dollars less a year than Juanita did, but it was true, she walked away from a lot. Still, Juanita could certainly have made the same choice. It seemed she had read Virginia's mind with her next comment.

"My husband would be happy if I went to part-time. But tell me, why does this choice always seem to come out of the woman's career? That's what I resist. It's a chunk out of my ambition, not his. Anyway, my kids have never known any different." She shrugged as she said this, but her eyes were not impartial at all, they were pleading with Virginia to absolve her.

Virginia had ducked the moment completely, made some joke about Milo missing his hamster when he was away, not her. They'd guffawed together rather too heartily. Back in her office, Virginia had turned off all the fluorescent lights, and thrown open the windows (even though she could hear the steam heating bestir itself to thwart her). She couldn't seem to get enough light or air. The day before, she had counted her savings to see if she had enough to make it without Finley. Juanita's eyes went on pleading. *Well, my kids have never known anything different.* Virginia felt herself slide away from sympathy into the noise of conflicting emotions and an inner voice saying, louder than the rest, *Yeah, but you've known something different. We both have.*

Virginia's creative writing course meets in Franzen Hall, an industrial-age cement box built with the pipes exposed on purpose so that you feel at all times as though you were in a toilet tank. Her classroom is a windowless bunker that hisses strangely—the sound of gas leaking in. She looks around the room at the expectant faces—the young men in the National Guard and Marine Reservists who disappeared from her classrooms two years ago are coming back. They wear white T-shirts and answer her questions "Yes, ma'am." Their sisters and fiancées don't have to be told about the importance of language; they have men living to receive their letters. The peacenik with the supersaturated black hair and tattooed face thinks she is going to be shocked when he writes about ecstasy and raves, and he's disappointed when she's not.

Next to him sits a slouched down hip-hopper with his hat on sideways. When Virginia calls on him, he displays an involuntary tic; his face flinches and his eyes blink uncontrollably. He'll write a story about a mother who doesn't protect her son from the rages of his Vietnam vet stepfather. Then there's the contingent of whispering girls whose nipples are always hard because they persist in wearing flip-flops in winter. Virginia is always coaxing them to speak louder, to learn to occupy some public space, to be more than ornamental. To the side by herself sits the large woman with extremely crooked teeth and the voice of a seductress. She'll write a story about an eight-year-old girl suffering from a broken arm for two days because her parents can't afford serious medical emergencies. No one can tell Virginia the twenties are golden years, not in this demographic. Her students rescue alcoholic parents, work forty-hour weeks in pawn shops, or enlist and get shot at to pay for their educations. In the winter, their colds progress from basic congestion to bronchitis to walking pneumonia. She gives them extra chances to revise their papers even though it means she's correcting all the time.

This afternoon, the class will critique an abortion story written by one of the whisperers. Virginia does feel bad for reflexively thinking of it as an abortion story, but unfortunately there are certain hallmarks by now, the villainous boyfriend who won't come into the clinic with the woman, the inevitable comparison of the fetus to a pearl in an oyster, the tough pragmatic questions: "How could she have a baby when she didn't even know how to make a living yet?" Virginia knows the workshop becomes the safe place to talk about the taboo, but the students are sometimes so inarticulate, she has to hold onto the desktop and will herself to be patient.

"I thought this story was really relatable. I was like so into it."

Virginia has taken to sucking on lemon drops in order to keep herself quiet long enough for the students to find their way around in their thoughts.

"You got the woman's point of view down."

Mention of a technical term is encouraging. Surely someone will want the villain to have more dimension.

As though she were considering the question herself, Virginia asks, "Did anybody wonder why the protagonist was attracted to him in the first place?"

"I thought she should have gone over there afterward and torched his place," says Hip Hop, before slouching further.

One of the National Guardsmen shifts uncomfortably in his chair, then speaks abruptly. "We don't know what the circumstances were. Maybe the guy was using birth control and the condom busted. How do we know?"

The peacenik bestirs himself. "Yeah, we need more context."

Virginia pops another lemon drop. At last the conversation is underway.

After class, what troubles her is that the students accepted the heroine's absolute isolation without question. Virginia had to be the one to ask: "Doesn't she have family or friends that she can turn to?" Maybe it was significant that abortion hadn't been seriously represented on TV since the 1980s. She remembered *Hill Street Blues*, and *St. Elsewhere*, but her students didn't, and as legal challenges to *Roe v. Wade* increased, abortion in the storyline had been replaced by the convenient miscarriage. After all, abortion was a decision requiring personal agency, and like any other important decision would involve talking to friends—doctors and counselors even. Miscarriage just happened, in the privacy of the bed or the bathroom.

Virginia wonders if she has been friend enough to Charlotte and knows she has not. She imagines Darius has turned hard, hating the powerlessness he feels, the guilt, the recrimination. Charlotte and Darius are not a couple who will get over this by believing they will have a baby later. Virginia knows Nan will never pass judgment on Charlotte, but has she? For Jean, it's futile to pretend there will be anything left of the friendship but smoke and ash. Virginia has called Charlotte only once since all talk of a baby shower ended, and Charlotte complained the whole time.

"Darius shuts himself up in the family room with his laptop or his big screen TV on loud," said Charlotte.

Just hearing her use the term "family room" made Virginia feel sad . . . the sadness she pushed away every day about Finley, because he had been willing to try and fix things. When she spoke with Charlotte, she felt at a loss about how to respond anymore. The calls had been cyclical for so long. Before Christmas, Charlotte was drunk and crying because Darius had threatened to throw her out.

"Well, you know what Nan would say," Virginia told her. "The most dangerous thing a woman can do in an abusive relationship is give up all means of independent income."

It seemed like a big crisis had to hit before she and Charlotte got honest. There, she'd done it, she'd used the word "abusive." But it was a risky business. Because then as time passed, it became apparent that Charlotte didn't really want to talk about change, about going into rehab or getting a job or leaving Darius. Then there were so many fine lines to be mindful of: the fine line between inquiring about Charlotte's recovery and being perceived as invasive, the fine line between respecting her privacy and being just plain old co-dependent, between using black humor for relief and laughing at things that just weren't funny. Virginia was growing impatient. She'd read somewhere that alcohol robbed the alcoholic of autonomy. She'd told Charlotte, "You'll get back your energy. You've always had a lot of pluck." But Charlotte grew wistful and admiring, a volatile combination.

"You've got it so together, Virginia. I don't know how you do it. Raising Milo and teaching and writing." Here it seemed the only thing to do was minimize her own accomplishments, downplay her constructive passions.

"If I knew how to do it, I wouldn't be separated from Finley."

"Oh, you'll find someone better suited to you. You've always been so directed."

As though Virginia's self-doubt and financial worries were mere peccadilloes. It was a tippy pedestal, to say the least, and it would quickly seem unfair to Virginia that she was giving up so much of the precious little time she had after Milo went to bed. Really what she needed was a cruel sense of appraisal: This was a friendship based on old loyalties, not new ties. But she doesn't have it in her to make ruthless assessments; she feels too fallible herself. So, Virginia is stumped. Except to tell Charlotte over and over that she loves her even as she puts more and more distance between them.

With Milo at Finley's for the weekend, Virginia attends an old friend's wedding reception. Not someone she is super close to, but a family friend, and she promised her mother she'd go. She is glad for Tracy, really she is. Tracy has been tenacious about meeting men in a way that Virginia could never imagine. Tracy's Internet dating record showed Virginia exactly what she wasn't willing to go through—long torrid exchanges abruptly cancelled after Tracy e-mailed her photo. And Tracy wasn't bad looking. Still, she wouldn't hear a word from some of these guys. Brutal, that's what it was. There was no protocol of courtesy. You reduced yourself to being a rejected product. Virginia knew she'd never subject herself to it, but here Tracy was, married all over again.

The photographer in the ballroom looks like one of the three stooges. His pinstripe trousers are cut like grocery bags, and he is balding just enough that the pate of his head forms a perfect yarmulke. He is trying to get the relatives of the bride together for their family portrait but it's confusing. The bride's sister is a Hong Kong orphan who'd been adopted by Tracy's German American family. In turn one of her other sisters married a black man, and that man's brother married a hair salon blonde. The groom's family is swarthy French and most people assume they're Chicano. The groom's younger brother is a college-age anarchist who wears his hair punk blonde; high top sneakers flash white from beneath his tuxedo slacks. Virginia overhears the photographer speaking to his assistant. "It's like the Rainbow Coalition. I can't figure this family out. Let's just line them up by size, from shortest to tallest, and be done with it."

Virginia eats her scalloped cake and studies Tracy's mother, who is trying not to look at her ex-husband's new wife, but the woman is wearing a white satin suit slit up the back, and white suede pumps with jeweled flowers. How like Tracy's dad, Virginia thinks. Fathering children by three different women, then finding himself a fourth one with a Ph.D. and none of the bodily distortion of childbirth. And the new wife is clearly too old to have children; she may age, but she'll never warp.

Virginia stands off to the side behind the food table, thinking about the do-it-yourself divorce kit she picked up at the courthouse. Self-dissolution, that's what this kind of divorce is called, and here she thought she'd already been melted and evaporated down to a few hard grains. So much for the heat of passion.

A flower girl of about five runs by, her face streaming with tears, and dives into a rhododendron bush. Virginia is glad she and Finley avoided the formal fuss of a big wedding. At the time, Virginia was six months pregnant, and the family was just relieved they were getting married at all. With two weeks' notice, she and Fin married in their garden amidst the hollyhocks and fireweed. Picturing the openness of Fin's expression makes Virginia wince. He read Pablo Neruda's "Noche" to her in front of everyone: "By night, Love, tie your heart to mine, and the two together in their sleep will defeat the darkness." How could the ordinary have defeated their sense of love's mystery? Perhaps Tracy had it right; it was better to answer questionnaires listing favorite hobbies and favorite foods. Virginia can feel her chest tighten the way it does when the grass season gives her asthma, but there's no grass growing now.

At the bar she runs into Charlotte, who hovers waiflike in a sparkly lime green dress with long floating sleeves, but the set of her smile is clenched, and she is so thin, her jaw appears too large. For a flash second, it reminds Virginia of the illustrations of Mike Mulligan's steam shovel. Virginia puts her arms out a few strides before she reaches Charlotte and sees the fear dissolve from her friend's face. *Jesus,* Virginia thinks, *I'm not going to criticize you,* but before she can check herself, her eyes have done a quick double take on Charlotte's stomach.

Virginia hasn't called. She didn't call Charlotte the week of the abortion, and she didn't call when Nan told her the deed was over. She thought about calling, but she didn't. Like so many things, she compartmentalized it for later, and since later meant choosing between a bath or reading the paper—some scrap of time for herself—later never came.

"Hey, long time no see," Charlotte says after they've embraced.

"Yeah, you know how it is," Virginia says. "The papers never end." She decides not to mention Milo.

"You sound just like a professor now," says Charlotte.

"Hey, I'm only a lowly lecturer."

"Oh, you'll get your book done. Then we'll all watch you on *Oprah*."

At what point over the years did Charlotte's compliments start to sound more like barbs? Virginia sighs aloud.

"I'm sorry I haven't been in touch. Single-parenting is much harder than I imagined." Ouch. Exactly what she didn't want to say spewed forth by accident.

Charlotte's pallor whitens, and she touches Virginia's arm. "I've been thinking about that. How hard it must be."

Virginia nods, relieved to be acknowledging what she can, her friend's sorrow, even though a voice in her head chants, not *that* hard. Charlotte's voice shifts. Brightly, brittlely, she speaks.

"Do you remember that time we watched the fireworks from the roof of the dorm? With Nan and Tasi?

"Yeah?" says Virginia, not sure where this is heading.

Charlotte sets her finished glass on the linen tabletop. "Tasi kept saying the fireworks trails reminded her of spermatozoa. But Nan didn't agree, and you said, that's because they're swimming in the wrong direction."

Charlotte's barky laugh is too loud, and Virginia can hear the forced heh-heh-heh of her own longer than she likes.

"Yeah, that was funny. I'd forgotten that."

"Listen, Darius wants to get out of here, but call me. Okay? And we'll get together."

"Sure," says Virginia, "I'll call," and she waves several times as she watches her old friend cross the room, knowing a ritual of protection had transpired between them. She wouldn't call Charlotte but she would honor loyalty, and maybe even for the next ten years when they saw each other at functions like this one, they would still declare their intentions to call. The poignance is there, in the way Charlotte keeps turning and waving from different stopping points across the ballroom, a little parade wave, as though the big crowded room were a diorama of time full of all the people they'd met together and all the selves they'd once been.

Virginia turns toward the window and the cold sun of March. It's not a good day for thinking. She tries to remember the requirements of the self-dissolution divorce, but all she can think about is the way Fin touched her after they'd taken their vows, as though she were too clean, as though he were waiting for the squeak his fingers would make on a too-clean surface, and he'd smelled like new straw, like something the green had not quite gone out of, the sun's warmth not yet left.

A man in a silvery Italian suit smiles at her as he takes an apple from a table centerpiece, a huge cornucopia overflowing with fruit.

"What's better? he asks her, taking a bite out of the apple. "To swallow a whole worm or half a worm?"

"Half a worm," she says, shaking her head.

"No, the whole worm. That way, you'll never know you swallowed it."

She nods and looks out the French doors again, disengaging in case the man wants to move on. But he stays where he is, crunching away with a zest she finds amusing though not necessarily attractive.

"So," he says, again between bites. "Is this a happy occasion for you?"

"Not particularly, I mean I'm glad for Tracy. But I'm in the midst of a divorce."

"What's the matter with your soon-to-be-ex?"

"He's a money addict. He can't get enough of everyone else's money."

"Most men have to go bankrupt in order to become human, or lose the woman they love. That's why they're so willing to go into therapy when it's too late."

"Is that theoretical knowledge or field-based?" asks Virginia, smiling wryly.

"From the trenches," he says. "Definitely." He wipes the juice from his mouth with the corner of his expensive sleeve and studies Virginia. "So, are you feeling available yet?"

"No," she answers quickly. "I'm not that frisky yet."

FINLEY

∿

Ice Cube Trays

In the dark foyer, Milo stands, hugging his backpack and taking in the beige Teflon-coated carpet and the tweed modular couches that came with his father's apartment. The vertical blinds over the sliding-glass door seem to partition the room in shadow. Finley hits the light switches. No better. The glare bounces off the white linoleum of the kitchen. Fin hates institutional white, its grey-blue cast—no tinge of sand, taupe, lemon, or almond—a white never touched by the heat of day.

He chose the apartment in a fatalistic frame of mind. He'd built so many of them in his early twenties. There were only a few floor plans, really. He rented the place the way men buy jeans or T-shirts; once they know their size, it's basic—stack 'em up and rack 'em up at the register. He'd been entirely focused on leaving the house intact so Milo wouldn't have to experience the break-up of his parents piece by piece; he'd failed to hold this moment in his mind. Here, he hung pictures: pen-and-inks of trains, biplanes, and tugboats by a friend of his whose work sold big at the maritime galleries. He picks Milo up now to show him the pictures, then walks through the place opening every door, noting their hollow-core flimsiness, and with the flick of every switch feeling how unlived-in the space feels. The apartment smells like enamel, acrid and bracing, not like the rich lived-in air of the Victorian he and Ginny had lovingly restored. There the air changed from room to room: cornbread, chili powder, lavender, and cedar. It still stung him to think of how fast they'd had to sell that house. Briefly, Finley entertains the notion of smoking a pipe like his father in order to give the apartment some distinct odor—bourbon and cherry wood—but it makes him feel instantly foolish. When he shows Milo the twin bed he managed to stuff into the one bedroom by putting his own dresser at the end of the hall, Milo places his hand atop the bedside table and turns bravely toward his father.

"We could get a turtle."

Yeah, thinks Finley, that would make the place homier, some tiny reptile to scuttle against the stones at night. "Sure," he says, "there's enough room for a turtle."

Later, while Finley fixes French toast and bacon, Milo sets his things out on the coffee table—Pokémon cards, Pokidex, magnifying glass, plastic spy glass (collapsible), and a flannel Crown Royal bag filled with marbles. That will go over well at school, decides Finley—only the best Canadian Whiskey for this child's parents while they argued themselves sick over who was responsible for what last fall. Next, Milo produces a paperback book of mazes; a plastic baggie filled with pencil sharpener, shavings, and the stubs of pencils; a small drawing pad his mom had tucked into his stocking at Christmas; and several large bolts and nuts that Finley had given him because of the quiet pleasure Milo derived from screwing and unscrewing them. The careful arrangement on the table is uncharacteristic of Milo, and Finley wishes suddenly for all the old crap to trip over, the everyday obstacle course of laundry strewn with Hot Wheels cars, Play Huts drooping under the weight of blankets, action figures to step on like Batman with his spiky head at six AM, Ginny's books in haphazard piles along with all those magazines she subscribed to for every neighbor kid's fundraiser, and the band aids strewn over the counter, and the soap in the bottom of the shower, and the bath mat in a wad—he misses the whole chaotic mess. It's as though Milo is living in a terrible visual silence in this apartment and trying not to disturb it.

Finley turns his head back to the stove too quickly and dings his temple on the corner of the cabinet door. Son of a bitch, it hurts. As he rubs his head and turns the spitting bacon, he finds himself crying. He can swallow back the sounds but the tears are copious. He can't do this to Milo. This isn't like being a college kid who finds the impersonality of it all wildly liberating. The layout of the apartment building in Finley's mind is like a stack of ice cube trays; he sees Milo frozen in their grey-white cubicle.

"Hey buckshot," he calls out with desperate cheerfulness, "want to go bowling after we eat?"

When Milo has finished his before-bed bowl of Cheerio's and climbed beneath a comforter sewn with fishing line, Finley stares at himself in the reflection of the sliding glass door. His hair has grown out into an unintentional mullet and his shrunken maroon T-shirt pulls across his chest. He decides he looks like an ad for a cut-rate furniture warehouse.

Finley looks up from the book in his lap and listens to Milo draw a long shivery breath. He misses things about family life he hadn't known he'd been aware of—Ginny and Milo's sleeping sounds at night. He remembers the last summer they visited his parents on Lake Chelan, a family reunion when Milo was two. His sister and brother in-law slept across the hall, in the other dormer, his parents downstairs. Each family to its own room, the way they might have slept one hundred years before, when people had fewer things and more of each other. The night noises rise in his memory now. Auntie, with her pounding heels and ciga-rettes on the porch, and Uncle with his late-night thrillers, and cousins gone to bed with kites in their cribs, and Grandma with her prayers, and with Grandpa, the sound of pipe scraping.

Early in the morning, maybe five AM judging from the thin blue light, Finley woke to a toilet flushing, the lake lapping, the ceiling fan paddling the air, and Milo's breath chug-a-chug-chug-ging as sure as *The Little Engine That Could*. He turned to Ginny then, and after one kiss, they took each other like a sudden draught, heads thrown back to welcome the tremor, the last taste. Then from the dark came a quick and singing voice, asking another voice to answer his. Finley sat up quickly to cover their leapfrog limbs and wet moons, saying, "Goodnight son" with love and finality. And Milo rustled back down into the warm nest of his parents' breathing.

He misses Ginny's passion, her indignation, even though it meant he could never watch the news without her constant editorializing. She wasn't just opinionated; she was fiery. Literally. She had a habit of picking up the kettle with a dishtowel and inadvertently dragging it over the burner. She'd trail flame on the way to the kitchen sink. When Ginny was harried or tired, baggies melted onto burners, spatula handles melted onto frying pan edges, or she simply let the water burn off beneath the steamer until the whole house smelled of scorched beets. She was a freaking fire hazard. Odd what makes you love a person later. Once she cooked the asparagus with the rubber bands on and didn't discoverer it until Finley remarked on the bitterness of the vegetable. Man, how they laughed when he speared a rubber band with his fork.

On impulse, Finley picks up the phone and dials Ginny's number, banging his thumb rhythmically against his kneecap as he listens to the repeated tone. She doesn't pick up until the third ring, then sounds immediately alarmed.

"Is Milo okay?"

"Yeah, he's fine, Ginny. We went bowling. Listen . . . I don't think this is good for Milo, you know? Hanging out with me in a bachelor pad. It's not homey."

"So make it homey." Her tone at least isn't caustic, only brusque and matter-of-fact.

"No matter what I do, Ginny, it's going to be what it is."

"And what's that, Fin?"

"A storage unit, Ginny, it's a storage unit." He is surprised by the stoniness of his delivery; he meant to sound evenhanded, pragmatic even.

"Too bad you didn't think about that before. If you hadn't borrowed so much against the old house, we'd still be living in it."

"I'm not going there, Ginny. I'm calling about Milo."

"So . . . what are you saying? You want to visit with Milo here on your nights?"

"Yeah. That's the idea. The mediator told me about it. It's this new thing called birdnesting, where you don't displace the kid."

"What about me, Fin. What about displacing me?"

"Can't you go to the gym or something else you want to do? Kind of like your night out?"

"Tuesday is a week night, Fin. I'm grading papers."

"Well, you could come over here and correct papers. I could give you a key." A stunned silence follows and Finley finds himself stunned as well.

"That's too weird, Fin. I'd probably be snooping around in your stuff. I couldn't help it. And what about Nature-girl. She might not like it."

"She's history, Ginny. Okay?"

"Should I say sorry?"

"No, you can leave that to me. That's my role, isn't it?"

"I'm not going to react to that, Finley. Really, I'm not. Anyway, I still don't think I can do it. Why don't you take Milo out to garage sales? Let him help you decorate."

"Yeah, I'll end up with another rubber trout that sings 'Don't Worry, Be Happy.' Remember that thing?"

"Yeah, I do."

"He must have pushed the red button a thousand times to see that fish wiggle and sing."

"I gotta go."

"Okay. . . ."

"Night, Fin. Kiss Milo for me."

"I already did."

"Bye."

Finley looks back toward the sliding glass door and watches his reflection mouth "bye" to a dial tone. "Love you, too, honey," he says out loud. The man in the furniture ad wants a beer bad, a beer and some TV, but Finley stares him down hard and prevails. He cracks his book instead: *Divorce Is Not the Answer.*

Mr. Vacation

Tasi has a meeting on Monday morning with the communications director and the account executive. Her stomach still feels like boat bilge, but she thinks she can get through it. She feels better anyway than Charlotte, who had her uterus scraped. But to Tasi's way of thinking, Charlotte made the right decision. Tasi has never heard a labor story that made her wish she'd had children. She can't think of anything more demeaning than labor, to have that many people see you so out of control.

In the recovery room, Charlotte cried awhile.

"It's over now. It's done," Tasi said, patting Charlotte's back.

"I didn't really want the baby . . . not unless Darius did, too . . . but I hate to kill anything . . . I couldn't even kill a fish . . . when my dad used to take me fishing . . . I couldn't even kill the fish I caught."

"Charlotte, something dies every time we sit down for dinner. We just don't have to think about it."

Charlotte looked at Tasi imploringly and gave a little, sniffly laugh.

Tasi stood, brushing her skirt down reflexively. "I saw Key lime pie in the cafeteria. That's your favorite, isn't it?"

Back in the world of consumer public relations, the communications director has called a marketing meeting. Mr. Firmani is a portly man, prone to taking Friday afternoons off to golf with his wife. He wears jerseys with Ralph Lauren polo logos that unfortunately cling to his pectorals, such as they are, shaped like teats and resting on his tummy. When Tasi comes in he is on the phone with doggy day care about his Corgi's medication. It would be easy to write Mr. Firmani off as a prick, which he is most of the time, except when it really matters. His son died in one of those freak military training accidents, and sometimes Mr. Firmani's liquescent blue eyes water and overflow while he is talking about database management or press kits. He always keeps right on talking, and though it is really disquieting, they have all gotten used to it. Mr. Firmani goes to great lengths to retain his employees.

The meeting starts off with the standard berating about vague reporting on time sheets and the importance of justifying billable hours according to procedure. Peter gives her a quick glance, his eyebrows raised, but Tasi senses a tightness in his smile; it isn't the usual conspiratorial bemusement. Mr. Firmani's assistant, Pauline, has dyed her hair a saturated shade of maroon, and Tasi finds herself staring at how pale Pauline's face looks by comparison.

Mr. Firmani wants to see the thumbnail sketches Peter is working on for the new BP logos. He is in an irritable, dismissive mood. "That's not a classic look, Peter. It's outdated. They're coming to us for an updated look." Tasi's turn is next. She's in charge of the Imperial Cruises campaign, and Mr. Firmani wants to hear about media pick-ups. Tasi has taken a mother-daughter angle with the recent round of press releases. She assembled some multigenerational testimonials: "My mom wanted to take me on a special trip before college but she also wanted to feel safe and pampered." Or "My mother can't get around like she used to. The nice thing about a cruise is that it makes the logistics of travel so easy." Then she documented the rise in the number of women traveling. *Good Housekeeping* gave Imperial Cruises a blip in the travel column and several newspapers picked it up for their family travel sections. Mr. Firmani is pleased.

The next item on the docket is the upcoming trade show for the Public Relations Society of America, where, for three nights and four days, Tasi and Peter will dine and eat breakfast together without anyone batting an eye. Last year, Peter stuck the tiny mini-bar bottles between her toes and painted her nails; she used the hotel blow dryer to fluff up his pubic hair. For weeks after, they would punctuate the end of their business conversations by asking: "Did you want a blow dry with that? Or maybe a pedicure?"

While Mr. Firmani is speaking, she tries to catch Peter's eye. He smiles at her but the look is wistful, not at all naughty. He is holding his hand up beside his face for Mr. Firmani to notice.

"Yes, Peter."

"I won't be able to make the PRS conference this year, but Rachel Polizotti, one of our lead designers, has requested permission to go."

"And why won't you be able to make it, Peter?"

"My daughter has developed diabetes and until things have stabilized, I think I belong close to home."

"Understandable, Peter, understandable. Tasi made an early travel request so I am sure she can accompany Ms. Polizotti."

Tasi nods. Her face feels like frozen meat. Her heartbeat is the tenderizing hammer. Peter is looking at the papers in front of him. He doesn't look up until the meeting's conclusion shortly after, and then the face he turns to her is a pathetic appeal. "What could I do?" it seems to say.

Tasi shoots him a stun-gun look, then marches to her office. After closing the door, she looks around for something to break. One Christmas, her brother Bayard gave her a vinyl paperweight that looked like a crumpled 1040 form. She picks it up and briefly considers the glass wall behind her desk that overlooks Cherry St. from seventeen floors above, then she considers her computer, but since it has a flat screen, it wouldn't be very satisfying, and by then, the very act of considering has robbed her of the impulse. She slumps into her desk chair and puts her head into the crook of her elbow like a child stuck in a school desk who has no other way to hide from the teacher.

The ending with Peter was always a foregone conclusion, she knows that, but she thought her pragmatism had somehow safeguarded her heart; she thought Peter would give notice on his tenancy there. Okay, so his daughter had diabetes. That was serious. Probably played on all his guilt, too. But didn't Tasi deserve better than to find out in an offhand fashion that the affair was over? Weren't they friends? Tasi always imagined the relationship ending with some rueful humor and some tender acknowledgment at the same time. Not like this. Publicly. Strategically set up to offer no acknowledgment at all. Did he really expect her to return to the flat, fake surface of collegiality?

She wouldn't have described the feeling that came next as pain nor would she have described it as anger. She is engulfed by a roaring white heat with the same suddenness it takes to light an acetylene torch. Peter is a hider, goddamn him. Like her father, he wants to hide from any kind of emotional intensity. Tasi blurs into a frenzy of activity. She checks her e-mail. Nothing. She checks Peter's office, not there. She sees him standing in front of the conference room, about to go in with a client. He holds up a finger and says to her, "I'll be with you in a few minutes." The client looks at him approvingly; Peter smiles at Tasi, the very picture of a congenial business associate. She strides back to her office and grasps the paperweight in her hand, turning it over briefly to examine its leaded underside.

Back in the hallway, Pauline tries to say something to Tasi, but Tasi marches on, the secretary's head turning to a maroon smear in her peripheral vision. The conference room is glass, a protruded bay window into the hallway. Tasi stops before the window, the paperweight dangling in her hand. Peter's portfolio case is open on the table, but no one is in the room. She retraces her steps back to his office.

"Where is Peter?" she demands of his secretary, smacking the paperweight down on her desk.

Esther wheels her chair back on its plastic mat. "I think he just stepped into the men's room for a moment."

Tasi strides on, through the reception area, past the elevators, toward the door with the little gold man pasted on it like a target.

She swings the door so hard it bangs against the wall and both men at the urinals jump. Peter's head whips around and his face is anything but convivial now, a mixture of shock and chagrin that gives Tasi a shudder of pure intoxicating rage.

"Don't think you can hide from me, asshole."

"I'm not hiding, Tasi, I'm in the men's room."

She laughs, watching Peter shake himself in agitation while the client fumbles so hard she can hear the change in his pockets—both of them hunch-shouldered as they try to stuff their dicks away.

"I don't care if you're on the right hand of God, you owed me better than to end it that way." She registers a figure in her peripheral vision, someone behind her opening the door and letting it close again.

"Please Tasi, I'm with a client."

"You're also with a lover, Peter, a former lover. Maybe your client should know how you treat people."

"Tasi, we agreed—"

"We agreed to treat each other decently, Peter, so that when it was over, we could at least return to being friends."

"Tasi," he says, his voice wheedling, "I meant to—"

"Meant to," she spits back at him, "I hope you pissed yourself all over."

She exits the bathroom with the same satisfying crash of the door and runs into Mr. Firmani so hard she bounces off his chest.

"Tasi," he says sternly.

"All yours," she says waving gaily. "The bathroom is all yours." By the time she arrives at her office she is giddy with exhilaration. It takes her a moment to locate her purse which is sitting on her chair beneath the desk. As the elevator descends, she finds herself mouthing her lines from the bathroom, as though she had just pulled off a performance of a terrifically important scene.

The adrenalin surge carries her all the way home where it beaches her like a critter spit out at high tide. She dumps her keys and purse with a clatter and stands in the foyer as though she were waiting to be invited in. Looking around the apartment, she doesn't like what she sees. Too much like a Sharper Image catalogue. She'd wanted to avoid the prissy and perfectly coordinated shades of single women's homes, the beds done up with huge shams, chenille throw pillows, and gargantuan flowers printed upon the spreads. Quite intentionally, Tasi's house looks safe for boots, a man's boots to prop up on the cocktail table or stick off the end of the couch. The problem, she decides, is that it looks just as intentional as the white and flowery fu-fu homes: black leather sling-back chairs and a chocolaty leather couch, Navaho throw rugs. She read somewhere that single women compensated for the difficulty of setting up a dream home without a man in the picture by obsessing over sheets and their thread count. Tasi sidestepped that by renting an apartment. But the only thing she truly cares about in the place is her grandfather's big walnut desk with the strip of green leather down the middle and the brass handled drawers.

She retreats to her bedroom with its surprising splash of yellow, the bedspread a solid expanse of sun with a woven seashell design, the headboard and end tables white wicker. Tasi purposefully expunged the tasteless past from her current swank apartment. Her dresser holds the requisite amount of memorabilia: a picture of herself in her mid-twenties with her two brothers at Whatcom Falls; a formal picture of her parents in their best against a swirling blue background, a miniature Doric column laden with flowers beside them. Her mother's smile is brave and bright, former captain of the girl's baseball team, nicknamed "Sparkplug," by her sorority sisters. In her father's eyes she sees that familiar glint of deflection—Air Corps cadet who came home after his brother was killed and ran the family car dealership with a tire iron beneath the cash register. His smile is small and protective; Tasi knows that the hand at the crook of his mother's elbow is there for prudence. He is afraid she will fall down. Next to the photo, Tasi keeps the beveled glass box her mother gave her one Christmas, a box full of glittery sand which when turned reveals new combinations of shells.

She lies on her back on the bed with the little box in her hands. After a few moments, she sets it beside her and she presses the button on her blinking phone machine.

"I'm not going to fire you over this . . . this . . . extremely unprofessional conduct. I pressed Peter for some background and I have to tell you . . . it's not worth it. I'm putting you on a disability leave for depression, that's the best I can come up with. Now, you'll have to sign some paperwork with Pauline [Beep, Message deleted]."

"Hey Sis. Bayard here. We're really looking forward to your coming up on Saturday. Dad's been after me to stock all your old favs—Hawaiian Punch and Heath Bars. Let me guess. You stopped eating that junk twenty years ago . . . Oh, well. You'll have to eat it now. Mom's not doing so hot . . . she's really unsteady on her feet, she's . . . she's losing her ability to walk. Dad wants us to go through some legal stuff. Anyway, call me if you want . . . I love you [Beep, Message saved]."

She hits the replay button and gets up off the bed. Next to her sink is a black iron rack for jewelry. She has to lift several gold chain droplet necklaces before she finds the necklace that Bay had made her—a shiny black kukui nut flanked by ceramic turquoise beads and chains of tiny bells strung at even intervals that make a sparkly little jingle when she walks. After putting the necklace on, she strips out of her work clothes and wraps herself in flannel pajamas.

Bay had made her a lot of things that she no longer had—a rope hammock, leather sandals, stoneware salt and pepper shakers—all products of the communes on which he had lived, East Wind or West Wind, she can't remember the name now. For egalitarian societies, there certainly seemed to be a profusion of offshoots, discontents intent on making an even better, better society. Tasi knows she has been snarky about his ventures as have her other brothers—Paul, who sells antiques and assesses estates for a living, and Simon, who is a commercial real estate broker. Bay was the family weirdo who started out studying environmental science but dropped out of college when he fell in love with a single mom—Shannon was her name. She had such great breasts she could wear silk scarves for halter tops and even the dreadlocks that hung from her head like trails of turds could not detract from her airy, cherubic beauty. Bay had followed her to the commune in Missouri where he became a "meta parent" at the commune day care, building a pen of beans for the tangle-haired trolls to play in, children who seemed dressed perpetually in wool vests or their underwear. Tasi marvels that he came home at all during those years when every reunion in Seattle must have felt like an assault on his manhood.

He fought back with good humor and relentless political tirades—"I'm trying to live outside of a tyrannical capitalist model. It's a pretty revolutionary idea when you think about it—to forego private income in favor of shared wealth. It's not some whacked out hippie idea." He used terms like "relationship orientation," "clearness session," "co-counseling," words that his brothers would repeat skeptically when he left the room. Bay's sincerity was itself almost tyrannical; he'd explain the composting toilet in excruciating detail to anyone he felt needed an example of "sustainable living."

Ultimately, his stay at the commune crashed in an ugly, distinctly un-utopian fashion with two of the moms warring over his affections and seeking allies in the community. The winter he left the commune, he didn't come home for the holidays, and Tasi saw keenly how she and her brothers vied for her father's approval. She understood then that Bay was the strongest of them . . . because he could stand apart, not only that, but he honored their mother's work in the kitchen, in the garden, always volunteering himself to move furniture or visit the nursery with her. With her other brothers, it was all about status, and status was conferred by the world outside the home, the world her father belonged to. In a rare moment of frustration, Bay once told her, "I know I just don't measure up, but I don't care, really, because I'm trying to find a new way to measure."

Tasi hasn't thought about her brother Bay in a long time. Peter's exit seems to be making room for it, or maybe it's that Peter and Bay are so clearly men at the opposite ends of a spectrum. In any case, she needs to hear a man say, "I love you," and mean it.

Before Bay quit at the organic food farm and moved back home, he was always living in someone's unfinished attic or falling-down guest house, bartering his board for construction work while attending drum circles or taking classes in naturopathy. Tasi asked Shannon why Bay didn't become a naturopath, or start a business of his own. "He's not into that whole achievement thing, he's not into becoming something. He wants to be who he already is." Tasi had scoffed inwardly. She, too, wanted to be who she already was, which meant driven and competitive as well as creative. Yet as the years passed and lovers did not turn into husbands, Tasi admired Bay's loyalty. He stayed in touch with Shannon and attended her son's high school graduation even while dating other women, all of them single moms too. Maybe her brother Bay was a one-man social program. But he was single again and didn't want to be.

Tasi wishes she knew what went wrong; Bay was so heartbroken when each relationship crashed. Maybe the women realized that Bay wasn't going to come up with an achievement plan of his own, nothing anyway that his father or brothers could comment upon. To be sure, there are things to consider about why neither she nor Bay have been particularly successful at relationships, only now Tasi feels too tired.

The heat comes on and the curtains stir. Tasi watches them in a fixated stupor, without comprehension, as a child will watch a mobile before sleep. She feels vaguely sexual, but too languid to do anything about it. That's the way it was by the pool in Las Vegas, too, watching the hawks move on the thermals above the hotel roof, Peter dozing on a chaise lounge beside her, his lower lip pooched and glistening, a relaxed hand resting over his penis, swollen as a crookneck squash. She remembers the rose pink sheets they made love on before dinner, the way he feel asleep with his nose against her neck, the small puffs of his breath beneath her ear. At dinner, she'd gaily told him what she always said to her friends: Who needs Mr. Right when you've got Mr. Vacation? And he'd laughed merrily. Familiarity breeds contempt, that was the French maxim. She and Peter were free of all that banality. All that dependability. Well, she thought now, dryly, Mr. Vacation cancels; there was that.

JEAN

∾

Sealed Boxes

In her free time, Jean reads the *Western Garden Book*. No case histories there, no revisions of diagnoses and treatment. Tim and she used to have a big garden with raised flower and vegetable beds. For fencing, they used old fishing nets and she would twist shells and driftwood into the web. She could grow Sutter's Roses five feet tall, her favorite for their saturated yellow and their lemony smell. Now, she takes care of basic shrubs and groundcover though she is slowly tearing out old juniper bushes and replacing them with heather. This morning she spliced a hose into four-foot lengths and staked a birch tree that had nearly pulled up in a high wind. Between chores, she reads the *Western Garden Book* and lingers over sentences like these: "After a tree has become established, it may grow satisfactorily with no further nutrient assistance. If it continues to put out healthy, vigorous new growth, fertilizer applications may be a waste of time, effort, and materials."

She still hasn't unpacked her boxes beyond bedding and kitchen, though she has organized them, dumping the book boxes in front of the bookshelves and the CD's in front of the entertainment center. It seems there is nothing she can listen to safely, without thinking about Tim. Every now and then she takes something out of one of the knickknack boxes, examines it like an ancient artifact, and puts it back. This morning, a bud vase from Charlotte, Portuguese or Spanish, that consists of five fat little vases in a ring, all connected at the base with a sixth sitting atop the crown they make. Charlotte has a good eye for things that are simple but unusual. For years, Jean used the bud vase to hold her nail file, clippers, scissors, tweezers, and razor. Now she wipes a bit of newsprint from the white glaze to be sure it will come off, then rewraps the vase and submerges it beneath a layer of foam peanuts. Beneath that Jean finds a rock. After returning from a trip to the Lopez Island, Charlotte had handed Jean a wave-polished agate, round as a full moon, white as an egg, and pronounced the gift "ovulation rock." When Jean first started the fertility treatments, her friends had been so optimistic for her, they called constantly; they buoyed her spirits. Virginia and Finley were trying too. For a couple of months, she and Ginny made jokes about their bodies, about the "tit fairy" who came in the night and made your husband happy. They fantasized about their children playing dress-up together, leaping through sprinklers together, picking berries together. A year later, Virginia was pregnant while Jean had just joined the I.V.F. sorority in Dr. Daubresse's office. She remembers the news from Nan, too, the solemn way Nan had said "I don't want you to hear this from anyone else," as though she were announcing a death and not her own pregnancy. Jean marvels that her friendships with them survived.

For awhile she felt like the eighth fairy godmother in Sleeping Beauty—the old unhappy fairy who arrives late and gives the child a curse. She knew her friends weren't keeping away from her maliciously. They needed each other so they could laugh about how often they had to pee, and how much their lower backs ached and how horny they were. If they included her, their solicitude made her mad, their carefulness charged the air; if they excluded her, she felt her grief denied, her loss unacknowledged, and she became mad all over in another way. Her grief was so black it was viscous; it was tar; she choked on it. Comparing it to depression was like using the word discomfort to describe disembowelment.

When Jean lost the one I.V.F. pregnancy that took, Charlotte thought to be consoling: "Probably there was something wrong with the pregnancy, Jean. I really believe that whatever was meant to happen happens." Jean had nodded numbly, needing her friend's comfort, hating the tired platitudes. If nature hadn't intended her child to survive did that mean she wasn't allowed to grieve it? She wanted to shout: Are birth defects meant to happen? But she didn't. She got quieter and deeper, like a U-boat patrolling alone. She sealed herself off and kept her distance from them all. She did manage to stop by Virginia's house after Milo was born. Jean was shocked to see Virginia looking so dark grey, so puffy about the eyes, and Virginia seemed visibly relieved to hand Milo over to Jean, sinking back against the bed buddy with her arms crossed beneath her swollen breasts. As Jean rocked and observed Milo's scrunched-up face, she concentrated; she tried to breathe with him; she caught herself believing that her body's proximity to the baby's might stimulate hers in some hidden way, that if she ran right home to Tim and made love, her body would hold onto the next child, just as she held onto this one. After the I.V.F. miscarriage, Nan had called.

"I'm not even going to ask how you are," she said.

"You talk. I'll listen," said Jean. "That's all I can manage."

"Well," said Nan, "There's nothing anyone can do or say that's going to be right, but I'm still going to call."

And Nan did call, faithfully, even though her son Luke was two years old before Jean laid eyes on him, and by then he didn't seem to have the same effect on Jean. The day she met him, he had smeared himself in pudding and his diaper reeked of poop. Though there was that moment, when all cleaned up he had waddled over with his squared stance and stroked Jean's chest admiringly. She felt the tar rise in her throat again, thought she might choke on it, but Nan had scooped Luke up and Jean had walked to the door, the two of them together keeping the visit blessedly short. After that, Nan had proposed the girls' night out plan, sans children, and Jean had slowly rejoined her friends.

She walks to the patio door now, opens it, and heaves the ovulation rock into the bushes. She is just closing the lid on the box when the phone rings. It's Nan, calling to tell her there's a job opening at the hospital.

"Let me guess. County designated mental health professional." Jean had done it for six years, arrived at the hospital every day to evaluate patients—people in crisis—and serve as a liaison to social services and respite care.

"That's it."

"I don't know. I'm pretty happy with the shrubs and the broken toilet complaints right now."

"I'm going to keep telling you anyway, whenever there's a job opening. You seeing anyone?"

"I'm maybe attracted to someone. Here in the complex. But I don't know."

"Don't try to know. What's he like?"

Jean laughs and finds herself toying with her cigarette ash against the glass rim of the ashtray. "Not my type. He's got this short ponytail even though he's in his forties, though he is in pretty good shape. And this Wild Bill Hickok moustache, kinda that Southern rock vibe—Lynyrd Skynyrd or the Allman Brothers or something. And he's got a kid."

"Perfect," Nan says.

"Don't say that," Jean replies. "Just don't."

There's silence at the other end while Jean asks herself if she has any right to be so thorny. Nan has tried hardest to understand.

"I'm sorry, Jean." Nan says in measured tones. "That was thoughtless. But I'm not saying it like I think kids are some panacea. I am raising a teenager after all. I said it because I think you have a lot to offer."

"Thanks, Nan. I'm sorry I'm so touchy. It's just. . . . Has Charlotte gone through with the abortion?"

"Yes, she did . . . last Friday."

"Dilation and extraction, isn't that what they call it when they use forceps, when they remove the fetus in pieces?"

"Yes, that's the procedure. In nursing school, I was told that the fetus is unable to feel pain until the twentieth week, at least that's the consensus among physicians."

"Do you believe that?"

"No." Coming from Nan, the word is heavy, square, like a brick.

"That's it, then." Jean lets a pause engulf her. "Do you expect me to stay friends with her?" she asks, experiencing an unexpected rush of adrenaline.

"I don't expect anything, Jean. I wanted to give you some closure." Nan's voice is soft but steady.

"Closure is a therapy word; it's not a reality."

Jean hears Nan take a deep breath and realizes she isn't going to respond to the rude comment. Jean thinks back to the year Luke was born, the way Nan absorbed her grief. She resumes, more neutrally.

"I think about Charlotte, a lot. Recently I remembered this trip we took, with our husbands, sailing in the San Juans. The boat was chartered and there were a bunch of other couples. One night, Charlotte and I got pretty hammered and we were laughing and carrying on. I guess our memories of college did exclude Tim and Darius, but Timmy didn't care. He could handle it. But Darius's mood got progressively darker and by the time he said goodnight, it was clear he was disgusted. That night, as I made my way to our cabin, I could hear them talking. It's not like teak is soundproof. Charlotte was saying, 'I'll be a good girl. I promise.' It made me sick to hear her say that."

"She's dependent, Jean. Her life is filled with fears you don't have."

"I'll try to remember that, Nan," Jean says, before she signs off.

Jean pauses and puts a plate in the sink. Maybe it's true. Maybe it's explanation enough. She asks herself daily why she can't find an iota of compassion in herself for Charlotte. She worked with mothers who were on methadone, mothers who made mistakes and OD' d. She believed them when they told her they loved their children, when they took out their wallet inserts and cried. She remembers now the fourteen-year-old girl who was sent home with twins. Her mother was supposed to help, but she went away for the weekend and one of the babies had a fever, was admitted to the hospital with hypoxia. Severe dehydration. How preventable was that? A nurse had called the house a few days after the girl was discharged from Labor & Delivery, but that was all the support she got till she became a part of Jean's caseload. The baby would be a vegetable all his life, yet she hadn't faulted the girl.

She knows she is supposed to elevate service to others above her own self-interest; that's in the National Association of Social Workers Ethics. But all she thinks about is how easily she could have arranged the paperwork, could have had another MSW at the Birth Center on Day One to arrange the transfer of legal rights. It's a tape that plays over and over in her head, the one in which she gets to pick up the infant and carry him out of the hospital, lay her cheek against his downy scalp and feel the steady beat of blood beneath the fontanel. But she has another tape, one of Charlotte on the table, Valium drip in place. Charlotte doing her best imitation of protoplasm. She pictures some hard-bitten nurse with magenta lips—the type that doesn't believe in painkillers.

Jean doesn't believe Charlotte should be allowed to block it all out. She remembers the famous Nilsson pictures published in *Life Magazine*, April, 1965, the cover shot of the thumbsucking fetus illuminated against a shimmering lace of amniotic sac, its moonstone eyes staring out. Anybody would have called it a baby, unless of course they intended to get rid of it. Jean has been hurling baby books from her boxes and putting them in the Goodwill pile. Still, she paused long enough to read that most women feel the baby's movements between sixteen and eighteen weeks. Would Charlotte feel a kind of movement, too? The Nilsson photos were that first window into the womb—like that first picture you see of the *Titanic's* lower deck, children pressing the rail, or of the Holocaust children waiting in gas chamber lines—it becomes a window that will not close.

Jean is lighting her second cigarette when there's a knock on the door. It's Reio, bigger somehow now that he's in her doorframe, and she instinctively steps back.

"I saw you out there with the tree, so I figured you were home. I didn't get your home phone the other night, and I didn't want to call you on the complaint hotline."

"Un-hunh," Jean replies, caught in the middle of taking a drag.

Reio cocks his head down and to the side, something falcon-like but endearing in his gesture, "Is this all right?"

"Oh yes, yes it's fine. I would have given you my personal number, but we got on to the snake and all."

"Oh . . . good," he says, unembarrassed in his relief. He looks around for a moment, the taupe leather couch and loveseat incongruous and blob-like atop the orange carpet. He scans the boxes, the small photos on the mantel, the blank walls. She's been here three months. "I don't think I should offer to help you move in," he says with a slight smile.

"That wouldn't be wise. I'm trying to decide which boxes should remain sealed forever."

"Choose the heaviest ones," he says, and she finds they are staring at each other again in this frank open way that seems to bring with it so much consideration and so much certainty.

"Did you come over here to ask me out?" she says to him finally.

"Yeah . . . yeah," he says slowly as though he can't remember how he planned it. "This may sound forward, but Tor and I are going to the coast for the long weekend. There's a family beach house in Moclips. We go a few times a year. I was wondering if you'd like to come with us." He sniffs a few times after he says this, like his nose is some major distraction to him, like it's what he's really thinking about, then he adds, "You'd have your own room, of course."

Jean has been holding onto the kitchen counter with one hand. She lets go and brings her hand to her face, touching the side of it unconsciously, as though trying out how it might feel to someone else. "Are you sure this isn't your need for the Big Brother/Big Mother program?"

"No . . . I like you." There's no sniffing this time, and his look is brazenly earnest. It makes her chest hurt.

"We've only really talked once."

Reio looks down and away, then back at her with a touch of impatience. "Have you had any really bad dates?"

"Who hasn't?" She scoffs protectively. Where is this going?

"Did you need to go out more than once?"

"No." Her laugh is incredulous.

"I like you, Jean. I already know that."

He writes down his number on the scratch pad in the kitchen. At the door, as he turns to say goodbye, she puts out her hand, and it lands on his chest, squarely over his heart, a gesture that both holds him at bay and holds him there, where if he were to drop his head he could kiss her. Instead, he presses her hand against his body for a moment, then opens the door.

CHARLOTTE

～

Shelter

*D*rink. Clink. Schlunk. Ice against my lips. Our hearts are like *cell phones—no apparent line of connection—but ringing suddenly in public places. You speak words of love on hotel shuttles, next to hot dog stands, riding on escalators, anywhere you can be sure of interruption. The red roses you left me are brilliant as maraschino cherries, as brilliant as stubbed toes. You see, it all goes back to gore with me. Think of souls only. Drink. Clink. Schlunk. One floor up, ladies and gentlemen, preemies to the right, wriggling feebly in their incubators; one floor down, ladies and gentlemen, don't look too closely in the jar. Think of souls only. Light a candle in the bathroom and watch its flame lick your face in the mirror. I returned a soul to God. I returned a soul to God so Darius and I would not harm it.*

The nurse made sure I understood—always the danger of perforation. Yes, always the danger of perforation. She was talking about the uterine wall, I'm not. Pierce my heart, hope to die. Puncture me. Drink. Clink. Schlunk. One time Darius yelled at me: "How long will it take you to kill yourself at this rate?" Alcohol. Alcoholism. The slowest bleeding out in all the world. He can't make me go into recovery. He doesn't get to be the hero in the script.

Tasi came to the clinic. She picked me up. She was kind to Darius, took his hand. He nodded his head in deference to Tasi when she brought me to the door. Old world values showing. This was something for women to live through with each other and men to respect from a distance. He took my elbow; he plumped my pillow. There is no morality in love, not for those to judge on the outside, only true contrition. After Irene was born, Nan said, "Find a man you don't have to forgive. Don't put yourself in the position of asking the question "Can I forgive him? Can I forgive him?" But I had to answer yes, over and over, yes. Didn't I? If I wanted to see my daddy . . . I had to answer yes.

Nan says we'll take a long walk soon, when I feel up for it. She's worried about my depression, though every call she asks how much I've been drinking. Every call, I answer like I'm still capable of counting, like I'm filling out the yearly health care questionnaire. Drink, clink, schlunk. Here's the weekly average. Too much. Okay. Too much all the time, just the way I like it.

Darius is gone now. Malaysia for two weeks. He'll call me every few days. He'll tell me: "Love you. Gotta go." It didn't take me too long to understand about Darius, to understand that I'm not his only lover. But I'm the one with the house; I'm the one to be jealous of. After his first trip to Hong Kong, I figured it out. Not from anything he said, it was nothing we spoke about. There is always the risk of perforation. He was asleep in his clothes, as though he had fallen face forward on the bed and not moved. There were leaves stuck to his socks when I took his shoes off, bent like flames around his black heels.

Baby was my clandestine love. I spoke to Baby about Darius and what we needed to do. Be a good baby I whispered, the fat, jolly kind of baby who sleeps through the night early, smiles early. Wish I hadn't waited till you had a brain. Wish I had done it when you looked like a boiled peanut with flippers. At five weeks you would have had no brain. Did I owe you an explanation when you grew a brain? They made me do an ultrasound . . . to determine gestational age. I kept my eyes shut tight. No snapshot for later. No book of firsts.

Women are drawn to Darius by the heat and force of his confidence, repulsed by his cruelty. The trick to staying with him is learning to love the cruelty, to find what lies beneath it. This is how I've outlasted the others. Think of souls only. In the beginning, I had *hopes of healing him. How cliché. Evidently, I still had those hopes a month ago. Until he yelled, "We're not having a baby, so get it out of your head."*

What he meant was "Get it out of your body." Always the risk of perforation. Once upon a time, I was attracted to him for his tough-ness; I can't despise him for it now. I was envious that he could filter and select and discard. The whole unexpurgated world seems to flood me. Drink. Clink. Schlunk.

Motown songs. All the ones that start with "Baby, Baby." For a while you were my clandestine love. But I had no right asking you to be my ally in winning your father over. Maybe you would regret being born? Maybe later you would turn on me, because he couldn't be won over. Maybe later you would ally yourself with him, dance to the sound of change in his pockets. Bells are ringing. Listen to them ringing. For awhile you were my water baby, floating above a pink coral reef, a crenellated placenta blooming bright in a salt water tank all my own.

Someone banged on the glass. That last fight with Darius. He held his hand up: Stop. No more arguing. "It is your decision," he said. He would send me checks every month. Where had he moved us already?

"Right. You could put us on an automated payment plan." I yelled everything. "The fetus has a face already. She can frown or smile." While we were arguing, Baby was kicking, curling her toes up and down, rotating her feet, her wrists, pressing her lips together. Darius held his hand up. A smack to the glass. All still. He could do it; he could shut us out. He could put us on an automated payment plan and think no more about it. Wave, baby, wave bye bye now.

I liked Darius's elegance and formality in the beginning; he didn't expect to understand me though he promised to protect me. I like shelter. I wouldn't want to be all worn out like Virginia. Once when I told her she must miss her friends, she said, "Hell, I miss myself." I like shelter. I know that's selfish of me, I suppose, that he gets to be the one to solve the problems, but fifty years ago that would have been part of my charm, it would have been essential to my femininity, and now what? Am I supposed to be ashamed of it? Fuck you, Jean. You can keep your social worker assessments to yourself. If I.V.F. had worked for you, you would have had a doctor pop off a few embryos. Who are you to judge me? I can't help it that you're so unhappy with your life.

The doctor told me he wanted me to quit smoking so he could put a Norplant in my arm afterwards. Stupid me. I'd told him I'd missed a pill or two. "I don't want to see you in here again," he said. Who is he to judge me? Some man. Who the hell is he to judge me? What do they say in the military . . . mission aborted? Why don't they say life aborted? It's in the paper every day. Every fucking day girls and boys shipped off. No one debates infanticide, but these are mother's babies, mother's babies who have fully formed arms, legs, and brains, at least until the explosives tear them apart. Here's an arm. Wave, baby, wave bye bye now.

I asked Baby for a sign. Tell me you want to be born. You are the one after all who chose, not me. Under what impulse, after all this time? The book told me: "Six or seven days after fertilization the egg embeds itself in the uterine lining." At twelve weeks, all you made me feel was sick. I sat in the car at the doctor's office unable to get out. Roll down the window. Sick. Sick. Sick. That night I dreamed of those wasps that lay their larvae inside the shell of another insect. When the larvae hatches it proceeds to eat the host insect alive from the inside. I saw myself on the high metal table, heels in the stirrups, a large noxious insect crawling forth from my body.

I wish we could ride. Make this go by fast. The Husquevarna sits in the garage now. Darius is too fancy for it now. Used to be we'd drive to the Okanagan on the Cascades Highway. And stop at Newhalem, the Seattle City Light Company town, little white houses all the same, the park a saturated green. An old black loco-motive that used to haul timber. Kids pulling the rope on the bell,

*clanging it like crazy. Wooden plank swings and probably the last
metal merry-go-round in the state, the kind we used to run round
till we tripped and got dragged. Gravel in the knees. It was worth
it. That day there was a girl lying down on the go-round with her
head hanging off the side. Remember when it used to feel good to
get dizzy? Drink. Clink. Schlunk.*

*Children kept piling out of cars with parents the size of boulders
who piled food on picnic tables: women carrying flat pans full of
white cake, and green plastic salad bowls full of potatoes and men
hauling propane barbeques and ice chests. If America is fat, it looks
happy. Darius bought me a lemon-lime push-up popsicle as long as
my arm; it tasted like Janitor in a Drum, like Pine Sol.*

"You have some."

"No here, you have some." And we laughed.

*Why do I think now about the girl with blue baubles in her
hair? Why do I remember what happened while Darius was in
the bathroom? The girl's father wore a flowered bandanna tied on
his head in a way that made me think of Black mammy dolls. He
opened the door to his truck, a pale green Ford oxidized to chalk,
turned sideways, and let his bulk fall out. He was huge, dark, and
curly and if he'd stepped out close to me, I would have avoided
looking at him. But from the other side of the truck, a girl of six or
seven and slender as a straw reached out the window of the truck,
punched the big button on the outside handle, and swung herself
to the ground when the door released. She was wearing pink clown
knickers and a white tee shirt and her hair was held in up by big
blue plastic baubles. "Take my hand, Marla," her father said when
she appeared on his side. And she began hauling on him as if he
were an anchor that could be pulled up. "No, Dad, buy me something at the market."*

*Back on the bike, the wind funneled up the gorge and pressed
against us. The dark dolomite walls narrowed as we pass beneath
them—walls of opportunity for hydropower. The highway dipped
and twisted; conifers consumed the foreground. We climbed. Beyond*

tree-line. *Above Rainy Pass, the glaciers gleamed. The mountains were black spikes, black spires, black bells. The sky incredulous blue. Think of souls only.*

Drink. Clink. Schlunk. I see us now. A big-chested man with a boy's slender legs, and a younger woman with her hair in a braid riding with her head pressed between his shoulder blades so she could keep her eyes open. I like shelter. Darius was the human battering board, my fortification against the wind. As we descended, insects cracked against his teeth and forehead. He shouted at me to lean with him on the curves. I had to close my eyes to make myself do it, lean with him even though the wind was blowing the same direction as we were leaning. Remember when it used to feel good to get dizzy? I heard him shouting again but I couldn't make it out. I pressed my ear to his back and felt the vibration of his bellowing.

A dirt road appeared. He cut the engine and rolled the Huskie off the highway. "Hold the bike," he told me, nearly knocking me off to get his legs over the seat. He pulled his shirt off, cussing, stamping it into the dirt. His belly was covered in welts, erratic star shapes swelling up, pink against his tan skin. A large wasp had crashed into his stomach. The air had beaten it back against his skin over and over.

I could hear water, not the far off skesh-skesh of irrigation birds in the orchards, but running water. Follow the sound to the source. Darius behind me cursing. No merciful shadows yet from the black and purple buttes, just heat and chewed down brush, sage to grey and mauve again. I stripped my shirt off and dipped it in the river. I bathed his welts: dipping the shirt, wringing it, laying it over the stung skin. Saying the sweet things you say to soothe, to move the mind from pain to lyricism. "Shhh," he told me sharply. I took up the cloth, to make it cool again, but he stayed my hand when I came back to lay it over the welts. "Enough, enough, I'm all right." But I could see the swelling, pink stars on a lattice of lash marks.

"It will hurt less later if we take care of it right now."

"Just let it be," he said, and this time there was a serrated edge in tone.

I walked away then—always the danger of perforation—followed the trail to an empty power station above the river. A one-room shack built on a boulder really. Clumps of cottonwood drifted in and out of the window frames. I like shelter. Prince Albert tobacco tins littered the ground; one steel-toed boot was setting off on its own. I should have heard Darius's footsteps but the low buffeting of the wind in the gorge created an undertow of sound. "Sorry," Darius said, in a flat speaking voice. I didn't answer. It was too late. I'd already learned about him. Darius is victimized by comfort, fears it as disablement. "Sorry," he said again. I let him follow me into the shack.

If I had known how much time would pass before I heard that word again, I would have savored it. I would have shaken myself from the drowsy fragrance of hillside flowers smelling like warm toast spread in butter and honey. I would have said thank you, I'll need this moment later. But his desire for me was too intense. No pauses. From the floor, all I could see in the windows of the power station was mist, the mist that rose above the precipitous drop, rose and folded back upon itself. He thrust into me; I gripped his back. Hold me from the edge, where the bad story eddies and whirls, where I have thrown it to tell itself to itself.

Groggy and sullen with each other in the heat, afterward, we cracked a beer and drank it in the shade. "On vacation," we said to each other.

"What time is it?"

Answer: "Beer-thirty."

Too much all the time, just the way I like it.

Back on the motorcycle, we stopped only where the road came to a hard left beside a stand of poplar trees, our turn north toward the Okanogan Valley. There Darius rolled the bike toward a shrine, a simple cross in memory of a driver gone over the edge. Remember when it used to feel good to get dizzy? Propped against the simple cross was a portrait of our faded savior, a rosary, and an empty bottle of Johnnie Walker Red. But everything was tipped way back, 45 degrees, because the shrine itself had played a part in saving another wildly careening life. Darius is this to me. A shrine to some death he endured prevents my own.

It took two days to winch my cervix open. Rods. Laminaria. They told me the seaweed was spongy, gentle. Gentle like a bulb of bull kelp shoved up there. They told me the twilight sleep might affect my memory. Drink. Clink. Schlunk. Nothing affects my memory. I have made a shrine, too. Next to my bed, a bud vase. A white and pink flower.

Darius wasn't complicated until I tried to love him, tried to give him back the pleasure he gave to me. He couldn't stand for me to touch him unless he was already growing hard. He had to grow hard inside too. One night not long after we were married, I went into the bathroom for cold cream, crossing behind him. He had his feet planted in front of the toilet bowl, a towel over his shoulder. I wasn't thinking, I went on talking, found my Oil of Olay—spread butterfly wings with my fingers over each eye then drew them under my jaw where the slightly bumpy skin is. It wasn't till he said, I'm going downstairs, that I realized what was missing: no sound of his splash in the bowl. He couldn't urinate in front of me. The patter of my voice must have felt relentless, not kindly, not familiar.

He did try to make love my way. He lay on his stomach, his long arms stretched over his head off the bed and into the air, his elegant fingers slightly curled inwards, his feet off the other end in overly arched suspension. I would start by sliding my fingers over the ridges between his toes, then sweep his whole body with my fingers, carefully, as one would brush rice grains from a table. Gentle touch didn't arouse him. The bad story eddies.

"Can we just pretend we've made love now?" he asked when I reached the bend of his neck.

"Sure," I said, "we'll snuggle up and pretend it's afterwards." But he would rise up and touch only my sex and take me hard, and I *absorbed his force, telling myself that he had to do it this way first, without feeling, in order to do it at all. Afterwards he told me, "Too many years of working sixty-hour weeks, too much time with pros-titutes in Hong Kong, Seoul, Tokyo." Think of souls only.*

"Don't worry," I said, "feelings are like wires; they can be reconnected."

The more I gave, the more I served as reminder of the wound and the less he could abide me. In the dark, I tore myself from the bed, trailing covers as I made my way down the hall. As I cried, I could feel the tiny blood vessels around my eyes breaking. I felt his weight as he settled on the mattress, head in his hand "I can't stand it, he said. "I'm paralyzed by your crying." And after a long while in which I did not speak, he said: "I'll tell you something now and you can decide whether to stay."

His face was in the dirt for a long time. The bully child held him down with his face in the dirt and later, after they had got his pants down and dropped the lit matches, after they poked the marbles in with their thumbs, when they were done they turned him over and he knew it was better to have had his eyes pressed shut.

He was eight, stripped, and tied to a tree. He could see his shoes flung only a little away from him. If he tilted his head, he could see down to his penis bent like a sippy-straw, waving a little. An hour, then another, before he saw someone coming. His brother's eyes ran with tears as he tore across the field. His father had said, "Darius will have to learn to deal with bullies," but he couldn't have meant this.

His brother ran like a stick-figure on uneven legs to keep from tripping over the clumps of weeds. He ran to keep back the sound of Darius's voice like the squeaking of a mouse closed behind a child's hand. He ran to keep back the twilight, but winter silvered even the horizon and thickened to a shimmering line.

He had to slap Darius to make him blink because his eyes had gone glassy, as though frozen open by the cold. And then Darius was freed and wrapped and led home by this brother who never once looked where women always look.

Six weeks now since the abortion, and I keep telling Darius the depression won't come back. I have to promise it away for him. "Better every day," I say. I am his affliction; the depression is mine. I don't want to do anything most days, because the things I want most to do something about belong to the past. I drink. Too much all the time, just the way I like it. Drink. Clink. Schlunk. The bad story eddies.

When he is home, he hides from me in the house—weekends in front of his computer screen which lights up his blue face, smoke-puffed and ghoulish. Even his skin has a pewter cast to it. I bring him warm milk and whiskey and try to coax him into taking breaks. "I have to work," he says sternly to the terminal. He's mad at me all the time but who is he to talk? He drinks his whiskies every night.

"Maybe Nan is right," I offer. "Maybe the anti-depressants would help me stop drinking."

"Try something," he says.

"I'm thinking about it."

After making us some dinner, I make a nest in the bed—magazines, cigarettes, wine, popcorn—and I wear my unsexy knee-sagging sweatpants. I like shelter. When he comes to bed, he complains of ashes and kernels and salt in his sheets. We shake the covers and smooth them again, and although I am smiling, he refuses the gaiety of an old gesture: lovers making a bed. If I tap on his back in the night, he turns to me like a man rotating on an axis.

When Tasi brought me home from the hospital after the abortion, I found a little satin bed jacket, laid out next to the pillow. I'm wearing it now. Who even knows what a bed jacket is anymore? I imagined how carefully Darius made the choice, how carefully he'd avoided negligees and teddies, how refined and austere he must have seemed to the saleslady as he made his wishes clear. "A convalescence," Ah yes, she got it. His sweetness is like the candy I used to make with my mother, dribbled in designs on snow, breaking the minute it is lifted from the cold.

NAN

∾

Last Resort

Nan is sitting on the couch at Virginia's looking out the window at the knobby apple tree branches and the drip, drip, drip of rain off them. Over the phone Nan and Virginia had concluded that no one else was coming to girls' night out so they decided to forget babysitters and let their boys play. Now the women are comparing notes while Luke and Milo's dinosaurs embark on an epic journey; away from the volcano seems to be the theme.

"So, "Virginia says, crushing pretzel bits between her teeth," Tasi told me that Charlotte was paranoid we were all going to sit in judgment on her as though we had nothing else to talk about. Tasi said she'll be here next time, but she wants to wait till Charlotte calms down."

Nan nods. "Tasi has to drive up to her parents' in the morning anyway. What about Jean?"

"Jean knew I couldn't *not* invite Charlotte, and even though I told her Charlotte wasn't coming, she wanted to avoid the outside chance of running into her."

"Yeah, that'd be like a demolition derby at this point."

"You got it. But that's not the reason Charlotte gives. Charlotte told me that right now social occasions risk her new-found sobriety." Virginia raises her eyes as she says this.

"Has she gone into rehab?" asks Nan, her hand frozen in midair.

"No, but she's seeing a therapist." Virginia laughs roughly. "She's always seeing a therapist."

"I know, but you've got to keep hoping." Nan looks at Virginia reproachfully, yet smiles as she shakes her head.

"So, we're down from five friends to two." Virginia turtles down into her sweater and stares at her feet

"Yep. Maybe we should sing Diana Ross. Where did our love go?"

A commotion is heard from the family room, and Virginia shouts from her post on the couch. "Milo, remember you said you'd share your dinosaurs." Then she turns to Nan. "I'm just going to bring the bottle to the table."

"You do that, Ginny," says Nan, leaning back and stretching.

When she comes back from the kitchen, Virginia sets the wine bottle down on the coffee table with a thump, as though making an announcement.

"So what do you really think, Nan, about Charlotte's abortion? Should she have done it?"

Nan pauses, drawing her fingers over her mouth as though feeling for her own expression. "I don't really know. I don't think alcoholics make good mothers, and I don't see Charlotte changing."

"But didn't it bother you, how late she let it go? I mean, isn't that the big debate, when personhood truly begins?"

Nan laughs, a short woeful sound. "Life starts when gamete meets gamete. You can't draw a line and say well this is where it's human, or this is where it feels pain or has consciousness." Nan no longer seems to be looking at Virginia; she's focused on the blank oblong of carpet in front of the fireplace. "But that's not what I think we should be talking about. Human beings aren't like fish or sea horses. They don't get out of the egg sack and just swim away. It takes years and years of commitment to raise a human being."

"No shit, Nan," Virginia says, jerking her head in the direction of the boys' voices.

"I'm just as pro-choice as you are, Ginny. But in an ideal world, women would make the decision early."

"And Charlotte didn't do that."

"No. She didn't. Denial in a word. It's a powerful thing. When I first started practicing as an RN, I'd meet women twenty-three weeks pregnant who claimed they didn't know it before then. Why? Because they were able to push it out of their minds until their tummies popped out. Women come in to ER's at full term complaining of abdominal pain. Well, the only thing that removes that kind of abdominal pain is delivery." Nan punctuates her comment by smacking the couch arm.

"Charlotte's in denial about a lot of things." Virginia sighs, and they both let the time pass, then Virginia rouses herself. "So, Nurse Nan, you don't have any answers."

"Nope. Not really. Legal abortion is better than the alternative. That's all."

Virginia twists around inside her sweater as though scratching an itch. "I don't think Charlotte and I have much in common anymore, even before this situation. I'm not drawing a dramatic conclusion. We've been drifting apart for awhile."

"I didn't think this whole thing had bothered me that much," Nan replies. "I mean it wasn't easy being between Charlotte and Jean, and I think it's sad and all that, but last night Irene made some snotty comment about abortion and I slapped her." Nan pulls at the curls on the side of her head alarmingly. "For the love of God, why did I slap her?"

"What did she say?"

"She said I should have aborted her."

"That's a rough thing for a mother to hear. Nan, cut yourself some slack."

"Irene stole Clay's pain-killers for some deadbeat guy and lied to me about where she was going. She told me she was spending the night at her girlfriend's." The whole story comes somersaulting out, and at its conclusion, Nan puts her head between her hands.

Virginia leans forward and rubs a little circle between Nan's shoulder blades. "Irene's behavior was atrocious, Nan, not to mention dangerous. You reacted to the danger, like a mama bear, gave the cub a swift cuff."

"But she's sixteen. She's going to test me all the time. What am I going to do? Slap her every time I think she's out of line?"

"Of course not. You're a terrific mom."

"I should have contacted her father when she was ten. I should have made his parents give me his info. Then Irene wouldn't need to feel loved by all these huffy-puffy boys."

"Nan, what good would hauling a recalcitrant dad into the picture have done Irene? You let his parents know the door was open. He chose never to walk through it. Besides she has Clay."

"She doesn't have Clay. Not really. It's too distant between them."

"What did he do last night?"

"He stood outside her door and talked to her until she let him in. Then he coached her on how to break up with deadbeat. He was a saint." Nan reaches for Virginia's hand.

"So maybe some good has come of this."

"I still can't forgive myself for slapping her."

"Okay, maybe you shouldn't. But I think Charlotte figures into this."

"How?"

Virginia pauses but holds her friend's gaze. "C'mon. You fought to keep Irene and raise Irene, no matter how hard that was. That's not the choice Charlotte made. Next your crazed teenager gets smart-ass about abortion. The connections are obvious to me."

Nan smoothes the curls at her temple and laughs, her familiar full laugh. "Can I write you a check now, Virginia?"

"Too bad I didn't become a psychologist. I'd be making a hundred an hour instead of this crappy lecturer pay. Don't worry, next week, it's my turn."

"How are you and Milo holding up?"

"Jesus. I hope we're getting a break between viruses. School is a goddamn petri dish. I feel like *Diary of a Mad Unwife.*"

"Is he sleeping better?"

"No, he still has those night frights. At school the kids were having a major disagreement about whether kings and queens were real so the teacher settled it by talking about the royal family. Then some older kid at recess tells him about Princess Di. Just what I need for him to hear—about a mother who leaves the father and then dies in a car crash. He's been totally clingy. He doesn't even go to birthday parties. Finally he asks me, "Mommy, why were they telling the princess to die?!""

"You're kidding? Sorry, I don't mean to laugh. I remember in nursing school, they told us not to say Barium Dye around children."

"Yeah, perfect. Bury and Die."

"Poor little guy."

"This is just not the story he needs to hear right now."

"You know, in play therapy kids can work a lot of this stuff out, Ginny. Hasn't your pediatrician referred Milo for therapy?"

"Yeah, but I can't keep him well long enough to get there."

Nan leans her head back against the couch cushions and lets her eyes loll towards the ceiling. "On second thought, Ginny, maybe we need play therapy. Hours and hours of it."

The next morning when Nan wakes up—everyone is at work or school as usual. There's a sticky note on the newspaper from Clay that says, "Sorry, sweetie. I love you." She's muddling this one over when she sees the headline: "Sniper Kills California Doctor Who Performed Abortions." She stares and stares, immobile until finally she hears a crunching noise and realizes it is her own teeth: clenched. The headline could as well read: Sniper Kills Doctor Who Delivers Babies, Saves Preemies. Dr. Theodore Pagosian, shot at his kitchen window. For a sliver of time she puts herself outside her own kitchen window, lives in the eye of the sniper, gazes along the clean smooth line of the barrel, Pagosian easily between the sights, moving only a little as he swayed from sink to dish rack, the curtain ruffle at the edges of the scope. Nan swings her forearm across the counter top, chipping cereal bowls as they dump into the sink. Then she smacks out of the kitchen in her slippers. If her eyes for a moment had belonged to the sniper, her voice was still her own. How could anyone believe they knew the will of God with such certainty? How could anyone construe it to mean killing? Thou shalt not kill. Who shall smite another down and still feel on the path to righteousness?

She shuts her eyes and she is in Dr. Pagosian's house, the house that will never again be safe, nor any home his children make, always the specter of their father falling, none of them believing—did you hear that sound? Not even he heard it. Out the kitchen window his wife sees the yard—the bird houses their youngest made, the tilting swing set, the holes the dog keeps digging, the daisies cut back for winter. It is no longer and can never be again merely a view; it is the last thing their father saw before he was felled. Now everywhere his wife walks, she follows the bloodstained prints of his shoes.

Nan makes tea to ward off the cold stillness she feels, eats toast that crumbles like pressboard in her mouth. Outside in her own yard, the leaves are strewn about the huckleberries like clothes thrown haphazardly about a room. A motley of colors backlit by spider webs and a chill sun. She just sits. The phone light is blinking and she knows Becky or Elaine or one of the other nurses has already called. But she is not ready yet. Her every internal thought starts with the phrase, "How could you?" It's not a new diatribe. And she knows lumping all pro-lifers into a category with the assassin isn't fair. She wants fewer women to abort, too, but where are the measures that would make it a less punitive choice? Why aren't pro-lifers supporting nationalized day care, universal health coverage, higher minimum wage? For that matter, why weren't the liberals demanding it? Nan looks down at the threads of terry cloth hanging off her robe that make it look like a cat's scratching post. Because we're tired, she thinks, tired of defending the laws that keep abortion legal, tired of fighting this same battle over and over. Meanwhile, fewer doctors are willing to teach these procedures in medical schools and plenty of med students don't want to learn them because they have no intention of becoming target practice. Nan doesn't stop shaking her head until she catches her reflection in the window.

The way Nan sees it, courage is in short supply these days. With liability suits foremost in so many people's minds, cover your ass medicine often prevails. Early in the week, she'd taken orders from a young doc who'd decided to do everything he could to save a preemie at twenty-two weeks. After fourteen years as a nurse, she knew the survival rate of preemies at twenty-two weeks was zip; a few survive at twenty-four weeks but they're badly damaged. Nan had offered to speak to the parents with the doc but he took it as a slight. "No, I can handle this one myself. Thanks all the same." Handle it?

Instead of palliative care this infant was hooked up to every device in the preemie ward and fifty thousand dollars got spent. For what? Where was God's mercy at times like these? Who was to say they knew it? It was a tricky business being a nurse in Labor and Delivery. You were on the front line. Should the doctor perform a crash C-section when no heartbeat could be detected with stethoscope or Doppler fetal scope? The ultimate judgment was the doctor's, but it was the nurse's job to put him on red alert.

Nan wishes she could call her father; sometimes in dreams she still dials his number. She wishes he were sitting before her with his long serene fingers laced together, listening not just with his face and eyes but also with his shoulders and hands.

Her father had the stories she needed, the ones that didn't fit categorical thinking, and he was gone. In the last years of his ministry and the first years of her ministrations as nurse, she'd had enough wit to collect some of his stories, to stand by him and listen intently while he filled the bird feeders or opened a can of fruit cocktail. Now the stories returned at odd times and not always piecemeal.

There was the girl in the parochial school kilt and Peter Pan collar who told him about her sex ed class, a curriculum titled: "On a Date with Jesus." In class, she'd piped up and said "If I was on a date with Jesus, I'd put out. I mean, he's Jesus."

"You must have been a most popular girl," her father had said, chuckling.

Then there were the less amusing stories—the twenty-one-year-old with three kids readying for her fifth abortion, obviously unwilling to see her priest but still seeking confession somewhere.

"My husband doesn't like birth control," she told him. She actually blushed saying it. She'd put her legs in the stirrups for an abortion how many times? Nan's father had reminded the woman gently that prescriptions for the pill were widely available and undetectable.

"It's against my religion," she said finally.

"But isn't having an abortion against your religion?" he had asked.

"Yes," she said, grave-faced, "but if I take the pill, I commit a sin every day. This way it's only a few times a year."

"Hopeless," her father said, affably. "You can't get inside that kind of logic."

"I would have told her abortion was meant to be a last resort," said Nan. Her experiences as a resident assisting doctors were fresh in her mind.

"Your mother would say 'whose last resort?'" he reminded her in his cheery brisk way. His demeanor always seemed to match his bow tie.

Another memory attached itself to this one, the morning Nan had told her mother she was pregnant with Irene, that the father of the baby was taking off to fish in Alaska forever. The rhythm of her mother's spoon in her coffee was unbroken—ching, ching, ching it went.

"Well, it's only a baby, honey. It's not like a baby will ruin your health."

Her mother's reaction was at once entirely disappointing and completely reassuring, but what had Nan expected? Hazel had been a nurse at Tacoma General during World War II when penicillin was so scarce that families had to pay before the nurses could administer the medicine. That was the kind of perspective she had on life.

There's only so much Nan can impart to Irene, though Irene's eyes went wide yesterday when she'd described an OB Infection Ward. She wants Irene to really get it, that having an abortion was not like getting a flu shot. Nan picks up her dishes, then reaches for the paper, but its back page is stuck to the mat by a glob of jam. Luke. She drops the paper in favor of refilling her coffee. There are things Irene can't understand: that pregnancy becomes a community you share with women you don't know; you feel yours progressing parallel to theirs—not just the people in your Lamaze class or the doctor's waiting room—the ones on your weekly route: market, pet store, pharmacy. The gal in the auto parts store who isn't even showing yet tells you her due date. Sometimes people recognize Nan, especially if they've had more than one child at the Birth Center, but that isn't the kind of moment she's remembering.

The pet store owner had smiled at her belly and then back up to her face. It was not at all offensive. "I'm going to be a granddad soon," he declared, then told her about his daughter. "I'm the one who is going to have to breathe into a paper bag when she goes into labor," he said cheerfully, ringing up a bag of millet spays for Irene's cockatiel.

Nan remembers how months later the pet storeowner had anchored her checkbook to the counter so she could write the amount one-handed while Luke at four-months-old wriggled in her other arm. The owner was known for giving copious advice about pet problems on the phone or while standing in the aisles; he made veterinarians last on your list. Nan has always liked Magnus—something kid-like in the gaze of his magnified eyes behind the square smudgy glasses. She asked him cheerfully, "How's your grandbaby?"

His body jerked suddenly as though he'd been brusquely unplugged. "Oh," he said, still smiling, "we lost her. Something about the vessels of the lungs and heart, not strong enough when it came time to function on their own."

Congenital heart defect, cardiopulmonary, Nan thought reflexively, maybe myocardial ischemia. She nodded, not breaking his gaze. Luke had grabbed a rawhide bone out of a basket and was pressing it to his tongue. She let him.

"Two days," he said. "We had her two days, and they were the best two days we've ever had as a family, and the hardest."

Nan could hear the gratitude in his voice, deepening it. He was leaning against a stack of dog food bags, his eyes reddening.

"I'm very sorry," she said. "I can't imagine anything harder." It's not his sorrow that has jarred the memory loose—Nan sees human suffering on a weekly basis—it's the gratitude, the gratitude for two days of his grandbaby's life.

Nan heads to the laundry room intent on making something else roil and churn. When Clay bought their new laundry machines he chose the industrial size, vats the circumference of semi tires. She appreciates his "let's take care of this once and for all" approach, but it also means that every member of the family waits until they're down to the last pair of underwear before washing anything. On the domestic tally sheet, it is Nan's job to grind the clothes through and Clay's job to fold it.

Nan opens the dryer and stuffs a hand in. A warm, tacky substance coats her fingers. She bends down, looks in. "Oh, please."

She bangs her head against the warm enamel. The dryer smells vaguely minty and is smeared on every surface she can see with gum. Clay has reminded her repeatedly to check the kid's pockets before tossing a load in.

Today, she was too damn tired. It looks like a whole pack of Trident went in, now yellow, gluey, and streaked. She separates the destroyed clothes from the ungummed, then racks her brain for a remedy. It's not like peanut butter is going to fix this. Squatting in front of the dryer, she tries removing the gum with rubbing alcohol, then bleach, and finally she eyes the gas can next to the lawn mower. The next hour she spends leaning inside the dryer and scrubbing upside down. She's pretty well asphyxiated herself and got it cleaned up by the time Clay, Irene, and Luke pull up the drive. She goes out to greet them with her highly flammable hair and red-rimmed eyes, ready for the simple human warmth they offer.

ơ

The Priest of Failure

Cedar Mobile Home Park really is in an old Cedar Grove, Tasi thinks, as she cruises slowly over another speed bump. In public relations, the difference between saying modular housing and trailer park is the difference between saying fresh Ahi and canned tuna. Cedar Park is the best of its kind. Gravel paths lead to a shallow lake with lily pads clustered at one end. At its center is an island covered by cattails and weeping willow. The move here was a recent one for Tasi's parents. Her father, anticipating paying $50K-$60K a year for her mother's care in a convalescent home, sold the salt box Victorian where they'd raised the kids. Now he and Winnie live in modular housing.

Tasi considers how easy it would be to be snide about the neighborhood—wooden butterflies attached to houses whose trade names were displayed on the front—Parkway, Hearthside, Villa West. She has entered the land of the miniature windmill, the poodle topiary, the white plaster swan. But she admires the senior citizens who run the voting station in the club house at election time; they're so cheery in their civic duty even if they can't hear you the first time you say your name and the conversation that follows is a yelled one. God help you if you actually want to concentrate on voting. All that racket causes you to punch your chad in frustration. But who else is willing to take up the task of democracy?

Each house has metal awnings jutting over shuttered windows, and that telling seam down the middle, and some, like her father's, have an aluminum tool shed. The colors are innocuous—shades of beige, brown, and rust. She looks for the occasional baby blue and lime green. Her parents' is white with orange trim, distinguished by a white-graveled driveway and a decomposing stump out front that will be filled with nasturtiums in the summer.

Tasi imagines her father alone here by spring, sitting on the porch listening to the drifty, random sounds of wind spinners and chimes, looking down at Mrs. Franken's zinnia patch and the saucy little gnomes she is fond of talking to like children. He'll talk to Bingo, their Jack Russell Terrier, and Flannel, the grey tabby who belongs to Tasi's mother. Tasi steels herself to step up to the astro-turfed porch, to walk the nubbed-down carpet to her mother's room. Instead, the door to the R.V. in the driveway swings open, giving her a start. Bayard springs out, wrapping her in an emphatic, breast-crushing hug.

"So, you're living in the Fleetwood," she says, when she can stand back from him. "I should have thought of that."

"I may even have to keep up Dad's membership in the Family Motor Coach Association." Bay's smile warms her. He has never had that chipped front tooth capped. Absentmindedly, he runs a thumb over his abdomen in a gesture that can only be described as teenaged. Her little brother by eight years, Bayard will grow rangy as he gets older; she can see that now, middle-age will not take the boy out of him. The T-shirt he wears beneath an open flannel shirt is thin enough to be almost transparent; his pants look like they've come off a Forest Service employee—pre-Grunge, pre-cargo pant chic—the word dungarees comes to mind. But Bay's charm has never failed to work on her. Not conventionally handsome by any means, he wears his dents and dings without shame—the slightly pitted cheeks, the broken nose that healed askant with a plateau. It's the bounce in his gait and the sincerity of his eyes that give him his youthful appeal.

"Actually, I'm thinking I might drive the Fleetwood to the Barter Fair on the east side this spring, that is, if Dad can get by without me for a few days."

Bayard's long Gallic face turns serious, darkening his hazel eyes. "You know, we're talking about moving Mom to a convalescent care home on Monday. This weekend is sort of a last chance to visit with her at home." He registers Tasi's stricken look; she can see it reflected back to her in the deepening kindness of his eyes. "Why don't you come inside the trailer? If Dad hasn't come out by now, it means he didn't hear you pull up."

The inside of the Fleetwood is comforting in much the same way as a boat's galley—the reduction in scale gives the impression that all needs can be met just within this small space; the rest isn't needed. Tasi and Bay scoot around the built-in window seat till they can see each other across the table.

"Yeah," he says. "She really can't walk anymore, and last week she lost control of her bowels. Parts of her brain are shutting down, that's how Dr. Hasagawa told me to think of it."

"Does Dr. Hasegawa know what's going on yet? Whether it's Alzheimer's or those . . . what do you call 'em's? . . . T.E.A.'s?"

"T.I.A.'s, transient ischemic accidents."

"Small strokes, basically, right?"

"Right. They can't diagnose Alzheimer's for sure unless they can do an autopsy of the person's brain. So it still may be that she's got atherosclerosis causing the T.I.A.s"

"Oh please Bay, speak English."

"Sorry. I'm starting to sound like Dad. Hardening of the arteries in the brain causes the T.I.As. Anyway, she's still on the meds to dilate the blood vessels and now she's on this new med, Aricept. It's supposed to slow down the progression of Alzheimer's."

"Doesn't sound like anything is working, if she's in bed."

"Nope." Bay studies his hands, scrubs his buzz-cut hair with them. "Dad finally broke down and hired 24-hour help through Visiting Nurses. I offered to sleep in the room with Mom but he won't hear of it."

"How is Dad holding up?" Tasi asks.

"He's pretty grim. You know, tight, holding it all in, and rigid about the routines, man. But that's cool. I mow the lawn when he wants it mowed, and put the cuttings in the bags the way he wants 'em bagged. He walks Bingo at night. I think that gives him a little space. Larry Myers keeps calling him to go play nine holes, but Dad won't leave Mom."

"Are they still fighting?"

"Nah. There's no aggression in Mom anymore. Most of the time, she doesn't know who we are. She has these lucid moments where she knows she's losing it. That's the hardest part. Yesterday I could hear Dad talking to her, in his Billy Goat Gruff voice and he's saying, "Winnie, we all love you and we're keeping you safe." She gets scared, panicky. He comes to get me sometimes because she recognizes me the most often."

"I saw the pergola you built for her."

"Yeah, she liked watching it go up from her window. Hold on a sec."

Tasi watches as Bay carefully removes a tray of grass from his refrigerator, and begins fitting the juicer together. While a moment before she had been close to tears, she feels the old irritations returning. His careful deliberations have always driven her mad, the way he pointed out to Dad that the weed killer contained Dioxin, the care with which he lined up his phyto vitamins in the morning and extolled the virtues of seaweed and wheat grass as antioxidants. A few years back, he'd persuaded Mom to give wheat grass a try and the experiment had nearly killed her, what with Mom's terrible hay fever. Good idea, drinking grass. The doctor had to prescribe Prednisone to stop the hives and itching. Back then, Bay had seemed to Tasi in every way well-intentioned but foolish. She decides to make her way to the house before the old aggravations can gnaw at her.

Her mother is asleep when Tasi enters. She sits beside the spindle bed and looks out the dinky bedroom window where she can see a cedar tree's black outline grow furry in the twilight. It takes her a moment to notice Li, the home-health-care-worker who is sitting quietly in a chair on the other side of the dresser. For a moment, it seems the three of them are spellbound by the sound of their own breaths, like singers in a round listening for where they should come in. Then Li rises. Smiling and nodding, she slips quietly from the room.

Tasi studies her mother. Her head is bent downward, her chin rests on a billow of neck, rising and falling with her chest. Winnie reminds Tasi of a pheasant sitting its eggs. Her mother's hands rest on the counterpane; they are permanently puffy from use. She knitted all her life, until this year when she became too confused to count the loops and it made her cry. She'd taught Tasi as a girl to knit, to can, to make freezer jam, to pin a pattern. Tasi wonders now if she can remember how to do any of those things. She reaches over and switches on the light.

Her mother startles. Like a quail suddenly flattening its breast feathers, neck elongated and wobbling around, the eyes beady-bright but not comprehending.

"Mom, it's me."

Up close, Tasi's mother smells of dental plaque and Pond's cold cream.

"Oh, sweetie, I'm so glad you could come. I've been worried." Her mother doesn't let go of Tasi's hands, leaving her to stand uncomfortably bent beside the bed. "I've been so worried."

"What are you worried about?"

"Oh Hattie, you know. Don't pretend like everyone else. You've been reading the papers."

"Yes, it's awful, Winnie. I agree." Tasi has learned to follow her mother's lead; it's less likely Winnie will become agitated. Winnie lets go of Tasi's hands and stares straight into space.

"He's flying those F-14s now. What do they call them? Japanese Peril. Hattie, you know Lake Michigan in winter. Some of our boys aren't making the landing onto the carrier. Right off the end they go, dumped into the frigid water."

"Who are you worried about?" Tasi hopes it is her father. She would like to hear some fond words for him.

"Why, Papa, of course. Sometimes you amaze me, Hattie."

"What about Jack?" Tasi asks, her cheeks warm with the audaciousness of it, asking her mother leading questions because of what she needs to hear.

"Oh, yes," Winnie says slowly as if mulling him over. "He came after Terrence. In high school, I dated a fellow whose mother was crippled up with arthritis. He had to go home from school every lunchtime to feed her and help her to the bathroom. I stayed with him nearly a year because every time I wanted to quit, he threatened not to go home. So I had to go to the dance with him. Imagine, a whole year. I'd probably be with him today, if Jack hadn't come along and saved me."

"Saved you?"

"Jack knew how to have a good time." Winnie claps her hands together as she says this, smiling dreamily. It is more than Tasi could have hoped for. "He knew how to make things fun, and Lord knows, there hadn't been a lot of that in my life. I suppose I should have seen some things then, but I didn't." Her mother emits a sigh that goes from high to low, an ultra-feminine cooey sound. "Wheeoow." She looks at Tasi directly, "All you can do is go on your best judgment."

"That's true, Mom." Tasi says, absently. She is still contemplating whether she can turn the conversation back to her father, but feeling there is something icky and opportunistic about it.

Her mother surprises her, taking Tasi's face between her hands. "Don't you be anyone's second best," Winnie says, fiercely and abruptly. "Jack would have married Hattie in a second, but she wouldn't have him. Don't you be anyone's consolation prize. You hear me, Tasi. Be your own treasure first."

"Okay, Mom," Tasi says, shocked to hear her own name.

Winnie presses her hands down on either side of the mattress and struggles to sit up straighter. She seems exasperated.

"I know why he doesn't come see me. You don't have to say a word. Your father hates it when I'm sick." For a moment, Tasi pictures Charlotte, sitting in bed, wearing the satin bed jacket that Darius had bought as a gift,; then Tasi pushes the image from her mind and focuses on her mother's monologue.

"Hattie and I called our quilting group WORMS, Wives Of Retired Men. Oh, it's a terrible adjustment to make, when they don't have anyone around to boss but you. Jack doesn't mean to get resentful. He hates to see me cry. When you kids were little, it wasn't that he wasn't a good father, he was a very loving father. But if I was down, he wouldn't say anything, didn't want to tip the balance, I guess. Then I'd think he just didn't care at all. Men assume if you're down, you want to be alone when that's the last thing."

The moment holds more than Tasi can bear. She remembers the time she was crying her head off as a teenager and her father cracked the door to her room, confirmed she was there, and closed it again. The years of her mother and Aunt Hattie fighting over everything from jello molds to heirlooms. She pictures Trisha's petite face at that promotion dinner, Peter scooching his wife's chair in, running a hand across her shoulders. Tasi puts her head in her mother's lap and weeps to think this is the woman whose words she has dismissed for so long.

Her mother smoothes the hair away from Tasi's face and Tasi sits up. She reaches for a Kleenex on the night table. While she blows her nose, her mother looks dreamily out the window, then back to Tasi. Her eyes glittery, yet strangely opaque, Winnie points to the manicure kit and bottle of polish Tasi has forgotten in her lap.

"Are you the lady who comes to do my nails?" she asks.

Over dinner, it becomes clear that nothing really has changed between her father and her brother. Bay is still Jack's whipping post. Tasi can feel when it is time for Bayard to leave, time to go back to the R.V. Her father never has to ask. Instead, he clears Bay's plate before he's done eating, smacks the back door closed in the midst of Bay and Tasi's conversation, grumbles loudly about not being able to "find a damn thing," because the fridge contains one box of Bay's soy milk. Tasi knows the root of it. Bayard is her mother's emotional lover, groomed for that job from very early on, and later punished for it. Now he has come home to her, to be both resented and needed.

While Dad is rooting out the soy milk in the fridge amidst eight bottles of salad dressing each containing a half-ounce puddle, Tasi suppresses the urge to help him. She knows better. Her folks were born right after the Depression and rarely throw away anything.

"How do you stand it?" she whispers to Bay.

"It's hardest on him," Bay says shrugging, "All that tension in the body. We have our moments. He always kisses me goodnight."

She stares at Bay, studying him as though she could locate the source of his compassion. On the phone, Bayard said to her: "It's okay. I'm the one who should do this. Paul and Simon have got kids and you've got a high-powered job." The reversals of time stun her. She, the consummate businesswoman, has just thrown a rock straight through the middle of her career, while Bay's failure to achieve in recognizable mainstream ways appears a strange success; his irritating patience with the unenlightened strikes her now as supreme love. Bay, by outward appearances the priest of failure, wears it like his funky Salvation Army clothes and those earth shoes that give him the posture of circumspection, a person always tilting away from the present for the long-term view, wears it like what it is, a sign of God's love.

She tells her father she is going to visit with Bay awhile in the Fleetwood. He already has the TV on, news blaring.

"Well, I'll probably turn in early," he says. "Are Paul and Linda coming tomorrow or Simon and his family?

"Paul comes tomorrow Dad, Simon on Sunday," she answers gently.

He kisses her goodnight by the door, flipping on the floodlight in case she can't see her way ten feet to the Fleetwood. "I'm awfully glad you children are here," he says hoarsely, his eyes glistening like obsidian, brightly black before darting away.

"Of course, Daddy. I wouldn't want to be anywhere else."

"All right then. Good night."

As she crosses the driveway, a memory jars loose. She used to dance for her brothers and their friends in the garage. She'd seen the movie about Gypsy Rose Lee, read about Mata Hari. She could hear the cymbals even now and the drum leading up—ba da da, ba da da dum—to the moment Gypsy Rose flung a sequined camisole away from her body and all eyes flicked toward it, then returned to her opalescent breasts.

Tasi had been determined to have that same power even if her tushy was as hairless as the cranny of an apricot. So she'd danced her version of the seven veils on the splintery floor of the garage loft. Never mind that she had no veils. She twirled her T-shirt round her pointer finger, swung her hip out to the biff, boom, ba and released it with expert timing, turned her head emphatically to look down the length of her arm at some grubby neighborhood boy who could surely appreciate her bow-red lips, her kohl-lined eyes ablaze with black flames.

That was how her father had found her and spanked her, bellowed at the boys but spanked her, right then and there in front of them as they scattered. She must have been about eight years old, maybe seven. Her femininity was drenched in so much shame, she wonders now if shame didn't have a narcotic effect on her— secrets, hiding, and shame. Before Peter, there was the Fulbright scholar from Ireland whose wife could only visit at Christmas, and before him, the lawyer who liked bondage and saying "bad girl." She shakes her head at the memory and lets it click shut with the sound of the Fleetwood door opening.

The R.V. smells heavily of sandalwood and dope; bamboo flute lullabies of Japan play airily in the background.

"You gonna give me a break, sister?" Bay asks, half-holding the joint toward her.

"Absolutely," she says, taking it from him and puffing with a vengeance. "It's hard to find a bad influence anymore."

"Here I am," he says, sweetly.

Dope has a wonderful way of making all things equally absurd. Tasi barging into the men's room; Peter trying to stuff his wanger back into his pants; Her father's tantrum over the soy milk. Even clucking over her mother's cuticles. Tasi and Bay settle into the old conspiratorial stances of brother and sister, speak in the shorthand available to those of long shared context. He has opened them both a beer when Tasi blurts out that she just broke up with Peter.

"What's the matter with us, Bay? Why can't we make a relationship work?"

"I don't know," he says, hesitating, "In my commune days, I was so into concepts of freedom . . . it just became drift. I didn't want to tie Shannon down. I should have protected what we had . . . There were moments we were so sincere, so ready . . . but nobody tethered their end. It seems so stupid to me now."

"At least you tried something idealistic. Not me. I keep getting involved with married men. I've made a habit of never putting myself in a position where I have to rely on a man. No failure rate that way. This winter I had an endoscopy because of my ulcers and they photographed this ugly, blobby thing and did a biopsy. It flipped me out."

"Was it normal?" She can feel the intensity of Bay's gaze.

"Yeah, turns out it was. Just a bit of blown out stomach lining, but it got me thinking."

"Why didn't you call me? I want to know when stuff is going on with you."

"I figured with Dad and Mom you had enough on your plate."

"No way. Don't make that judgment call for me."

"Okay, I won't next time."

"Hey, there's some heavy shit that's going to come down this weekend."

"Like what?"

"Dad is going to talk to us about how he's disbursing the will. You know he's going to give us everything now so he and Mom can get on Medicaid by next year."

"So what's the big deal about that? It can't be much."

"It isn't, but it's not evenly distributed."

"What the hell?"

"Hold on. He's giving everyone a check for 10K this weekend, only he's giving one to each of the grandchildren. So it's not evenly distributed among the siblings, but hey, we're not trying to raise kids. Paul and Simon are."

"So what. I should be able to spend my entire share on Greenpeace if I want to. If he loves us equally, it should be divided equally."

"Tasi. . . ."

"Forget it. I want another beer."

"Well, I did ask Dad if we could have the Fleetwood and he said okay."

"We?"

"Yeah. You and me. We could take a trip together."

Tasi can't help it. She starts laughing. "When I'm eighty will you drive me to see the Grand Canyon?"

Bay is laughing too, even as he says, "Hey, don't laugh. I read about this tribe in China, the Na."

"Na Na Na Na," sings Tasi.

"Really. Brothers and sisters are the main social unit. They never marry or move away. Lovers come and go, kids come and go—"Bay is waving one hand in the air—"but they run the household."

"I'm going to remember you said this." Tasi's tone is taunting.

"Fine. Fine. I'm serious."

Tasi stretches her hands across the table and encircles his forearms. "Bay, it means a lot to me that you would say that. Really it does."

In the morning, her mother has a clear spell. She wants Bay and Jack to carry her into the living room so she will be sitting up when the grandchildren arrive. Tasi fixes her mother's hair so it won't be flat in the back and sits on the sofa with her, turning the pages of a photo album created before Tasi was born. At the turn of each new page, her mother speaks, more to herself than Tasi.

"Rose, she boarded at school with me, was a devilment to the nuns. I heard she passed some time ago."

Winnie smoothes the pages down and brings her face toward the face in the photo. "Aidée," she says, pointing at the hand-written caption, "That's the French word for help. We moved to Chicago together. She married a man she didn't like, too stiff, but we kept on. Our first-born weren't so far apart. But then I moved out West, and they discovered she had lupus. Poor thing. She didn't live to see her grandbabies."

Soon there's a photo of two people Tasi recognizes; she stops her mother before she can turn the page. It's of her parents when they were young and thin, standing together on a porch, black power lines criss-crossing behind them and dividing up the sky.

"He didn't want to introduce me to anyone," her mother says, tapping her nail against the bottom of the photo. Tasi looks closer. Though they were leaning against each other hip to hip, her father's upper body was as curved as a reed in a wind blowing away from Winnie. "I was the closet girlfriend," her mother says and laughs, holding her newly painted fingertips to her cheek, a despair made pretty.

The green velveteen of the sofa itches behind Tasi's knees and the room smells of the chalky mints her mother keeps in a blue bowl, but Tasi stays put, sensing that Winnie needs someone to do this with her, to turn the pages in her book of the dead. Yes, she thinks, we all want long life but we rarely stop to consider the length of loneliness.

VIRGINIA

∿

Immersion

When Virginia comes into the faculty lounge to get a cup of coffee, Juanita makes the mistake of asking how she is. As Virginia is talking about her two-week stint in viral hell with Milo, she sees her colleague Carrelos smile as he goes by, a tight smile that could easily be mistaken for wincing. Boring, it seems to say, how boring can you be.

Milo has been sick for so long that Virginia is starting to feel an almost biblical dread. Any day now she expects to be battered by dead birds falling from the sky or to gag on water turned to swine's blood. Milo threw up two times last night—in his bed and at five AM—then had diarrhea this morning. Option A says that the mucous from the bronchitis or sinus infection is irritating his stomach. Option B says that he caught yet another virus—maybe while they were at the doctor's office or the pharmacy getting the last scrip filled. Yesterday consisted of laundering, comforting, and cleaning up. This morning her mother agreed to come over so Virginia could manage to teach her morning class, though she'll have to cancel the afternoon one.

She resists the urge to stick her foot out as Carrelos goes by the coffee machine. It's not boring, it's grueling, she wants to tell him. If you've ever taken care of someone recovering from surgery, or someone not recovering and on the journey to death, you know what she's referring to—constant care compelled by love. You hold your baby and think, if you went into a coma and the doctors wanted me to leave you in a state hospital, I would devote my life to bringing you home and keeping you home, so you could die with dignity and love. Is that an achievement in Carrelos' book? You hold your baby and think about the lives of women and children before antibiotics; women rocked babies who were dying, and no matter how many nights these mothers stayed up, no matter their devotion amid staggering fatigue, they could not change the course of smallpox, cholera, pneumonia—they could only hold their babies closer and sing the songs that are prayers. It's not boring; it lets you know what your love means—the brutal strength of it.

Virginia's great-grandfather died of strep throat. Think about that, Carrelos. Almost no one makes the connection between common illness and mortality anymore.

Over the weekend Milo gets the intestinal flu, and Virginia gets it too; she goes down with him, sick ward time. Nan stops by bringing saltines, ginger ale, and popsicles. Virginia can hear her putting dishes in the dishwasher. She thinks she remembers her standing by the bedroom door and speaking. Twenty-four hours later, Milo and she are still in bed, feverish together, humidifier chopping water into white noise, Milo's skin so pale, with a sheen like mother of pearl in the darkening twilight. "Mama, Mama," he wakes in alarm.

"Sshhh," I'm right here," but it's not what he wants to hear.

"Where's Papa?"

"He's at his house."

"Does he know I'm sick?" Milo has propped himself up on his elbows and fixed his glittery gaze on her.

In the last two days of throwing up, she has not considered calling Finley, a major omission on her part, she can tell. The gulf of their separation hits her viscerally, as vertiginous a drop as that from the side of the mattress to the cooking pot down below. She cannot bear to gaze at it. The distance has dawned on Milo: now that you don't live with your father, it's possible to be sick, to hurt, to suffer without him knowing.

"I'll get the phone," she says.

Finley comes over right after work. He brings canned soup and vanilla ice cream. He and Milo watch *The Lion King* together. In the kitchen, Finley surprises Virginia with a new plan. "Look, we'll get divorced so you'll feel secure, okay? No one can ever come after you over my debts. You've already refinanced the house in your name."

She stares at him blankly. Who ever heard of divorce as a way to continue a relationship? He barges onward.

"Milo and I could still do our Tuesday night and every other weekend thing so you could write."

She looks at the suspicious dribble on her pink fleece bathrobe, thinks of the chalky marks she recently washed from the corners of her mouth. "Do we have to talk about this now, Finley? Really?" There's a twinge of condescension in her tone. It is not lost on Finley.

"Didn't we make a lifelong commitment?" he hisses. "I'm not some screwball loser!"

Sick as she is, she still has to admire his stance of righteousness; it restores a sexiness to him that all his defeat in the face of finances had destroyed. He's right, of course, where Milo is concerned. You don't get children out into the cold air and then start debating lifelong commitment. She's about to tell him she'll think about it when Milo calls from the living room.

Finley licks his lips. Virginia can tell he is debating something. When he offers to take the day off from work, Virginia understands that the larger offer is now enfolded in the smaller one, but she brushes him off, reflexively it seems. "We'll be all right." Finley turns away from her before she can take it back. Virginia sighs. Now that Milo is feeling better, all she can think of is a good night's sleep. She is counting on a good night's sleep.

At some point every parent knows how abuse happens. If they tell you otherwise, they're lying. Virginia hasn't slept through the night in two weeks, and even though Milo is over the stomach bug, his sleep cycle has been completely disrupted. As is her habit, she finishes grading papers about midnight, then she takes a bath, reads a magazine. It's either just as she is dipping down into sleep, or not long after, that Milo sits bolt upright crying. Except he's not really awake. Night terrors are not in the same category with nightmares. It's as though someone jammed a stick in the turning wheels of sleep and your child is frozen in fear yet unawake. Milo clutches Nunna, his stuffed rhinoceros, and screams, "I'm all by myself." His eyes are open but inward-seeing only and though his mother is sitting right beside him, he does not see her. The advice books tell her, "Night terrors are sometimes precipitated by traumatic events." Right, no mystery there. It's spelled: D-I-V-O-R-C-E.

Spock advises: "If your child develops an intense fear, or a number of fears, or frequent nightmares . . . you ought to get the help of a children's psychiatrist." This does not make Virginia feel better. Granted, she did everything wrong the first night. The more you try to talk to a child or engage a child having night terrors, the more agitated he or she becomes. She definitely talked too much, offering assurance as much to him as to herself: "Mommy's here. There's nothing to be afraid of. You're in your own cozy house, in your own cozy bed." This seemed only to ignite a wild fire in his synapses. She could hear his teeth clench, and he reared back from her touch as though he were seizing up. He looked up toward the ceiling blindly like Patty Duke playing Helen Keller in *The Miracle Worker*, crying out, "I'm all alone," screaming "No! No!" the way the protagonists of horror flicks do before the blob gets them. Despite her entreaties, she remained invisible to him and concluded in her despair that Mother wasn't enough, never could be enough, no matter her desperate attempts to comfort him.

This scene plays itself out repeatedly in the next week. Gradually, Virginia learns that probably all Milo hears is the tone of her voice. Therefore the tones of rising desperation are to be avoided. Eventually she discovers that if she calmly repeats the same few phrases over and over and keeps the hall light on, Milo will come back to himself, still frightened but not terrified. Finley points out that the more she tries to reassure Milo, the more he might become convinced that there really is something to be afraid of.

"Does he wake up screaming at your place?" Virginia employs a real hand-on-hip tone with him. She never calls his place "home."

"Yeah, but it doesn't sound as bad as what you're going through."

"What do you do?"

"I pat him on the back and the steady rhythm seems to soothe him."

"Oh. Well, that's certainly not in the books."

Her comment manages to be both a jab and a concession. When they were a family, she was always the one reading the parenting books and relaying the information to Finley. He was open to hearing her but he rarely read the books himself. He trusted himself as a reader of *situations* and often saw what she had missed. This time Virginia consoles herself by believing it would be different if Fin had to deal with Milo's wakings every night. And deal with it she does. Eventually, Milo plonks back down onto his pillow in a decisive gesture that reminds her of a dog circling around before it lies down, and that is that . . . until about three hours later when Milo sits bolt upright and it starts all over again.

Why not simply move him into the bed with her? Because the parent-educator at the divorce support seminar advised against it, said the child might blame himself for displacing Daddy. At 3:42 AM this matters not one wit, and at 7:30 AM, Virginia wakes to the sensation of two small hands cupping her face and Milo's burning blue eyes not six inches from her own. "I love you so much, Mummy," he says. At that moment, she doesn't care whether it is God's grace or neurological phenomena that prevent Milo from remembering anything of his nightly episode. Nor does he seem to notice that the pillow his head lies on is his father's. He is her sweet, serene, cooey boy.

During the day though, between classes, between conversations with students and colleagues, in some interstitial silence, she hears Milo's cry: "I'm all alone." And it resonates with the profundity of Genesis, how divorce creates the experience of separation, how little there is she can do to diminish Milo's perception that he is on his own . . . even when she is right there next to him. Suddenly, she pulls out her fusty desk chair, and, standing on it precariously, locates Finley's photo atop the bookcase where she'd shoved it. Gazing at it, she remembers that they promised to go through time together—now the very quality of time itself has changed for Milo.

After a month of disrupted sleep, Virginia loses her mind; stamina and reason give way to fury. It is not during a night-fright, but after, when Milo continues to call out to her from his room: "Mommy, I can't sleep." The nuances of what is the matter increase in intensity and frequency: "My night light isn't bright enough." "The covers are itchy." "There's something crawling on the ceiling." Virginia starts by calling from across the hall: "I'm right here, Milo. You're all right, Milo. Go back to sleep, Milo." This works, for at least five to ten minutes. But when it doesn't, she threatens to spank him; she yells and swears: "Goddamnit, Milo. Mommy needs her sleep."

His endless complaints continue: "I'm too hot." "Everything in my room looks too big." "The sound of the train woke me up." His comments should mean something to her—*I'm too hot. Everything in my room looks too big*—but she is too savagely tired to be alert to clues. At 3:30, she leaps out of her bed like a woman possessed, meets him full force coming across the hall, grips his arms and sends him stumbling backward toward the bed. "I can't sleep! I can't sleep!" he is shrieking in her face. Then she spanks him, without warning, without telling him she is going to. The advice books tell you to establish a three strikes system and name each step: this is a warning, this is a time-out, next will be a spanking. They tell you that so you'll hear yourself, so you won't self-immolate in a rush of pure incandescence and spank out of anger. Virginia spanks out of anger; she leaves welts.

"You stay in your room. You hear me? You stay there."

She lies on her bed, shaking with exhaustion, adrenalin, and sorrow. Through his wailing, she can hear him speak to her.

"Ma-ma, you spank-ed me to-o ha-rd. I ca-n't brea-the." His voice is raggedy with weeping.

She goes to him then, weeping herself, and when she puts her hand on his cheek, she feels how hot his skin is, so hot his tears feel cool to her touch. "Honey, I think you're sick. I think that's why you can't sleep. Oh sweetie, Mommy shouldn't have spanked you. You hug Nunna while I get the thermometer."

The thermometer beeps almost instantly. 103.5. Virginia becomes a frenzy of activity. Pulling off his pajama bottoms, cooling off his forehead with a washrag, going to get the Tylenol bottle, which she finds in its place in the medicine cabinet. Empty. A residue of purple gook in the bottom like crystallized honey. She begins her searching mantra: *Shit, Fuck, Jesus Christ.* That's how the first part goes. *Goddamn, Son of a bitch.* That's the second part. The first aid kit yields nothing but gauze and band-aids, then she cuts her thumb on a razor as she scrabbles through her travel kit. *Shit, Fuck, Jesus Christ.* She rips off some toilet paper to wrap it in. *Goddamn, Son of a bitch.* She can hear Milo crying, "Mummy, I'm sick. I'm sick."

What should she do? Drive to the 7-11? Ten minutes away. He could have a seizure with a fever this high. Go to the emergency room? One hundred dollar co-pay. Call Finley? No.

"Mummy, I'm si-ick."

Yes. Call Finley.

"Honey, come with me. That's right. Mama's going to pick you up. Yes. Even though you're a big boy, I'm going to pick you up. We're going to call Daddy.

Ring. Ring. Ring.

An accompanying incantation begins in Virginia's brain: *Oh, please for the love of God, please be there, Fin. I'll kill you. I'll fucking kill you if you're off fucking someone else.*

"Hello?"

"Fin, it's me. Milo is sick."

"Where are you?"

"We're at home. His fever's really high. He needs Tylenol but I'm out." She practically wails the last three words.

"I've got some, Ginny. I'm coming."

"Okay . . . okay." Tears are runneling down her cheeks.

"Ginny?"

"Yes."

"How high is his fever?"

"Almost 104."

"Use cool compresses, Ginny. I'm coming."

In the bathroom light, Milo's face is the color of anchovy paste. He's moaning now instead of crying. Virginia runs some tepid water in a Tupperware bowl, throws washrags in, and carries him into his room. She puts on Milo's favorite lullaby tape—Celtic fiddle and crooning—but he waves his hand in the air against it and curls into himself away from her.

Finley's tap on the door is percussive and quiet, a code in rhythm. He kicks off his shoes by the door, then pads down the hall behind Virginia.

"Hey Milo, I hear my boy's not feeling so good," Finley says, settling on the bed as Milo struggles up to hug his father. Finley gathers him up while Virginia measures out two teaspoons of acetaminophen. Afterwards, Finley rocks Milo by shifting his weight from one ham to the other, side to side. Virginia heads into the kitchen though she doesn't know why. She hears Milo's chirpy voice and Finley's rumble in answer: "Yep, Mama's here. Papa's here. Everything's going to be all right." When she checks back, their boy's head has fallen back against the crook of his father's arm. It makes Virginia remember the pictures taken in the 1930s by Hansel Mieth of cowboys with their children, the once a week they got to see them, the tenderness in those craggy faces; these were the pictures *Time Magazine* chose not to run when the feature was published.

Virginia feels weak and tingly as though Milo's fever spike were a peak climb and she'd just descended too fast from high altitude. The sky between the shutters is that bright first blue. When Finley slowly stands after settling Milo in the bed, she wants to hug him. No, that's not true, what she wants is for him to hug her, to absolve her of being such a terrible parent, to safeguard her against herself.

"I spanked him, Fin. He had a fever and I spanked him hard." They stand, crowding the doorway together, and she can feel when Finley turns to look at her, though he doesn't pull away.

"Well, Ginny," he says slowly, as if deliberating the risk, "we were better together. I know I did my share of wrong, but I still think we were better together."

The words Virginia needs collect like spittle in her throat; there's an ache she can't push her voice past. She stares down at Milo sleeping—ashen child, a Victorian shade of pale, but sleeping deeply. Reflexively, she reaches for Finley's hand, feels the heat of his palm, the grip of his fingers. As they step into the hall, hand in hand, Fin takes a step toward the kitchen while simultaneously Virginia takes a step toward the bedroom. Their arms draw taut. He takes a step towards her and they go slack. Neither of them lets go. She can feel him peering intently at her in the ambient blue light.

"What are you thinking here, Ginny?"

Oh please, she thinks, not integrity, not now. Couldn't Finley for once be one of those guys who just wants to have sex, delicious, comforting sex? Not a moment later, she is stricken by her love for him as though felled at the knees.

She wheedles. "I'm so tired, Fin. So down. I'm not trying to seduce you. I just need someone to hold me."

"I don't want to be *someone*, Ginny. It has to be me you want."

She waits before she speaks, because she knows he won't believe her if it comes too fast, and she wants to feel the words expand inside her chest before she speaks them. "It is you, Fin. And us." She can feel him peering at her though his face is sheathed by the shadow of the wall.

"It's not just because I can fix the garbage grinder?"

"No, Fin. It's because you . . . it's because I . . ." She shakes her head to clear it.

"There're a lot of reasons to examine," he says, resolutely.

"I know . . . I know. And if I could stop being so high-handed, I think we could talk about it."

"But not now?"

"No, not now."

He gives her a sidelong smile, pointing down with one finger. "There it is, Ginny, the threshold."

She looks down and sees that she is standing with one foot braced on each side of the doorjamb.

"Are we going over?" he asks, and when she picks up her foot he moves his body behind hers, joins her in this slow slide toward the old bed in the light of the new day.

JEAN

∾

Note in a Bottle

It rains so hard on the drive out to the coast that the water on the windshield is viscous as mercury and about as transparent. Tor plays the Red Hot Chili Peppers on his CD player—head thrown back, his socked feet bouncing against the seat in front of him. He sings off-key with the headset on: "Suck My Kiss." Neither Jean nor Reio stop him, though his singing is bad enough that they occasionally have to laugh.

The town of Pacific Beach is fairly typical for a beach community amidst closed sawmills and plywood factories: in front of the kite shop the wind socks droop, farther down main street the bumper cars cluster like black beetles in a swarm, and the arms of the taffy machine are suspended mid-turn. The placard in front of the gas station is lashed to a pole; it advertises "shovel rentals" and "good razor clamming." Reio tells her his forefathers were Finnish clammers, "a bunch of hobos really," who camped and dug clams and picked cranberries. "They made out okay, but one of the younger lads made a break for the shingle mill and married. My great-grandmother bought the property. Just a shack on it then. But you'll see. The house is nothing grand."

"Beach houses shouldn't be grand. They should be simple." Immediately, Jean regrets having spoken with such certainty. What if Reio's sisters have filled the place with tchochkes, silk flowers, and kitty rugs? But Reio simply nods, staring down the length of his arm and over the steering wheel.

The house is a weathered grey and white building that has been much amended; at the center stands a straight up and down house any child could draw, flanked on either side by additions with flat roofs, one of which encloses the walkway and a mud room, the other a kitchen. Beyond the house, the gray sky has lifted cleanly as a pot lid and between water and cloud cover, a seam of blue and gold shines irresistibly. Jean follows Tor around the front of the house while Reio lets himself in to turn on the water and flip the switches in the fuse box. It is then that she sees the house stands on a sandy knoll overlooking the dunes and a jetty wall. In the distance, she can see the Moclips River, and beyond that, the wild coast of the Quinault Indian Reservation.

Jean thinks briefly of lighting a smoke, as is her habit after a long car ride, but the air buffeting her face smells of spruce, shore pine, and salt. Tor is already down on the jetty wall, leaping off the far side of it, hooting and landing on all fours in the fine sand.

"Hey," Reio says, not wanting to startle her as he comes up from behind. "What do you think?"

"It's glorious," she says, looking over the spiky beach grass and scotch broom to the waves unfurling in long lateral lines of white. "I'm breathing it in."

Reio stands close behind her and points north, toward the reservation. "At night, you don't see any lights up that coast. They had a smart chief back in the 1950s, kept everybody out."

She lets herself lean a little against him, taking in the sensation of his voice and breath in her ear. Then his hand swings out in front of them. "In another month, you can see pairs of gray whales migrating north, calves and cows."

Just beyond the end of Reio's finger, Tor suddenly appears, a slender rakish silhouette making fast time toward the water. Reio steps adroitly down to the jetty, puts two fingers to his mouth and whistles shrilly. It takes another ear-splitting whistle before Tor slows in his tracks, moving ever slower as he returns to them.

"I wasn't going swimming," he laments from the bottom of the wall. "I just wanted to go to the beach."

"We got a car to unload, buddy," his father says, mustering a neutral tone. When Tor is enough ahead of them Reio turns to Jean. "I'd like to eliminate sentences beginning with 'I just.'" He shakes his head, smiling.

Inside, the walls are covered with tongue-and-groove fir, making it ambient like the inside of an instrument. Gold ocean light floods through the embroidered eyelets of the white curtains. A compass star quilt in faded shades of celadon and rose hangs over the couch, and above the hearth, a large black-and-white photo of a swath of beach dotted with tiny lights. "Kerosene lanterns," Reio says, reading the question in her face. "Sometimes clammers used them at low tide."

Jean hefts the bags of groceries into the kitchen, stepping on braid rugs the colors of shore grass in summer—straw, wheat, olive, and brass. A set of miniature ferryboats lines the windowsill. All the appliances are old—nothing to beep at her in this house.

Reio deposits her bag down the hall. "This is your spot," he says with a jerk of his head, dropping his own bag one-armed over the threshold of the room opposite hers. She follows his gesture to a sizeable room, running her hands along the dips in the scallops of the wrought-iron footboard while she takes in her surroundings. The bedspread is the color of tea-stained muslin, a ribbon motif in rose and maize; at the bottom of the bed stands a blanket chest, a fat urn painted on its crackled front. "It's lovely," she says, turning, but Reio has already gone.

She steps over to a strangely narrow armoire. Opening its doors, she sees the hooks that must have held necklaces—pearls or garnets or rose quartz beads—perhaps Reio's mother's—and the shallow felt-lined drawers. Without thinking, she pushs the lift-up top and there suddenly she is, her face in the mirror, the broad planes of her shtetl-Jewish ancestors and the deep set dark eyes. She studies the question they seem to be asking: "Will you know who you are when you give up your suffering?" She hears Reio's steps on the porch and realizes that if she makes love to Reio, it won't be because she is trying to have a baby. Her grandmother used to tell her, "Smile when you look in the mirror," which her cynical adolescent self had dismissed as American boosterism, more high school pep rally. She tries it now, a careful, inviting smile, then snaps the lid shut when she hears Reio call her name.

Down on the beach, Tor runs a quarter mile ahead of them, skittering back and forth across the sand like a rolled coin. Entire flocks of Dunlins take to the air in front of him.

"He's a spirit set free out here," Reio says.

"I can tell."

So far, Tor has kept his distance from Jean, directing his comments to his father, occasionally eyeing her. She knows there is no use forcing anything. If she tries too hard with him she will only earn disdain and derision. So, she is surprised when he races up to her shouting, "Jean, you've got to see this. C'mon!"

Where the high tide line has dried on the sand, Tor has found a desiccated sting ray, wingspan about six feet, its body a leathery brown. The orbits of the creature's eyes are stretched ovals, a ghoul mask looking up from the sand at her.

"Wow," she says, "that's a big one."

"And look at this. It has teeth on its tail."

She kneels in the sand with Tor, fingering the thorn-like teeth that barb either side of the tail.

Reio strolls up but stays back a few feet, watching them.

"Quite a find you got there," he says.

"Yeah, Dad, you don't find one of these very often, do you?" Tor is skipping in circles around the animal.

"Nope, they're creatures of the deep."

"Let's turn it over," Tor says, his eyes now on Jean.

"There will probably be some kind of worms or maggots attached to its underside," she says matter-of-factly, but when Tor reaches for the ray's wing, she gets a hold of it with him and helps flip the animal, which lands with a puff of stench and sand.

"Gross!" Tor shouts, entirely pleased. "That is so disgusting."

After that, it appears Jean has passed the initial test in Tor's mind, and he has a new idea for her every minute. Back at the cottage, he wants to play Pictionary and draws in an emphatic, stick-figure, comic book style that gives him an edge over Reio and Jean—Tor draws heat lines, sound waves, speed waves, the biff, boom, and pow of impact. She recognizes "speed bump" and "cough drop" right away. When she compliments Tor on his animated drawing skills, his smile shines and he offers to make her a flipbook in the morning. While she puts the kitchen stuff away, he seems to be chattering non-stop—"Can we light a bonfire? Last year we made the best. Can we make S'mores tonight? How many Hershey Bars did you bring? Can we go to town and get a stunt kite? Man, they are so cool." The prospect of so much fun seems to overload his circuits. Jean watches in amazement as Tor stuffs his head into the cushions of a swivel recliner and runs circles around the thing. Reio seems non-plussed.

"Horizontal hamster wheel?" she says quizzically to him as he hands her a glass of wine.

"Yeah, he's wired all right. He can catch flounder with his feet at the mouth of the river. He feels 'em and then he scoops 'em up. Takes pretty quick reflexes."

"Remind me not to play mumblety-peg with him," she says, setting a pot of chili to warm on the stove.

Once enclosed, Tor seems to run everywhere; he twice catches his feet in the pedestal base of an end table, sending the lamp flying, until finally Reio picks up the table and stuffs it up against the arm of the couch. To Jean, the picture is getting clearer. Guidelines for diagnosis of Attention-Deficit/Hyperactivity Disorder (ADHD): "Often acts as if driven by a motor, often runs about or climbs excessively in inappropriate situations." She halts her mind with a sip of wine.

Reio is on the couch helping Tor untangle his headset. Once that is accomplished, Tor sits on the couch intent upon his Game Boy, feet bouncing against the cocktail table.

Reio shakes his head as he approaches the kitchen counter.

"Game Boy is the only thing that goes as fast as his brain. It seems to give him some relief." He winces as he says this, and Jean looks down into the silverware drawer.

"Here," he says, putting out his hand for the knives and forks she just counted. "I know what you're thinking. He's already been diagnosed hyperactive. Believe me, we've gone the distance with all that."

"Was it any help?"

"Not really. They put him on Ritalin for awhile, but it just dumped him down every day. Didn't matter if it was the short-acting or long-acting stuff. He'd come home from school and blowout, melt down, sobbing and locking himself in his room."

"Yeah, that's called the rebound effect."

"I don't care what it's called. I took him off that shit." Reio is standing with his elbows on the counter, staring right into her, a dangerous edge in his voice.

"How do you think he's doing now?" she asks quietly.

"He's getting by. He can do the schoolwork. I just have to sit with him at night while he does it so he doesn't skip steps or skip problems."

"That's great you do that. You know, hyperactive children aren't medicated nearly so much in Britain. Maybe he'll grow out of it."

Reio's face softens. "Well, I grew out of it. When I was a kid, I was always scrazzing around. I drove everybody crazy. My father gave me a drum kit cause I used to sit there pounding out rhythms on the table with my hands while loosening the chair struts with my feet."

"Really? You're a drummer?"

"Was. I played in Canada for years. The band did cover tunes—Springsteen, The Pretenders, Lynyrd Skynyrd. We played those mill towns in the prairie you can smell before you get there."

"Why don't you set up a drum kit for him?" she asks, nodding her head towards Tor.

Reio strokes his moustache and laughs. "What kind of manager are you? You can't exactly play drums in an apartment complex, can you?"

That night, she puts on her new nightie, tiny blue cornflowers on white cotton, feeling that somehow she matches the room. She wishes Reio had kissed her and is relieved he didn't. It's clear they both feel slightly sheepish about taking turns in the bathroom, but afterwards, he hugged her in the living room, not a polite or restrained hug either—it was plank to plank. She went up on her toes so she could lay her head on his shoulder and let the weight of it go. But when she turned toward his neck, pressed her forehead against his skin, he broke the embrace, setting her a little back from him by her shoulders. She saw then that his face was full of hurt and ruin, and her hand sought his.

"Well," he said with a sigh, "okay then." And he let her hand go.

Afterwards she lies in her bed listening, vigilant to every noise in the house, the waves a background texture of sound, the pipes pinging as they cool. She waits for the squeak of a door and is mad at herself for waiting, as though she and Reio were in some corny Western where everyone says goodnight but finally one of the fated pair in flannel appears like an apparition in the doorway.

She wakes alone in the morning, chilled by fog, and rises to close the window.

When she comes into the kitchen, Reio is already at the stove making pancakes.

"You want chocolate chips in yours?" Tor asks brightly. He is at the kitchen table with paper and pencil in front of him, though he mostly seems to be sharpening a pencil down to a nub.

"Definitely," she says. "I wouldn't want to miss out."

Jean takes a mug down from the cupboard and fills it. As she is exiting the kitchen, Reio surprises her. "Good morning," he says, leaning down to kiss her on one cheek and then the other as European families do. She flushes with a sense of well being, then takes her mug to the table where Tor sits, still and alert as a little fox.

"What are you making?"

"Well, it's not finished yet, but I'll show you." He takes the Post-It pad he was been drawing on with his now equally tiny pencil and bends it so the pages flip through his fingers. Jean sees two stick figures move jerkily to throw javelins at each other, pick up the javelins, plant them into the ground, and swing around mid-air on them.

"That's amazing," she says. "You make them look like they're going around."

"Tell me something you want me to draw. I can do it."

"How about a surfer on a wave?"

Tor pauses for a moment, looking toward the ceiling. "Huh," he says, "I don't think I've ever done that before."

While Reio puts the plates on the table, he and Tor argue because Tor wants to wear his headset during breakfast.

"Give me one good reason why not?"

"Well, it's rude to Jean, for one."

"You don't care, do you, Jean?"

She puts up her hands. "I'm not getting into this, Tor."

Reio waves the spatula in the air for emphasis. "Maybe you need to go chill out for awhile, Tor."

"Maybe you do, Dad."

"When you're not in my face, I'd love to."

"You're the one jumping all over me," Tor says, but the pitch of his voice drops, and he slides back into his chair.

Jean folds the B-section of yesterday's paper flat, "Here," she says, pushing it toward Tor, "the funnies."

He makes a noise in his throat while folding a giant wad of waffle into his mouth. He eats with his head slung low over the plate, shoveling it in, and reading the funnies up close.

As Reio serves her, they exchange a meaningful look. "Thank you," she says, when he takes his seat. She waits for him before taking the first bite.

"You," he says, an exaggerated glimmer of exasperation in his eyes, "are very welcome." And they smile at each other. Tor does not look up.

When Tor goes out to feed bread heels to the gulls, they linger over their coffee. Jean wonders if Reio will want to talk about Tor and tests the territory.

"You really keep your cool with him, you know. You avoid all the traps."

"I try to reserve our power struggles for the big issues. That's when I lose my cool," he says, raising his eyebrows. Then he turns his gaze back toward the beach where Tor is now flinging himself from the jetty toward the dunes.

Jean is sipping her coffee and taking in the view when Reio segues to the difficult subject, the one she was hoping wouldn't come up. Maybe it has to with the two of them watching a child leap off a wall repeatedly.

"So fill me in," he says. "How come you and your former didn't adopt?"

"We tried," she answers, sipping and delaying. "A few times. The adoptions fell through. It was too heartbreaking. I don't think it was what Timmy really wanted, and I felt guilty, so I let it drop."

"You felt guilty?"

"What are you, a social worker?" This gets a wry smile from him.

"I want to know about you," he says seriously.

"I didn't want to have a baby for a long time, and he did. I took Women's Studies in college when Betty Friedan referred to the homes of married women as 'comfortable concentration camps.' The worst thing that could happen was to get trapped with babies, to wind up without serious work."

"But you became a social worker."

"Yeah, but I had an abortion in college and couldn't conceive when we wanted children."

"I'm sorry," he says, looking down into his hands and rubbing his knuckles.

Jean can feel the old ache in her mandible joint and puts her hands to her jaw as she waits for him to say something else, some stupid meant-to-be-comforting bromide that will annihilate her attraction to him. But only the sound of the waves buffets between them.

"Some things you don't get over," he ventures. He turns, his head slightly toward her, meeting her gaze.

"No," she says simply. Suddenly she sweeps her hand across the air and laughs. "Yeah, but I've been wallowing in it. The worst was at Christmas, after I bagged my career. I felt like a walking cautionary tale: 'Look what happens when you put your career first.' I was baby-hungry in a way that was insane."

She looks down into her lap, thinking about Charlotte and the abortion, about whether she should tell him now or save it for later. What could she say, really? I wanted my friend's baby and she wouldn't give it to me?

"Maybe that's behind you now." Reio says. His hand is on her shoulder.

"That's possible." His saying so makes it seem like a possibility anyway, but without meaning to, she shrugs, and he lets his hand fall away.

"Babies are wonderful. They also grow up and insult you." He nods in Tor's direction. "And if you've done a good job, they leave you."

His words seem to let the bone-white light of the sea bleach her mind. She hasn't allowed herself to think this way, that there are people her age ready to arrive at the end of child-rearing, that there is no shame in it. When she puts her hand open-palmed into his lap, he takes it. "It's good for me to be reminded of that," she says quietly.

"Anytime," he says.

"I burned out on social work," Jean says, as though he'd asked the question. "You're supposed to refer people to service providers but the non-profit agencies are disappearing. Maybe I could have stayed with it if I'd had any sense that the system would improve. Instead of a safety net, we've got a sewer grate. It was the same story over and over again."

"Yeah, federal monies get cut. Medicaid reimbursements fall short. That's the trend," Reio says, swirling the last of the coffee in his cup.

"Right. My job with Visiting Nurses got phased out," she said, her eyes rolling upward as though she were looking into the top of her head. "Then they restructured and offered me a new one— higher case load, lower pay, no benefits. Job-hunting was something else. Not a lot of places want you when you've got seniority."

He nods. "Too high end on the pay scale."

"I call it the young, green, and grateful syndrome, because that's who they want."

"The Indians like it when you're older," Reio says. "The government is happy to send me to deal with them. So is the apartment manager gig full time?"

She is grateful for the way he phrases it, so it doesn't sound like 'what's a smart girl like you doing in such a crummy job?'

"The job doesn't have to be full time. I mean so long as I run the office and keep the debit-credit ledger, my rent is free. But I've been doing extra landscaping, vacuuming the halls, that kind of thing on an hourly wage. I don't have to."

"You got something else in mind?"

She considers making another joke, but something stronger in her warns against it. She doesn't feel criticism coming from him or the need to have her status reflect on his. His tender and steady gaze conveys regard, and she knows she has been ducking the question with everyone else and is now equally interested in her own answer.

"I can't go back to social work full-time, but there are . . ." she stumbles, "there are focus groups for kids with mental health issues . . . at family service providers. Some of them produce 'zines, journals, web pages, videos. I'd like to get some art therapy training, I guess, go back in at that level."

He smiles at her, nodding. "I bet you'd be good at it."

"Whew." She leans back and stretches. "I haven't answered this many questions seriously in a long time."

"Let's go to the beach," he says, pulling back his chair.

That night, she comes out of the bathroom to find Reio leaning on the opposite wall. It confuses her momentarily. "I'm not waiting for the bathroom," he says, moving toward her with his hands held open. He kisses her in the hallway, tentative kisses made tickly by his moustache. She is holding her toiletries bag in one hand and she lets it fall with a thud. Before long they are pressed against each other in the narrow space, smothering their laughter in each other's necks. When it seems like neither of them can breathe, they stop kissing to make a parody of their own love scene.

"Is this the part where I pin you to the wall?" he whispers.

"Oooh baby," she says, giggling and slinging a leg around his backside. Then breaking off again, each looks in the other's fully incredulous face, open to beauty and belief.

At about 6:00 AM, Jean sneaks across the hall to the bathroom, intending to return to her room. She is startled to see the back of Tor's head at the kitchen table. He is sitting where his father usually sits and staring fixedly at the monotone gray of water and sky beyond the dunes. Relieved that he didn't turn and hear her, she slips quickly into the bathroom.

Later, when she comes alongside the table, she whispers, "What are you doing?"

"Just sitting," he says. His tone is flat, disengaged. She notices that he has made a pot of coffee, and she goes to get a mug.

"How nice you made coffee."

"Dad showed me. So I could make him coffee on the weekends."

Emphasis on the word "him," she notes. Jean has been warned about the territorial wars in the land of stepmothers, and she has to admit she is glad that Tor's mother is out of the picture, though she feels guilty about it. After all, the woman is a drug addict. Anyway, Jean won't have to endure another woman's insecurity about the inevitable comparisons: there will be no envy, no bitchery, no subterfuge through the poor kid. Jean can stay clear with herself, too. No martyrdom about Tor's mother not thanking her for shuttling him to baseball games or taking him to counseling or nursing him through the flu. But addicts often resurface. People clean up. Jean has to be prepared for that.

She wraps the afghan from the couch around herself and sits at the table.

"Now I get to see your real face," says Tor.

"How's it look?" Jean cups her hands around the warm ceramic and ignores the taunt in his tone. Tor's own lips are puffy and the creases across his cheeks made him look younger than twelve.

"Older," he says, studying her seriously, "but not bad."

"Glad to hear it," she says, smiling at him, then breathing into her mug, disappearing into the vapor of a long, hot sip.

"Will you get me some cereal?" he asks abruptly, before she can put her mug down again.

His tone is a little surly, and he barely glances at her before staring back out to sea. Is he testing to prove her the dupe or protecting some greater need?

"Sure," she says breezily, walking over to the cupboard. "What kind do you want?"

She puts bowl, spoon, milk, and cereal in front of him, then offers him a glass of juice. She can feel his gaze on her as she does these things, the urgency in his waiting.

"Thank you," he says solemnly, when she returns to her seat, his dark eyes aflame with intensity, the way they were when she first met him crouched around his little fire. She knows then that the request was an echo that emanated in a wrong place and time, sees in his face how much he wished over the years for an every-morning-mother to pour his cereal though it is irrevocably too late now, just as it is too late for Jean to have a son. But they can play at it, if she delivers to his need and he to hers without too much acknowledgement, without making it self-conscious. She sees that in this way they can become friends.

"Shall we see if there are any cartoons on?" she asks, moving across the room to pick up the remote and flopping on the couch. "You can never be too old for cartoons."

By mid-morning, Tor is rocking out with his CD player, the recliner squeaking from the exertion of his feet pressing against the floor. "Let's head out," his father says, giving the chair a hearty spin to get Tor's attention. He turns to Jean. "I'll take Tor into town. Give you some space. He's been wanting a skim board real bad."

Within seconds, Tor is raring to go. He stands by the front door kicking his feet toward the far wall, seeing how far his flip-flops will fly.

"Out," Reio says firmly.

It doesn't faze Tor at all. "See you later, Jean Bean," he calls cheerily as he opens the door.

In parting, Reio again kisses her on both cheeks, but with their faces close together, they pause, and each unintentionally makes a throaty sound, then they laugh at the simultaneity of it.

"More later," Reio says.

"Bring me a cinnamon roll," Jean says smiling, pleased to set him to a lover's task.

"Big and gooey. You got it."

After the car tires have crunched away on the gravel road, she stands in the hallway, feeling the bend of her body towards Reio's room, running through a list of justifications. It's the only room in the house she hasn't seen, and it isn't like she's going to search his suitcase or read his journal. Maybe she just wants proof, to see, now that the darkness has receded, their impression on the bed or to find some lingering scent in the air. But he has made the bed—Scotch plaid comforter pulled taut—and the only scent is of fir paneling and wallboard heater. Still, on the bedside table, she finds a photo, black and white in a brushed chrome frame. It must be ten years old: Tor slung on his father's hip, his head thrown back in laughter, his toddler tendrils of hair spread on the wind, a Botticelli boy. Reio is wearing a Greek fisherman's cap, woolen braiding above the brim, his eyes crinkly with the shared joke. Jean wipes a coating of dust off the photo with her shirt tail, looks at it more closely, tries to look at it with the eyes of the woman she is certain took the photo. There must have been love in the gaze, yes, this is after all the moment the woman chose, the laughter between father and son forever silvery in the frame.

Jean slumps on the bed, lets the photo rest on her knees, feeling herself suddenly excluded from this father-son bond, perhaps even as the woman herself had. Well, someone always feels excluded, don't they? Isn't that the reality of having a past and not pretending it away? The boxes she could neither unpack nor give away. The white stone of Charlotte's she had thrown into the rhododendron bushes and later retrieved.

The anger toward Charlotte had served a purpose. She sees that now. Like booster rockets, it had propelled her through an atmosphere thick with memory. If she had splashed down in flames, still she had splashed down, and now she was back in the present of her life, a life that promised to be chaotic, that promised to swing from joy to ache. But the years with Timmy could be telescoped, could become one photo of a faraway time, on a dresser like this one, not something Reio would ever ask her to put away, though she might someday on her own.

What about the photos of Charlotte back home? Would she put them away? It depended. Jean couldn't do the Christian thing, the forgiveness thing, the resolve all your bad feelings thing. Jews didn't believe you had to forgive the unforgivable, but that's where she was stuck. Her grandmother used to say, "Two Jews, three opinions." Were Charlotte's actions unforgivable? If Jean reached down deep, she knew she'd lost respect for Charlotte a long time before the pregnancy, sitting in the living room with the newlyweds and realizing she'd never have a real conversation with Charlotte in Darius's presence, convinced Charlotte had put away her best self to lead a partial life, convinced that now it would all have to be nicety and pretend, because if Jean were real, it would test the limits of their friendship. Instead, the test had been deferred, and now Jean understood that she had no respect for Charlotte, not just because she wouldn't have the baby but because she hadn't claimed her own life either.

That was the crucial inequality between them, and Jean didn't feel you could have a true friend unless you felt equal. A true friend functioned like a compass point in orienteering, a chosen benchmark above the tree-filled valley, a fixed point one could navigate by. If it weren't for her friends, how many times might Jean have chosen badly? Oh all right, worse even. But Charlotte had ceased to be that kind of friend. She had over time become the example of failed dreams, of repeated poor choices, of retrograde tendencies. The person about whom Jean could say: "At least I'm not like her," to herself, as often as she liked. Jean saw how useful Charlotte was to her, how she too, hoarded an unexamined attitude of moral superiority. If that was why Darius suited Charlotte, Jean had to admit, it was also part of why she remained "loyal" to Charlotte. She saw now that if she gave up hating Charlotte, she'd have to give up that attitude too, and that wouldn't be a bad thing.

She could hear herself telling the story differently now, the story of what had happened when she'd asked her friend to give away her baby; she could hear there was a more sympathetic version, a version that incorporated Nan's view that Charlotte's assessments of herself were what mattered, or Tasi's view that dependency was a temperament; a view in which forgiveness was not central, but release was. Maybe out here with Reio and Tor, she could release Charlotte, could hope some good for Charlotte, could recognize Charlotte's suffering without making it her own.

That afternoon, the three of them head toward the river, where the high tide has reached its peak, forcing the river to flow backward into the estuary. Though the day is gray the sun threatens to burn through, the sky shimmery thin in patches. Gigantic cedars on the bluff above the river have been torn by storms and tossed sideways, their tips crossing like staves in battle. Tor is yelling ahead of them, "I see something! I see something!" He runs into water above his waist and comes back out with a bottle in his hand. There he stands until they can catch up to him, turning the bottle in his hands.

Jean expected a beer bottle or maybe a wine bottle with a pirate's note scrawled by a child's hand.

"What is it?" Reio asks, hand extended when he sees Tor's stricken face. The tip of the cork has been covered in red tape. It's a large pale green bottle, rings die-cut on the neck and an oval where a product label would have been. Powdery gray ash and chips of white appear as Reio turns the bottle sideways in his hand.

"Jesus," he says.

"Read the note, Dad. Read it."

Reio slowly reads aloud: "Please don't separate us. If found, please put in the outgoing tide. Signed, Ed and Darlene."

"They're crematorium ashes," Jean says, putting her hand on Tor's shoulder. He leans toward her and she lets her hand travel across his back until she has her arm around him.

"Unbelievable," Reio says solemnly. He tilts it bottom end up to check for a trademark symbol, but there is none.

"Give it to me," Tor says suddenly, breaking away from her. "I found it."

"It's all yours, son." Reio puts his hands up when he lets go of the bottle.

Tor walks down the beach away from them, until he becomes a silhouette in the reflective light, a green willow stick of a boy, long-waisted as he will never again be in life. He cradles the bottle in his arms, head tilted toward it. Jean wonders who is in the bottle for Tor. His mother? His child self? And she thinks of Charlotte, not with the old anger but with a quiet sense of loss, one she knows will diminish over time. Reio's eyes never leave Tor, and to Jean each of them seems fixed in their own histories of hurt and loss, the too-bright sky like the flash of an over-exposed photo. Tor runs swiftly into the surf, runs on legs that bound as though the earth were a springboard. Cocking his arm high and leaning back from the waist, he sends the bottle spinning and glinting in the newly breaking blue. Reio is hooting and hollering. "Atta boy. Put 'em back where you found 'em!" Jean doesn't see where the bottle lands, only the pull of the tide taking it back out.